THE NE
LOOKED O   ER AT
THE COP.

"I don't want to fight you on this. I want to work with you. Team up again. I think it's a dynamite idea. What about you?"

Broskey sighed. "I don't know, Jake. We might have ourselves a serial killer out there. We might not. It's too soon to tell."

"But if there *is* a pattern killer out there, Kev, we could work on nailing him together. This time, I can play it your way, the cops' way. I'm not talking just newspapers here. I'm talking book. I'm talking TV rights. I'm talking movies. Wouldn't you like to see someone play you in a movie? Roy Scheider? Burt Reynolds? Sally Fields?"

Broskey blinded.

"Hey," Jake said. "She's very versatile."

Broskey glanced at his watch.

"I just had this creepy thought," Jake said. "The next victim, I mean, if there *is* a next victim, could be in this bar right now."

And she was . . .

ON THE EDGE

ED NAHA

POCKET BOOKS

New York London Toronto Sydney Tokyo

An *Original* Publication of POCKET BOOKS

POCKET BOOKS, a division of Simon & Schuster Inc.
1230 Avenue of the Americas, New York, NY 10020

ISBN: 0-671-66622-3

First Pocket Books printing June 1989

10 9 8 7 6 5 4 3 2 1

POCKET and colophon are trademarks of
Simon & Schuster Inc.

Printed in the U.S.A.

For
C. A. Rabin & Suzanne

With very, very special thanks to
Harvey Klinger, Jane Chelius, Linne Radmin, and
the cultural icons of Los Angeles

One

The midday sun filtered through the window, settling on the front page of the *Los Angeles Tribune*. PIT BULLS TERRORIZE TINY TOTS! A shadow fell across the paper as the intruder took in the layout of the place.

He sat in the brightly lit living room and took a deep drag on his cigarette. Bad habit. It excluded you from being served quiche in some of the lamest restaurants in Beverly Hills. Coke was fine. Liquor? No problem? But Marlboro Lights? Forget it.

He took another puff. Oh well, he had a lot of time to ruin his lungs. He'd started smoking a year or two ago, after Janet left. Just a few a day, at first. She had left a pack behind. He still smoked her brand, although he was up to a pack and a half daily now.

Sometimes, for perverse pleasure, he'd take a deep breath and feel the junk rattle around in his lungs. It sounded a little like a leaky concertina.

He stared out the window. What the hell; if the cigarettes didn't do him in, the smog would.

He took another drag. There was that concertina sound. He took solace in the fact that he wasn't a jogger.

Hated bicycles, too.

1

He made a move to flick the ashes on the floor. He glanced around. No ashtray. She had probably been a health nut. He walked over to the open window and tossed the cigarette down to the street below, nearly burning a particularly muscular bicyclist. The rider swerved in the street and looked up angrily. The man in the living room grinned and flashed Mr. Muscles a peace sign. Two points for the Lazy-Boy team.

He slowly walked around the room. How did a woman her age afford this kind of place? Terribly deco furniture. Top-of-the-line stereo, compact-disc player, VCR, oversized TV.

When he was in college, he was happy with a battered black-and-white Sony TV and a stereo he had inherited from the kid who ran the bookstore.

The stereo shorted out a lot, sending waves of static over the speakers. You'd have to slam the side of the amplifier with the flat of your hand to make a Santana record sound like a Santana record and not like the soundtrack of *Godzilla.* The FM portion of the set was beyond comprehension. For years, he thought the title of the Sammy Davis, Jr., tune "The Candyman" was "The Handicapped." "Who can make an ashtray? The handicapped can."

He padded softly around the room, taking care not to touch anything.

Ah, to be young, affluent, and hip. He sighed.

Alabaster bookcases, filled with the kind of touchy-feely stuff he'd gotten used to in L.A. Ramtha tomes. Tarot stuff. Thirty-seven pounds of Shirley McLaine. Books with titles like *Smart Women, Foolish Choices, How Men Feel,* and *Women Who Love Too Much.* He tried to count how many titles had personal pronouns in them but lost count after twenty.

Video collection. *Crimes of the Heart, Sophie's Choice, Out of Africa.*

She was probably very intelligent. Good student most likely. He glanced at the fully stocked liquor cabinet and again at the books. Liked to have a good time. Liked to feel that she was above the norm. He spotted a folder on the bar.

2

A program from a seminar: *Past Lives, Future Glory*. A name tag was next to it. "Hi, My name is *Missy*."

She was the kind of young woman who would adore L.A., the largest collective case of arrested development in contemporary America.

He moved to the fireplace. He glanced down. Phony logs. He gazed at the mantelpiece. Framed pictures. An older couple with a dog. "To Missy. Merry Christmas. Mom, Dad, and Caesar." Another photo of the same couple with the girl. She was younger then. Maybe sixteen. Still pretty, though. White skin. Freckles. Red Hair. Green eyes. She must have driven the boys wild in high school. Probably the kind of girl who didn't notice it, though. The photo caught her in a natural, unassuming pose. The parents were stiff, conscious of the camera. The girl, however, was completely at ease.

She would have been the type who was at ease anywhere, he theorized.

Another photo: Missy in a bathing suit. Two-piece, string-type bikini. Very recent. Good figure. He leaned closer to the photo. From the background, he could tell it was taken at the marina. Not far from her apartment. Two miles. Lurking in the shadows behind her, two potbellied lounge-lizard types with wigs that merited a carpet cleaner tried to stare down her bikini top. The girl, however, frozen in Kodachrome time forever, seemed blissfully unaware of it all.

He smiled to himself. She probably knew the guys were there and couldn't care less.

"Good for you, Missy." He smiled.

He caught a glimpse of himself in the mirror behind the photos. He winced involuntarily. His brown hair was too long and tinged with white. His eyes were showing the wear and tear of long hours and short paychecks; heavy-lidded, crow's-feet-encased. His face was beginning to show the ravages of happy hours that went on for days. What the hell was he doing prowling around this apartment, this homage to free-spirited times? He glanced at Missy's photos again. Young and proud of it.

He heard a sound from the bedroom.

His concentration faltered. He remembered Missy as she was now. Nude. Spread-eagled. Battered. Blood-soaked. Clawing at the crimson-spattered sheets.

He reached for the cigarettes in his shirt pocket. They weren't there. He glanced at the end table next to the snow-white couch. The pack stood leaning against a brass lamp. He walked over and retrieved it.

Getting sloppy.

There was something about this one that rattled him. It just felt a little too squirrely. Nothing he could put his finger on, though.

"Lieutenant?"

Broskey turned around. Two older forensics men stood in the doorway of the bedroom, sweating in their lightweight suits. Two young plainclothesmen stared out from behind them, in Duran Duran outfits. Broskey stared at the younger cops, cursing the day "Miami Vice" ever hit the tube. None of the four seemed too upset by the mess inside. Clinical detachment. Either you had it or you broke.

Broskey slid the pack of cigarettes back into the pocket of his short-sleeved shirt. He knew what they were going to tell him.

The heavier of the forensics men, a crew-cut grimace built onto a barrel-shaped body, chewed on a slice of gum as he spoke. It was like listening to a cow. "No sign of forced entry. Dusted for prints on the windows and the doors. We have a heap of them but I have the feeling—"

"Most of them will be the girl's." Broskey finished.

"Autopsy will show more, but right now looks like she's been dead a good twelve hours."

Broskey nodded. "Died about eleven last night. Chance of latent prints?"

"We picked up a couple around the face and the breasts."

Broskey nodded. They probably wouldn't do much good. Unless the guy was a local or on the FBI list, it would be slow going trying to trace the prints. There were 17,513 police agencies in America. Three thousand counties. Exchanging information wasn't the easiest thing in the world.

4

"Neighbors didn't hear a thing," one of the plainclothes-men added.

"I'm shocked." Broskey smirked. "Sexual?"

"Yup." The heavier of the two forensics men nodded. "Don't know whether it was post-mortem or ante-mortem, though."

Broskey entered the bedroom. A small wave of blood stained the pale green wall above the headboard of the bed. What was left of the woman's face was smothered beneath a pillow.

"Nasty way to go." The heavyset man sighed, checking the notes. "Bruises on the breasts, heavy bruises on the vagina." He pointed to a beer bottle already placed in a plastic bag. "She was . . ."

Broskey waved a hand. The heavyset man lapsed into silence. Broskey lifted the pillow from the dead girl's face. The heavyset man continued, still pointing at the bottle. "Probably used it on her head as well."

A stocking was wrapped around the woman's neck. Broskey couldn't help but grimace, remembering the fresh-faced sixteen-year-old in the photo outside. "This guy didn't take any chances, did he? I'm surprised he didn't nuke the place."

"Maybe she just picked up the wrong guy at the wrong bar," one of the plainclothesmen offered. "You know how college kids are. Pretty girl. Shows some leg. Teases some geek. Brings him home. He comes on strong. He won't take no for an ans—"

"Yeah, probably all her fault," Broskey said, flashing the plainclothesman a Medusa look. "How old are you . . . ?"

"McDonald," the plainclothesman said, a dribble of sweat sneaking from beneath his moussed-up hair.

"How old are you, McDonald?"

"Twenty-seven, Lieutenant."

"Twenty-seven." Broskey nodded. "Keep your fantasies to yourself until you're at least thirty or have kicked MTV, okay?"

Broskey walked around the bed. He got down on his knees and glanced under it. Torn panties. Dress. No brassiere.

He stared at the bedspread. Tiny red roses. Stained. "Semen?" he asked.

"Uh-uh," the heavyset man replied. "Not a hell of a lot of physical evidence around, other than that."

"Saliva?"

"Throat, breasts, ears, vagina, feet. We swabbed."

Broskey blinked. "Feet?"

"A passionate man," the heavyset man said, with no trace of irony in his voice.

Broskey felt the hair on the back of his neck tingle. There was something about this . . .

He walked to the bureau. Purse in place. He took a pen and opened it. Wallet inside. Cash.

He turned to the four men. "Okay. We have a very ugly homicide. Sexual assault. No robbery. No forced entry. Someone she knew or worked with."

The second plainclothesman consulted his notepad. "The victim—"

"She had a name, didn't she?" Broskey snapped, staring at the kid's haircut. The haircut probably cost more than Broskey's suit.

"Yes sir. Patricia Sharone, age twenty-one. Student at Bay City College. English major. Born and raised in Washington. Parents still live there. Moved out here three years ago. She had a part-time job at Music Max, a rock club on Pico."

"What shift?"

"Night. I think."

"All right. Get down there. You have the outfit for it. I want to know who she hung out with, who she worked with, who she liked, who she disliked, how she got along with the patrons."

"Yes sir."

"Oh, Officer McDonald?"

"Yes sir?"

"You might want to check out her class schedule at the college."

"Yes sir."

The two plainclothesmen left the room in a hurry, leaving Broskey with the two forensics men, veterans of the limbo

6

known as homicide. Although he was only thirty-eight, Broskey felt more at home with the older guys on the force than with the embryonic supercops. The heavier of the two men, Goldstein, chuckled out loud.

"You don't like that kid much, do you, Lieutenant?"

Broskey fished a cigarette out of his pack and lit it. "I don't dislike him. I hate his attitude, though. If someone does somebody's mother, it's a crime. If someone does a pretty woman, she's the cause of it all. Tell me the logic in that?"

Goldstein shrugged, chewing his gum furiously while smelling the smoke from Broskey's cigarette.

"I hate the way he dresses, too," Broskey muttered, imagining McDonald driving out to the campus with a loud Phil Collins tape playing in the car. Wimp rock. One notch above the Eagles and the stuff they piped into dentists' offices.

Goldstein's nostrils flared; he was reveling in the cigarette odor.

Broskey exhaled. "It's a filthy habit, Goldstein. You should be proud that you quit."

"Oh, I am, sir," the sergeant said mournfully. He spat out the gum into his hand. "But I wish they'd invent a sugarless gum that didn't taste like shit."

"One hurdle at a time," Broskey said.

"You know, Broskey, you could add seven or eight years to your life if you quit smoking."

Broskey nodded. "I could add ten if I quit this job." But why bother, he noted mentally.

He headed for the front door, surprising a uniformed cop in the hallway. "Get the gurney in here."

He jogged down the stairs, wheezing slightly. Maybe sugarless gum was the answer. He stepped outside into the bright sunlight. You could smell the ocean seven blocks away. He gazed at the trim, tan, and vacant faces of the onlookers standing behind the police barricades. In an hour or two, they'd forget the crime and would be back to their volleyball games in Venice.

He climbed into his car and sat for a moment. He

shouldn't have snapped at McDonald. He bled to reporters like a verbal hemophiliac. Let the papers think it was date rape. Let them think it was a simple lust murder. Broskey couldn't figure out why exactly, but he just had this feeling that whoever did Missy had done other women as well. In spite of the violence, the rage . . . there was something methodical about it.

Something too neat.

He found himself getting angry on the girl's behalf. He had to be careful about that. That made for a bad cop—Broskey smiled to himself—but a wonderful human being.

Broskey glanced at his Mickey Mouse watch, a gift from Janet. Maybe he'd knock off an hour early today. His stomach didn't feel so hot. It never felt that great, but today it felt like he had hamsters wearing cleats jogging around his intestinal track.

"All units," his radio squawked.

Then again, why knock off early?

"Possible hostage situation on Pier Street."

Broskey sighed. He heard a black-and-white unit respond. He picked up the microphone in his car. What the hell, he *had* majored in psychology.

"Broskey, here. I'm on my way."

He pulled the car slowly out of the apartment complex. Pier Street was near a pretty good pizza parlor, he remembered. That would settle his stomach.

Within minutes, he pulled up outside a two-story beach house, one of those quaint gingerbread types built for the very rich in the 1920s, owned by middle-class stiffs in the sixties, and now renovated by the nouveau blow-dried in the eighties.

Two black-and-whites were outside the house, the uniformed cops crouched behind them.

A woman in an aerobics outfit with a hairdo that made Cyndi Lauper's look tame was clutching a similarly clad eight-year-old girl while shrieking at the police.

"He's shooting! He's shooting! He's insane! He'll kill me! Kill my life! My life!"

Broskey grimaced, suddenly remembering the sound of fingernails on a blackboard. He slid out of his car and duck-walked up to the black-and-whites.

"It's all right, lady," he said calmly. "Who's shooting?"

"Who the fuck are you?" the woman demanded.

"Lieutenant Kevin Broskey, ma'am."

"Well, it's about time!" she said. "These . . . these . . ." She motioned to the uniformed cops.

"Policemen," Broskey interjected helpfully.

"Ball-less cowards," she continued, "are letting him . . . kill . . . kill . . ."

"All right, ma'am," Broskey said in a soothing tone. "Who's inside—"

"He's *killing* . . ."

He looked at the little girl. She stuck her tongue out at him. He thought briefly about the advantages of birth control. "Are there any more children inside?"

"No," the woman answered.

"Relatives?"

"No."

"Pets?"

"No."

Broskey winced as a *pop, pop, pop* sound echoed from the house. The woman wailed, causing him to wince a second time. He glanced over the hood of the police car. Sounded like a handgun. Twenty-two, maybe. "Who's inside, ma'am?"

"My husband Arnold! He's insane!"

"Uh-huh. Does Arnold have a last name?"

"Henry. Arnold Henry. He's insane. He's a *killer!*"

Broskey grabbed a bullhorn from one of the uniformed men. "Any shots fired in your direction?" he whispered.

"No, sir," the officer said. "When we got here, the guy was holed up in the house and this . . . lady was in the front yard with her—"

The little girl stuck her tongue out at the cop.

"—*kid,* screaming her head off."

"Get them into my car," Broskey said.

"Yes sir."

The officer ushered the woman and child away from the scene. Broskey picked up the bullhorn. "Arnold? Arnold Henry? This is Lieutenant Kevin Broskey. I'm here to help you. Can you hear me, Arnold?"

Pop. Pop. Pop.

"Now, Arnold. I know you're upset, but if it's okay with you, I'm just going to walk slowly up to the front door and come inside, okay, Arnold?"

Pop. Pop.

"Okay, Arnold? I just want to talk to you, okay?"

Silence.

"All right," came a voice from inside the house. "I'm done anyway."

Broskey heard the woman wail from inside his car. She sounded like a cat in a blender.

Broskey put down the bullhorn and walked slowly toward the house. He stepped up to the front door. Inside, he could hear an old Steppenwolf album blasting on the stereo. "Born to be wiiiild," the speakers growled.

Broskey eased his .38 out of his shoulder holster and knocked on the front door.

"Arnold? It's Kevin. Can I come in?"

"Sure. Door's open."

He eased the door open and stepped into a very classy setup, with a trendy southwestern design and paintings of cow skulls and nouveau Hopi grandmas. In the middle of the vast living room sat a sweating, clean-cut man, late thirties, black hair. He wore a faded pair of cutoffs, an ancient "Give Peace A Chance" T-shirt, and a head-band.

"Arnold?"

"The gun's on the table next to the door." Arnold sighed. "I'm finished."

Broskey gingerly pocketed the revolver.

"I have a license for it," Arnold said, nodding his head back and forth to the music.

"That's good, Arnold." Broskey eased himself into a pseudo-corral chair across from Arnold.

"Want to talk about it, Arnold?"

"Naaaah," Arnold said, nodding to the music. "Like a true nature's child, we were born, born to be wiiild," he chanted along.

Broskey got to his feet, inspecting the damage. The VCR had been shot. Four Jane Fonda aerobics tapes had been plugged, the TV set shattered. Compact-disc player blown to long-playing heaven. "Just stay put, Arnold," Broskey said, knowing the worst was over.

He walked into the next room, which was an exercise area. It was probably a library once upon a time when people still read. A very expensive electronic exercise bike was riddled with bullets, a rowing machine whittled away into Davy Jones's locker.

In the kitchen, the microwave, the food processor, and the cutesy electronic clock/radio/TV were on death's door.

Broskey returned to the living room. Steppenwolf was on another track. So was Arnold.

"Arnold," Broskey whispered. "Let's talk about this."

Arnold Henry sighed, got up, and lowered the stereo. "I had to kill them," he said, tears dribbling down his cheeks.

Broskey tensed. "Kill who?"

"Not who, *what . . . them!*" Arnold said, gesturing to the house around him. "Those *things.* Those things that began taking over."

"Taking over . . . like in . . . your life?"

"Right on." Arnold nodded. "I mean, can't you see?" He knelt down in front of Broskey. "You saw my wife and my kid. Look at them! They're monsters! Monsters that were created by this . . . shit! My wife used to be a person, you know. A long time ago I was, too. Things mattered then. I met her in college. We believed in things. The earth. Peace. No nukes. We had ideas in our heads. We had love in our hearts. Remember Woodstock?"

"Couldn't make it," Broskey said.

"Me neither." Arnold sighed. "But it was a great flick. We got married. I got a job. Advertising. I got promoted. I got promoted again. Made a lot of money . . . and things changed. We had a daughter and we had things, too many things. And the things started to change us. The things started to make *us* things, too. We had no ideas anymore. We had no feelings. All we had was . . ."

Arnold gestured wildly, mutely.

"Things," Broskey noted.

"Right. Things. I mean, I started waking up in the morning and wondering, What for? I'd look at my wife and my kid and it was like *The Stepford Wives* or something. Do you know what it's like to come home from work and see your family dancing to a television screen?"

Arnold twisted his face into an expression only a gargoyle could love. "It was grotesque."

"I hear you."

"You're about my age," Arnold said.

"I suppose."

"Then you remember how it used to be. Robert Kennedy. Gene McCarthy? Peace now? Hell no, we won't go? *Lord of the Rings?*"

Broskey nodded as Arnold went on. "Well, I woke up this morning *missing* all that. I woke up, looked at my family, and missed what they used to be, what they could have been. So I came home from work early, found some of my old clothes, one of my old records, and assassinated the killers of my family."

Broskey slowly led Arnold to the front door. "The things."

"Exactly." Arnold smiled. "You understand, don't you?"

Broskey opened the front door and turned Arnold over to one of the waiting officers. There were two more black-and-white units purring in front. "I do understand, Arnold. I really do."

And he did.

"Do you think I did right?" Arnold asked, waiting for approval.

"In a very symbolic way, Arnold, you did the best any caring person could do."

Arnold flashed Broskey a wide smile as two uniformed cops led him to a black-and-white. Broskey sighed. They'd probably put the guy in a laughing academy for a brief stay. He'd lose his job and his family and find himself starting out all over again alone.

"He's a madman!" came a scream from behind him. Mrs. Henry was standing at the front door to the house, gazing at her shattered VCR and aerobics tape that would never see Spandex again.

Broskey watched the cop car housing Arnold pull away.

Maybe a laughing academy was a viable alternative to this little domestic scene.

"He's crazy! Totally insane!" the woman cried, rushing into the living room and yanking the Steppenwolf album off the turntable. She smashed it against her stretch-pants-wrapped leg, shattering it.

"He gets in these moods and listens to this old shit! I hate this shit! I hate it! Windham Hill Records? He wouldn't think of them! He's a fiend! I want him prosecuted!"

"Yes, ma'am," Broskey said, allowing two uniformed cops the pleasure of counseling the distraught harpy.

"All the time, listening to this old shit!" she screeched.

Broskey got into his car. An hour later, he was sprawled across the ratty couch in his rented bungalow on the Bay City/Venice border. He held a slice of cold pizza in one hand and a glass of vodka in the other.

The TV was on. The sound off. The picture of Missy that was taken at the marina was on the screen.

His stereo, the one he had owned since college, blasted Cream's *Disraeli Gears* album. The familiar guitar riff of "Sunshine of Your Love" cut through the room like a dull but reliable knife.

Broskey nodded his head in time, trying not to stare at Missy's picture on the tube.

In an instant, the guitar riff had faded, replaced by a wall of ear-shattering static.

Broskey sighed, tossed the half-eaten pizza and the half-guzzled glass onto the coffee table, and walked up to the amplifier. He slammed it with the flat of his hand.

The static dissipated.

When he returned to the couch, Missy's picture was no longer on the TV screen, replaced by video footage of a body bag being wheeled into an awaiting ambulance.

He was glad he had a black-and-white Sony. Somehow, it made it all less real.

He settled down on the couch and took a long hit of vodka. Ginger Baker embarked on a small drum solo, filling the room with a twenty-year-old musical frenzy.

Broskey would postpone reality until tomorrow morning when, as always, it would hit him right between the eyes.

Two

Kevin Broskey had a clock radio in his living room that didn't work. It told the wrong time and never seemed to zero in on one station. In a perverse way, he admired that clock radio. It had a mind of its own and wasn't afraid to use it.

Broskey didn't have to rely on the radio to wake him. His block was filled with small, cramped two-bedroom homes that usually housed ten people or more. Mostly Hispanic workers. Some illegals. They'd get up at five o'clock in the morning, turn their radios on at Panzer-tank volume, and prepare to meet the trucks that would take them to the unofficial day-worker spots on Olympic in West Los Angeles. Between the radios, the trucks, and screaming babies, Broskey would have had to have been deaf not to wake up.

And, there was Mrs. Ramirez next door, who would spend each morning screaming at God and the Blessed Virgin. Some days, God and the Blessed Virgin seemed to scream back. Visitations by long-dead martyrs and archangels were big at her house as well. Once, Mrs. Ramirez claimed she saw St. Theresa's face in a bowl of Jell-O.

To this day, Broskey couldn't watch Bill Cosby commercials without thinking of religion.

For Mrs. Ramirez, religion came in a bottle with a little

sticker that read "100 proof." What the hell, God works in mysterious ways.

Broskey lay, sprawled on the couch, still fully clothed, when the phone rang. He slowly slid off the chair and, sitting cross-legged on the floor, reached for the receiver. The mouthpiece still had pizza crumbs on it.

Mrs. Ramirez was shrieking at St. Anthony, something to do with the neighborhood cats eating the birds in her yard.

"Are you up?" said a female voice.

Broskey had to think about that one. "I guess."

"Have you seen the morning paper?"

Broskey shook his head clear, staring at the empty glass on the coffee table. He heard the tension in Sergeant Fine's voice.

"What time is it?" he mumbled.

"Six."

"Then I haven't seen the morning paper. I haven't even watched 'Captain Kangaroo' yet."

"Do you want me to tell you about it or do you want to read it?"

"Give me a minute. Hold on."

Broskey put the phone down on the couch and walked to the front door. Damn. He had fallen asleep with the door unlocked again. No matter, there was nothing much worth stealing in the house. He opened the door. A transient sat on the front step, reading Broskey's copy of the *L.A. Trib.* The transient didn't seem to mind the intrusion.

"Morning, Lieutenant," the transient said, flashing a jack-o'-lantern grin.

"Morning, Bud," Broskey replied. "Can I see that a minute?"

"Mind if I keep the sports section? There's a good article on that doubleheader yesterday."

"Keep it. I haven't followed baseball since the Giants left New York."

"I never knew they were there. I heard of the football Giants being there. But they're someplace else now."

"New Jersey."

Broskey fished in his pocket and pulled out a handful of

change. He handed it to Bud. "Here. Get yourself some coffee."

"Thanks, Lieutenant. Store-bought coffee is a lot better than the stuff you drink."

"No problem." Broskey returned inside, gaping at the headline: PORN QUEEN RAPED AND MUTILATED IN BAY CITY. There was a picture of Missy. There was a byline under the headline: Jake Mayer. "Shit," Broskey hissed.

He turned to the phone. "What the hell is this?"

"Turns out our co-ed led a double life."

"Why does the *Trib* know this and we don't?"

"He's *your* buddy," Sergeant Fine replied.

"Not anymore. How bad is this?" Broskey asked.

"A couple of night-shift guys said they could hear the chief reading it clear across town."

"Was he moving his lips?"

"Not funny."

"Let me shave. I'll get there when I get there."

"Don't panic, Lieutenant. I ran down the story. Your co-ed was an extra in an R-rated slasher film. Softcore at best. Lots of blood and bad effects. Let's just say the *Trib* exaggerated."

"What a surprise," Broskey replied. "We still should've known about it. Have officers McDonald and whatever his partner's name is . . . the Ken doll?"

"Bluth."

"Have them in my office in an hour. Andrea?"

"Yes, Lieutenant?"

"Thanks." Broskey hung up the phone and turned on the TV. The local morning-news program was showing the same footage of the previous day's crime scene. Broskey knew the routine. It would be shown all morning, probably all night, until some smart programmer could get footage of the dead girl from the slasher film. That would be coupled with interviews with shocked friends who were a) appalled over her death; b) more appalled over her double life; c) glad to be on TV.

He walked into the kitchen and turned on the hot water. He didn't have time for a shower. Taking a paper towel, he wet it and smeared it across his face. He tossed some shaving cream, strategically located next to the Oreos, onto his face and began raking off the stubble. The phone rang a second time. He pulled the phone into the kitchen and continued shaving.

"Broskey," he announced flatly.

"Kev?"

Broskey sighed. This was just what he needed. "What do you want, Janet?"

"Kev, why do you sound so upset when I call you?"

Broskey blinked, using a small mirror to guide the movements of his razor. Why did she think? She had left him, not the other way around, taking most of his furniture, his savings, and a good deal of his emotional stability. Plus, she had the habit of calling him at daybreak, before she could go jogging in her five-hundred-dollar sweat outfit. "How much do you need?"

"Two hundred. I invested my last paycheck in the Lemurian Stairstep Temple . . ."

"A pyramid." Broskey sighed. "You put your money into a pyramid scheme."

"Kevin, you're so earthbound."

"And you're broke, Janet. Pyramid schemes. Ponzi games. They're not investments. They're rip-offs. One of the oldest form of rip-offs in the book."

"But I was guided by—"

"Yeah, yeah, this week's guru. I can give you a hundred. I'm tight this week. I had to buy new tires."

"Thanks, Kevvy. Can I pick up the check at your office?"

He almost sliced his throat on that concept. "I'll have some one drop it off."

"You're a dear."

"A regular prince, I know. I gotta go."

Broskey hung up the phone and then took the receiver off the hook. Let it beep away in a perpetual busy signal. He finished shaving, wiped his face off with a dishtowel, and headed for the bedroom and a change of clothes.

He thought, briefly, of Janet before Atlantis, Ancient Egypt, Lemuria, Ramtha, loquacious Space Creatures, and a BBC documentary director named Fenton Ducke. She had been pretty special then, with a mind all her own. More headstrong than his clock radio. She had goals and ambition, a real powerhouse. They'd been happy for a while.

He smiled grimly to himself, lacing up his shoes. He'd pretty much forgotten what it was like to be happy.

He stepped out into the living room, passing by the TV set. The screen was full of snow. Happiness is fleeting, he surmised. Like the reception on his Sony.

He grabbed the half-eaten slice of pizza from the coffee table and chewed absentmindedly on it as he headed out the door. Bud was still on the front steps. "Here you go, Lieutenant," the transient said, handing Broskey a Styrofoam cup. "I got you a cup, too. I figured you didn't have any in the house."

Broskey looked down at the dirt-encrusted man. "Thanks, Bud."

He trotted to his car, hesitating for a moment. "Hey, Bud," Broskey called. "I've always been meaning to ask you. Where are you from?"

"Philly." Bud smiled proudly. "I was an investment counselor."

Broskey nodded. "Nice town," he said, getting into his car. "Nice job."

"Yeah," Bud said, lapsing into a Katharine Hepburn sigh, "but I ratha wanted to come out here and get a taste of the rally *good* life."

"Didn't we all," Broskey said, starting up the engine.

Ten minutes later, Broskey was seated in a smoke-filled room, next to Officers McDonald and Bluth and before the source of most of the smoke, a very irate Police Chief Donald Medega. Medega was chewing a cigar while guzzling Mylanta. His face resembled a Michelin Guide to facial ticks, each pockmark taking on a life of its own.

"There's no excuse for this," he said for the tenth time, pointing to the front page of the *Trib*.

"I know that, sir," Broskey replied.

"And he's supposed to be a *friend* of yours," Medega said evenly, his nostrils flaring.

"Past tense," Broskey answered. *"Was* a friend."

"Why didn't we know about this porno shit?" Medega asked with a crocodile smile.

"Well, sir," Broskey began. "The investigating officers were—"

"Ah, the Pep Boys," Medega said, glaring at McDonald and Bluth.

The two young plainclothesmen withered under Medega's gaze. "All right," Medega said, still smiling. "Here's what you do. You follow up your friend Jake's lead. You investigate our gal's involvement in this porno film. You interview the cast. The crew. Anybody involved with it. You see if there's a connection between the murder and the porn industry."

"But, sir," Broskey began.

"I don't want to hear it," Medega replied, the veins on his neck forming something resembling a penmanship guide. "We're going to have the mayor on our ass for this. She's sucking up to the moral watchdog bunch. She's pulling tit tapes off shelves. Rock records out of stores. Monitoring local radio shows. If it means taking a few days or a week to placate the moronic little twit, then do it. Just give me details on your plans within the hour. Our beloved mayor has called a press conference for ten. I'd like to have a rebuttal in hand by nine-fifty-nine. Got that?"

Broskey stared at the ceiling. He began counting the tiles. "Got that?" Medega repeated.

Eighteen. Nineteen. Twenty. "Yes sir," Broskey said.

He and the officers left the room. "In my office, kids." Broskey smiled to the plainclothesmen sweetly.

The two men followed Broskey into a small cubicle that boasted a door. That made the area an office. The rest of the floor had cubicles without doors. They were known as spaces.

The plainclothesmen sat down. "Sir," McDonald began, "I can explain."

"No, you can't," Broskey said, putting a cigarette in his mouth and lighting it. "You can try to explain but you can't really explain. You can't tell me why you neglected to pick up a small piece of information that, thanks to your idiocy, has now become a major headline. A major headline that's going to waste our time, our manpower, and our resources. A major headline that, in my humble opinion, is going to take us miles away from any leads that we *should* be following. A major headline that's going to attract every kook, every columnist, every commentator in Los Angeles County. A headline that's going to spawn think pieces in newspapers, fancy features in Sunday magazines, and titillating exposés on every TV news show in town."

Broskey took a deep drag. He heard his lungs squeak. "No, Officer McDonald, you cannot really explain anything to me right now."

McDonald gulped. Even his hair looked wilted. "Well, actually, sir, if I may . . ."

"Please, officer," Broskey said, holding his palm up. "Cease and desist. I am armed. No court in the land would convict me of homicide right now. I believe the term they'd use would be something along the lines of 'an exercise in Social Darwinism.' You know, eliminate the pinheads so the species can survive?"

McDonald suddenly found his shoes fascinating.

"Okay." Broskey sighed. "Within the hour, I want you to find out the name and location of the producers of this film epic. I want you to type up a step-by-step bullshit memo of how you're going to run this down. You *can* type, can't you, McDonald?"

"Yes sir."

"Good. Then your years in the Police Academy were not wasted. Now, get out of my sight for an hour. I want to rest my brain."

The two men shuffled out of his office.

Broskey sighed and slumped down in his chair. He had lost control of his life around 1956. Kindergarten took a lot out of him.

"Knock. Knock."

Broskey looked up. Sergeant Andy Fine stood in the doorway, a smile that hovered somewhere between amusement and pity on her face. "May I come in?"

"My cubicle is your cubicle."

The sergeant, a blond woman in her early thirties with the oldest eyes Broskey had ever seen, emptied two armfuls of stuff on his desk.

"What's this?" Broskey asked.

"The runny yellow gunk in plastic is eggs from the diner downstairs. I figured you hadn't had breakfast yet."

"Thanks."

"The semisolid stuff in the cup is coffee."

"What would I do without you, Andy?"

"Wither and die, probably." She shrugged. She pointed to two file folders. "I figured you'd be wanting these, too."

"Homicide folders?"

"Women victims. Ten in the last six months. Two unsolved."

Broskey flipped open the file of unsolved homicides. He glanced through them. "Bingo."

"Both students at Bay City College." Andy smiled sweetly. "I peeked."

"I knew it," Broskey said, unwrapping his nuked-out eggs. "We have ourselves a pattern here." He stuck a fork in the eggs. The eggs slithered around the prongs. He picked up a plastic spoon and began shoveling the eggs in. He took one swallow. "Christ! If we do have a pattern here . . ."

"We have one sick puppy on the loose." Andy nodded.

Broskey glanced through the coroner's reports. "Sexual molestation—"

"Preceded and followed by some violence."

"Necrophilia?"

"Doesn't seem to play that way. Both girls were killed either during or after intercourse."

Broskey frowned. The word "intercourse" made it sound so normal. "Nothing after their deaths?"

The sergeant leaned forward on Broskey's desk. "A lot of rough-trade stuff. Bite marks. Minor-league mutilation. The killings themselves, however, were pretty brutal."

"So I see."

"The apartments were clean as well. No signs of robbery. No forced entry. Everything was left untouched except in

22

the bedroom. They were pretty much trashed as a result of the killings."

"Have you told anybody about this?"

"Like who? The Hardy Boys? McDonald would only leak it to the press."

"I thought *I* was the only one who knew he did that."

"Broskey, even the janitors know he does that."

"Okay. Let's keep this to ourselves for a while. The chief is going to want us to play up the porn angle. And while our intrepid officers are hunting down T-and-A leads—"

"You'll make the campus scene."

"I've always loved the world of academia."

"You had four calls when you were in with the firebreather."

Broskey abandoned the eggs and concentrated on the coffee. For that, he needed the fork. "Who called?"

"Your wife."

"Ex-wife . . ."

"A rep from Geraldo Rivera's office. They're doing a show on snuff films."

"How timely."

"An Arnold Henry called from Saint Regis Hospital, woo-woo ward. He just wanted to say thanks."

"I hope he'll be happy there."

"And your pal, Jake Mayer called from the *Trib*. Wanted to know if you could meet him for dinner tonight."

Broskey pushed the gelatinous coffee down before it could evolve into an ambulatory life-form. If Jake wanted to meet him, it meant Jake had a reason. They didn't pal around much anymore. Not after the story Jake had written about Janet and the British fowl. It had been a couple of years since they'd spoken.

"Where does he want to meet?" he asked.

"A place called Music Max."

Broskey slammed his hand down on his desk. "That's near the Bay City College campus, isn't it?"

"A block away."

Broskey's face reddened. "He knows. He's made the connection."

The sergeant took away the alleged eggs and coffee. "I'll give these a Christian burial. What are you going to do about Mayer?"

"I don't know. See if we can use him before he gets a chance to use us."

"Nice trick. What about your other calls?"

"Tell my ex-wife I've died, Rivera to get a day job, and Mr. Henry that I may be sharing a suite with him soon."

"You got it."

"And could you get a time from Mayer for dinner? I don't want to talk to the jerk until I have to."

The sergeant nodded. Broskey watched Andy leave the office. He leaned back in his chair. Maybe rooming with Mr. Henry at St. Regis would be good for him. Get himself a prefrontal lobe job. His insurance would probably cover it. Concentrate on staring vacantly out windows. Waving bye-bye to passing strangers. It sounded like a good career move right about now.

He began counting the tiles on the ceiling. He knew there were a hundred and eighty. He counted them every day. Perhaps, one day, the tiles would surprise him and add one or two to their ranks. It would be their way of saying "Thanks for all your devotion." At any rate, staring at them helped him relax until the next disaster.

"Lieutenant?" came McDonald's voice. "We have that memo done up."

Broskey sighed and tore his attention away from the tiles. He had only counted up to sixty.

Three

Music Max was a solidly nondescript place on Pico
Avenue, the kind of loud, dark, transient club Los Angeles is
famous for. Start a club. Attract attention. Establish a
clientele. Have your rent raised six hundred percent. In six
months it'll be a Radio Shack.

Pico used to have a personality way back when, full of
stucco houses smushed against phony Tudor homes, hastily
constructed Spanish castles resting alongside a homesick
architect's Cape Cod dream. Now it was nothing more than
auto-clogged pavement. The kind of concrete alley that
would have felt at home in New Jersey, with mini-malls and
uninspired buildings lining its sides.

Joints like Music Max.

Broskey was on time, a useless habit in laid-back Los
Angeles, but one of the few good ones he had left.

He knew Jake would be fashionably late.

He nestled into a table near the corner of the bar and
ordered a double shot of vodka with a tonic chaser.

The bar area of the club was dimly lit, but it was clearly
obnoxious. Guys with tons of mousse mingled with girls
with tons of teeth. They spouted the latest buzz words and
talked about their future "agents," "deals," "options," and
"extra work."

The "dance floor" in the next room was dark and unimaginative, lit with lights that would have made any airport runway proud.

This evening, it seemed that the house deejay was pleased as punch to play the Billy Idol oldie "White Wedding" over and over again, with the bass turned up to King Kong volume. To Broskey's ears, it sounded like a Johnny Weissmuller film festival. Tribal drums. Elephant bellows. Little else.

He nursed his drink and thought about Jake Mayer. They had grown up together. Lower-class, New Jersey background. Both had wanted to leave Routes 1 and 9 and Standard Oil refineries behind from the time they were teenagers.

They went to high school together (Roselle Catholic, although Mayer wasn't Catholic, just a fast talker) and even attended college together (Newark State Teachers College, later renamed Keane College for no apparent reason. The twosome, from that point onward, had referred to their alma mater as the "Neat School").

After graduation, they had both decided to move to New York. Jake immediately gravitated toward journalism while Broskey lurched from job to job, dream to dream, refusing to pay attention to his teaching certificate. Eventually, Broskey drifted west and wound up attending the Los Angeles Police Academy. It was something to do, and his degree in psychology didn't hurt his chance for promotion. Jake had unexpectedly become a major force in journalism, constantly being wooed by big papers with big paychecks.

While Broskey had worked hard to establish a career, keep a marriage from floundering, keep his head screwed on straight, Jake had written books, hosted a late-night news show, and even guested in a few TV cop shows (playing himself, of course).

And now, Jake was the newest star in Los Angeles, where constellations seem to arise once every twenty-four hours. He was the street rat of the *Trib*, the lone reporter who seemed to enjoy poking journalistic sticks into the underbelly of the city. If there was dirt to be found, Jake would find it.

The amazing thing was that Jake Mayer never got into trouble for writing things that would have landed other reporters into slander city. Jake was, well, *Jake*. He charmed information out of people. The poor saps he screwed were almost proud to see their names in print under Jake's byline.

Broskey ordered an appetizer from the bar. They were supposed to be nachos but they looked like mutated potato chips. They seemed to be hemorrhaging as well.

The deejay began playing Talking Heads. The bass was still on rhino when Broskey heard his name being yodeled. "Kev-vin."

Broskey sighed, half expecting to see Tarzan, Jane, and Boy swing in. Instead, he was greeted by the compact, wiry, always animated form of Jake Mayer.

Broskey stared at his old friend. This was the guy who had broken the story of his wife's affair in the papers before Broskey had been aware of it. He had wanted to strangle Jake at that point. Instead, he canceled his subscription to the *Trib*. It seemed more constructive.

Eventually, when he renewed his subscription, he had to pay more for it.

Jake flashed his patented, boyish smile and held up two plastic knives like a crucifix in front of Broskey. "Here. You can keep me at bay with these."

Broskey rolled his eyes. Jake planted the crucifix in Broskey's alleged nacho pile and began writhing in front of the bar, clutching a bar stool. He began to screech in a Bela Lugosi accent. "I haff been twapped by de lonk arm of de laawwwww."

A woman on a stool next to Jake, who couldn't have been more than twenty, stared at the flailing reporter. "Are you having an attack or something, mister?"

Jake straightened up to his full five-foot-four-inch height and smiled at the woman. "Thank you. I'm fine, now. War wound."

"Sit down, will you?" Broskey said, smirking. "Before you get us thrown out."

Jake pulled up a chair and slid next to Broskey's small table. "They can't throw us out. You're a cop. You carrying?"

Broskey nodded.

"Kev-vin has a gu-un. Kev-vin has a gu-un," Jake began to chant. "I'm telling the bar-ten-der."

"Will you cut it out?" Broskey hissed.

"Have you fired that thing yet?" Jake asked.

"Nope."

"Kev-in is a wus-sy, Kev-in is a wus-sy," Jake chanted.

Broskey sighed. "Are you drunk?"

"Nope." Jake shrugged. "Not yet, anyhow. I'm always like this, remember?"

Broskey nodded, smiling. He *did* remember. Jake used to get away with the craziest stunts in school. It seemed that during their long friendship, it was Jake's job to get them into messes, Broskey's job to figure out how to get out of them.

"You still mad at me, Kev?" Jake asked, suddenly serious.

Broskey shrugged. "I hadn't really thought about it lately."

"It wasn't my fault," Jake said. "It was a good story. Plus, that director guy was parading your wife all over town. I would've hadda been Ray Charles to ignore that."

Broskey had never really thought about it from that angle. "I suppose. You have your job to do."

"Oh, thank you, thank you," Jake said, removing the crucifix from the oozing nachos. "I guess we can get rid of this, then. A cross wouldn't have worked on me, anyhow. I'm Jewish. Ever wonder about why all vampires are Catholic? I mean, you never see Van Helsing in those movies trying to construct a Star of David. Imagine if he ran across a Druid vampire. He'd have to lug Stonehenge over half of England. I wonder if they had trusses in those days? Can't you just see that big finale? Van Helsing comes lumbering up to Dracula's castle carrying these big stones. 'Stop, you inhuman fiend! I'll . . . aaaaarrrgh!' Dracula stands there, not knowing what's going on. 'Are you okay?' Van Helsing's lying there, squirming. 'Yeah. No problem. I think I tore something. You got a cold compress?" I tell you, Kev. People in Hollywood have no imagination."

Broskey began to laugh. It had always been impossible for him to stay angry at Jake face-to-face.

"Oh, my God!" Jake cried. "It's the laughing policeman! Didn't they make a movie out of that?"

"I don't know," Broskey said, ordering another drink. "I don't see many movies."

"Are you dating?"

"Nope."

"Why the hell not? Any woman in this place would fall over you. Of course, most of them have a bad sense of balance and it *is* awfully dark."

"What about you?"

Jake ordered a sunrise. "I was seeing someone for a little while. An actress. If you're taking notes about being single, put this at the top of your 'Don't Ever' file: Don't ever date an actress. It's like going out with Sybil. One day she's Gidget, the next day it's like hanging out with the Exorcist."

Jake ran his fingers through his curly black hair. "Now, I just date folks I meet through work. TV reporters. Dancers. That kinda stuff. People who don't have to take AIDS tests before they hop in the sack. I don't have all that much time, anyway."

"Me, neither."

"I could introduce you to some folks," Jake said. "You like people from Atlantis?"

"I never even liked watching 'Flipper.'"

"Ever learn how to swim?"

"Nope."

"I always thought that was a real clever move on your part. Coming out to Los Angeles, living by the beach, and not knowing how to swim. Showed a lot of insolence."

Broskey laughed out loud. "So I'm not real good at planning."

Jake stared at the dance floor. The dancers were working up a sweat now. Young bodies gyrating drunkenly to badly syncopated flashing lights. "You know," Jake mused, "one thing that amazes me about living out here is that you never see any truly ugly people. Everybody out here devotes their lives to looking good. They may not be able to read, they may not be able to make change in a supermarket, but they look great. That's one thing I miss about New York. You can walk down the street and see some real grunt mugs. Walk into a store and Quasimodo is your salesgirl. It makes you feel good, somehow. Like the world is balanced. Out here, though? Everybody looks like they should be on TV hawking Levi's or cologne or something."

He turned to Broskey. "Maybe that's a story. What does Los Angeles do with its ugly people? Do they kill them at birth? 'Mr. and Mrs. Jones, you're the proud parents of a ten-pound baby boy. The kid was ugly as hell, though, so we killed him. But . . . as a consolation prize, we have this wonderful Amana freezer for you. Tell them about it, Johnny!'

"And, if they don't kill them, do they make the ugly people live underground? In the sewer systems? Like alligators? I tell you, Kev, you inspire me. You really do. We're talking possible Pulitzer here."

"I thought you already had one."

"That was for a book, not my newspaper work. Doesn't count."

Broskey nodded, grappling inwardly with his sense of deep friendship and dread. Jake hadn't invited him to a bar, to this bar, to make small talk.

The smile faded from Broskey's lips. Jake noticed. The newspaperman slid down low in his chair. "Aha, I see a cop emerging. Before you ask, let me give you the answers. One: I knew the porn angle was bullshit on that co-ed murder. I ran it because it existed and it would sell a hell of a lot of papers. Two: I checked our obits for the last year or so and found two unsolved murders of campus cuties. They could be linked. Three: I don't want to fight you on this. I want to work with you. Team up again. I think it's a dynamite idea. What about you?"

Broskey sighed. "I don't know, Jake. We might have ourselves a serial killer out there. We might not. It's too soon to tell."

"What does your gut tell you?"

"Off the record?"

"Sure." Jake nodded. "Let me send the thirty-seven cameramen away." Jake motioned to several startled people at the bar. "Out! No cameras! Please!"

He turned to Broskey. "Better?"

Broskey managed a smirk. "I think we may have a sick one loose. But, as I said, it's too early."

"But you think . . ."

"Maybe."

"But if there *is* a pattern killer out there, Kev, we could work on nailing him together."

"Don't sound so excited."

"Well, in one sense, I'm revolted. In another sense, I'm looking forward to working with you."

"I haven't said yes."

"I know. I know. But remember how I scored back in New York with Son of Sam? That shit? Writing columns to him? Getting his Crayola'd notes back? The cops hated me. But if I had been allowed to work *with* them, we could have nailed the squirrely son-of-a-bitch weeks, maybe months earlier. Saved some lives. And sold some papers.

"This time, I can play it your way, the cops' way. I'm not talking just newspapers here. I'm talking book. I'm talking TV rights. I'm talking movies. Wouldn't you like to see someone play you in a movie? Roy Scheider? Burt Reynolds? Sally Field?"

Broskey blinked.

"Hey," Jake said. "She's very versatile."

Broskey glanced at his watch.

Jake caught the move. "Audience over?"

"I've got to get home."

"Why? You addicted to 'L.A. Law' or something?"

"No. I'm just tired."

"Okay. I'll let you go just this once. Next time, you'd better have a note from your mother."

"It was good seeing you again, Jake. I mean it," Broskey said, getting up from his table.

"Same here, Kev. And please don't be mad about that story back then. Old news. Yesterday's papers."

Broskey nodded, trying to remember the photo of Janet on the front page of the *Trib*. He couldn't. Right now, he couldn't even recall her face.

"Will you call me if anything pans out?" Jake asked. "I mean, I have a *lot* of connections in town. Real smarmy ones. You'd be proud."

Broskey looked down at the table, where Jake still sat. Mayer's face was an exclamation point with hair. He still looked like a short eighteen-year-old. "I'm not making any promises."

The enthusiasm in Jake's eyes refused to fade. "But you're not saying 'no.' "

Broskey pulled out a cigarette and chuckled while lighting it. "No. I'm not saying no. Happy?"

"Delirious," Jake said. "It'll be the Jake 'n' Kev show again. Think of the social repercussions."

"The mind boggles."

Jake downed his drink. "Come on, I'll walk you out. You still driving that piece of shit Toyota?"

The two men waded through the bar, bumping elbows with dozens of fresh-faced bodies. "No. The department gave me a car."

"What happened to the Toyota?"

"I totaled it."

"Drinking and driving again?"

"No. I totaled it with my fists."

Jake flashed Broskey an astonished look. "Divorce hit you that hard?"

Broskey nodded.

"Well, then a girl from Atlantis is definitely what you need," Jake said, swinging open the door. The newspaperman glanced inside the club one last time.

"What's up?" Broskey asked.

"I just had this creepy thought," Jake said, letting the door close behind him. "The next victim—I mean, if there *is* a next victim—could be in this bar right now."

Four

*B*roskey stared out the hole in the plaster that passed for a window in what passed for his office. Sprawl. That's all he could think about as Officer McDonald droned on. Los Angeles wasn't a city exactly. Not in the sense that New York and Chicago were. It was an architectural stew. Hundreds of suburban enclaves connected by serpentine roadways, monolithic high rises, and the occasional smattering of palm trees. It must have been pretty once, when citrus groves reached high into the sunlight, when one could hear the ocean's roar two miles from the beach, when trolley cars swung and swayed along reptilian tracks long before the days of smog, freeway snipers, and ten street-gang-related killings a day.

Somewhere along the line, Los Angeles had mutated, gone haywire. Roads were constructed with no thought to where they would lead. Homes were tossed up with little or no regard for style or location. Warehouses and office buildings were erected in the most unlikely of places.

For the most part, the city looked like a prized panel from an old Krazy Kat comic strip: angles and shapes gone wild.

Bay City had been intended as an antidote for all that, a slice of quaintness that bordered Los Angeles proper. But now, even Bay City was showing signs of progress. Crime was almost as casual there as in L.A.

From Broskey's window, facing east, you got a good view of the Big Sprawl. These days, about the only way you could tell the difference between L.A. and Bay City was by the color of the air. It was slightly browner in Los Angeles.

Broskey wondered why he stayed.

Well, he shrugged inwardly, it was probably because he had no place else to go.

McDonald was chattering away in the background. "The guy who produced the film is a sleazebag named Anson Rhodes. It was a softcore horror movie. *Sorority Babe Massacre*. He works out of a boat in Marina Del Rey. Does a lot of blood-and-guts movies. Also has a pseudonym: Raoul Delgado. Produces some hardcore porn. Out of state. We questioned him about the babe—"

Broskey stared at McDonald hard. The young officer coughed.

"—the deceased. He couldn't even remember her. He looked her up, though, and found her time cards. She had a bit part. That was about it."

"Fine." Broskey sighed.

"That's it?" McDonald asked.

"That's it unless you can tell me who butchered Patricia Sharone."

McDonald ran his hand through his crew-cut hair. He came away with a palmful of ooze. "Then I suppose that's it, Lieutenant."

Broskey slid into his chair and wondered why he hadn't taken a teaching job. Oh yeah, he remembered. The kids he'd seen coming up through college were assholes. He lit a cigarette and actually tasted the poison in it. Sergeant Fine entered the room, a cockeyed smile on her face. "Ready for this morning's installment of Looney Tunes?"

"You just missed him," Broskey said.

Sergeant Fine tossed a folder on his desk. "This little item makes McDonald look like 'Masterpiece Theater' material."

Broskey glanced through the file. "You're kidding me."

"Nope." The blond woman smiled. "Came down from the DA hisself."

"They're actually considering prosecuting this guy for manslaughter because he raised bees?"

"Read on."

"Okay. Juan Cuvallo lives next to Jess Rodriguez. Juan likes honey and raises bees. Some of his bees have the habit of gathering on the fence that separates Jess's house from Juan's. Jess spots a swarm of bees on the fence. He decides he wouldn't mind some honey. So he takes a cardboard box, sprinkles some sugar in it, and walks over to the fence. He tries to *scrape the bees into the box with his bare hands?*"

"Jess definitely wasn't think-tank material," Sergeant Fine pointed out.

"He smacks the bees. The bees get cheesed off and, understandably, affix themselves to his face, where they proceed to ventilate his mug. By the time the paramedics arrive, he's DOA."

"That's it."

"And the DA wants to prosecute the bees' owner for manslaughter?" Broskey muttered, amazed. "He doesn't need a cop. He needs Marlin Perkins."

He closed the file. "I can actually feel the brain cells dying."

The phone on Broskey's desk rang. He picked it up and held it slightly away from his ear, as if it possessed some exotic infection. "Jeez. All right. I'll be right down. Let me talk to the neighbor, okay? Keep her calm."

He hung up the phone. "We have another ex-co-ed," he muttered to Sergeant Fine when he was already out the door.

Ozone Avenue was as close as anyone would want to come to living in Venice without actually taking the plunge. Just a hundred yards or so from Ocean Front walk, it was a collection of fading bungalows and beach houses, bricked-in front yards, and cocoa-buttered sun worshipers.

By the time Broskey arrived in front of the flaking white,

two-story apartment complex, the body was already being hauled out on a gurney.

Broskey approached McDonald and Bluth, who were busily hoping the forces of gravity would suddenly erupt upon a bikini top worn by a dazed damsel sunbathing next door. A half pitcher of Long Island Iced Tea was by her side.

"Who ordered the body to be moved?" he asked the officers.

"I did," Bluth said. "I thought—"

"You what?"

"I thought . . ."

Broskey turned to the forensics men. "Alert the media, I think we have a first here." He returned his gaze to McDonald and Bluth. "Put your eyes back in their sockets and question the neighbors."

Cheshire-cat grins appeared on both their faces. "Yes sir." They nearly ran out of the yard, loving police work.

"What do we have, Goldstein?"

"A very dead young lady. Debi Noland. One *b*, one *i* in Debi. Remember when people used to spell their names normal?"

"What else have you got?"

"Pretty much the same MO as on the other girl. Sexual assault. Had her head bashed in with *this.*" He held up an old-fashioned music box. Wooden. Hand-carved. "Probably a family heirloom. It plays 'Thumbelina.'"

"Thank God it doesn't play 'Feelings.' Have you got her neighbor in tow?"

"Uh-huh."

"Lead me to Debi's room. Then I'll see the neighbor."

Debi Noland's studio apartment overlooked the street, giving her a nice view of the Pacific and a long stretch of Ocean Front walk. Broskey stared down the walk. Elderly couples huddled on benches, trying to catch some sun, feed some pigeons, and fend off the rantings of the druggies, derelicts, street crazies, and buzzed teenage gang members. Jugglers nearly collided with swamis who could read your fortune by squeezing your toes. Young men in business suits tried picking up dirt-encrusted bathing-suit beauties with enough holes in their arms to qualify them for spaghetti-strainer status. Lovely place, Venice. Everything was screwy. Most of the street mimes actually talked.

Broskey tried to ignore the blood on the walls and concentrated on the apartment. He produced a small plastic bag and a pencil and begin sifting through Debi's belongings, most of which had been tossed onto the floor when the bureau was kicked over by person or persons unknown.

A flyer from Ace Modeling Salon. Postcard from Arizona: "Miss you; love, Mom and Dad." Matches from Music Max. Uh-huh. Broskey walked over to the door. No sign of forced entry. Here we go again, he sighed. Photos of Debi, a full-figured blonde, probably a little too broad-shouldered to be a full-time model. Outdoorsy. Looked good in workshirts. Hair pulled back in a ponytail. Bay City College library card. UCLA library card. She worked hard for her grades. Textbooks from Bay City College. A photo of her and some long-haired guy. Broskey bagged everything and walked into the hall. Goldstein was there, his massive arms folded on his chest. He nodded toward a door.

"You're going to love this one. Samantha Rambeaux. Her friends call her Sami."

"Two *m's*, one *i?*"

"One of each."

Broskey stepped inside. A woman in her forties, with hair down to her waist and eye makeup that stretched nearly that far, sat cross-legged on the floor, swaying back and forth. The apartment looked like a storage facility for Woodstock leftovers. A collection of lava lamps, wind chimes, crystals, herbs, oversized pillows, and enough incense to qualify for an EPA summons made do for decor. Her makeup, and there was a lot of it, looked like a combination of a *Cosmo* cover and a flyer from Ringling Brothers' Clown College.

"Ms. Rambeaux?"

"Actually, I pronounce it Ram-bux."

The woman opened her eyes, which were bloodshot and dilated. Broskey wondered what herbs Sami had been snacking on that morning. "I'm Lieutenant Broskey. I was wondering if you'd mind telling me a little about your neighbor?"

Would she? The hyped-up woman opened her mouth and a flood of words emerged. After a few seconds, Broskey decided it would be useless to try to take notes. "She was a wonderful girl. A sweet girl. Like my daughter. Only I don't have a daughter. She was from Arizona, you know. Came out here to be a model. Couldn't be, really. Too big-boned. Healthy. She had beautiful breasts. I always admired her breasts. I wanted to have big breasts but I never did get around to having them. I wanted an operation, at one point, but I was warned off by my psychic.

"He's wonderful. He does psychic dentistry, as well. I had a toothache once and I went to him and not only did he cure my toothache but he changed my fillings into gold. I could give you his number—"

"Maybe he could work on my bullets. Look, about Ms. Noland."

"Debi. What a sweet girl. I mean really *sweet*. Very spiritual in an earthy kind of way. A real hard worker. She worked in the school library to put herself through school. I think she did some art-class modeling too, you know, life class? Very Rubens, that body. Such nice breasts. I was very envious. She didn't flaunt them, though. Not the type. Really *sweet*. Never dated much. She went out with this one asshole for about six months but he was an asshole, did I say that? Well, she came home one day and found him entertaining himself while watching an X-rated tape. They argued. Turned out the guy was a closet porn buff. She moved out of her first apartment. I think it was in West L.A. Can't be sure. Moved here. A great kid. Like my own daughter, if I had a daughter. I don't."

"But if you did, she'd be just like Debi."

"Right."

"No steady boyfriend. Did she cruise bars with any girlfriends?"

"No. No. She mostly kept by herself. She'd come over to my place for some tea and tarot but really never socialized that much. But last night? She didn't come home right after work. I always hear her come home at the same time. Well, she comes home a few hours later with a man."

"Did you see him?"

"No. But I *heard* him."

"What did he sound like?"

"Well, like a *man.* The two of them seemed to be having a good time. I couldn't hear what they were saying, after all I'm not a *snoop.*"

"Nor clairvoyant."

"Heavens, no. I've always wanted to be clairvoyant, though. Never did get around to developing that talent, but anyway. They were playing music. Laughing. Lots of laughing. Then I went into deep meditation, crystal healing, you know, it soothes the mind and the body."

Broskey stared at her kabuki face. Now if only it would teach her the proper way to apply makeup.

"Anyhow, I'm meditating and meditating. I must have dozed off. I woke up in the middle of the night. Wham."

"Wham?"

"Like something falling or something hitting the wall. I thought it was an earthquake, just a tremor. The whamming didn't continue and I went back to sleep. Then, this morning, I didn't hear Debi leave for school. I thought she might be sick."

Or still in with the guy, but you're no snoop. Broskey nodded.

"So I knocked on her door. The door was open and I walked in and found her or what used to be her. Her soul is now on a higher plane of existence."

Her body is a mess, though, Broskey thought. "Well, I appreciate your talking with me, Ms. Ram-bux."

The woman giggled. "Actually, it *is* pronounced Rambeaux, but I changed it for karma reasons. I mean, isn't it awful that I should have a name like Rambeaux because it sounds like the Stallone movie? Here I am so spiritual and he's so . . . so . . ."

"Unspiritual."

"Exactly."

"I'm sure there's a Zen-like reason for it, Ms. Rambeaux."

The woman brightened. "You know, you're probably right? Who am I not to go with the flow?"

Broskey nodded. "I'll have one of my men take your statement."

He left the room smiling. He'd give this one to McDonald. God, would he love to witness that pairing. Goldstein was still standing in the hall, chewing a wad of gum the size of a sweat sock. "She's a pip, ain't she?"

Broskey nodded. He handed the plastic bag with Debi's things to Goldstein. "Can you check these for prints?"

"No problem."

"And get Officer Bluth to run down Ms. Noland's last address. She had a boyfriend. I want to find out who he is and where."

"Suspect?"

"Probably not. He might be able to tell us about some of the girl's friends, though. I mean *that*"—he gestured to Rambeaux's apartment—"can't be the only friend she had in town."

"Will do. So, Lieutenant, what's our next move?"

"In terms of law enforcement? I have no idea. In terms of me, I want to take a long walk and get the smell of incense out of my lungs."

Goldstein sniffed the air oozing out of Rambeaux's apartment. "You'd have to walk to Afghanistan to lose that stink, Lieutenant."

Broskey walked out into the street and stared at the decaying elegance of the once proud beach homes. It wasn't the smell of incense he had to lose, it was the odor of death. Something very ugly was happening in his city. There was an animal on the loose that he had no idea how to catch. It went from neighborhood to neighborhood, house to house, and killed for sport.

Broskey walked down the street, stepping over a puddle of piss. Maybe he could put some of his old college training to use and outpsych the guy. Maybe he could come up with some massive shrink scam to shadow the shit's every move.

To do so, he'd have to toss the book away and play by some pretty unorthodox rules.

He found himself walking with his fists clenched.

Maybe to catch this guy, he'd need help. He'd need the kind of help that the department couldn't get him.

He stopped at a phone booth and watched two mimes argue over the possession of a hat. Dropping in a quarter, he dialed a number he hadn't used in years.

"Jake Mayer here," came a voice from the other end. "This is not a machine, but I have been known to beep for no reason."

Broskey found himself smiling.

"What the fuck are you laughing at!" one mime screeched at Broskey. The lieutenant reached inside his jacket and flashed a badge at the mime.

"Holy Jesus shit!" the mime said.

And Kevin Broskey began to laugh.

Five

The Bay City Palisades used to be the nicest spot around. Main Street, in this oldest section of the town, was situated directly across from a small, rambling public park, which, in turn, stood towering some two hundred feet above the roaring Pacific. It seemed that on every block there was a massive colonial home that was used as a haven by the city's elderly.

Morning used to bring the oldsters to the park, where they would carefully nurture the pigeons, the gulls, and the flowers. Lunch was taken on a park bench, catered by one of the numerous homegrown shops on the thoroughfare. These days, the few elderly residents who braved the park had to dodge and duck Walkman-powered joggers, escape drunken derelicts, and step gingerly over rivers of piss.

As for the Palisades themselves, about a third of the cliff face had made an impromptu visit to the beach parking lot far below during a particularly bad rainy season in '83, thus changing not only the shape of the park but that of about fifty autos.

The whole area, these days, was sort of like a perky portrait of a leper colony. Bright but decaying.

Broskey sat in Café Parc and waited for Mayer to show. Café Parc was one of those trendy restaurants that specialized in Continental food served cafeteria style at astronomical prices. Eggs florentine was sold by the gram. Most of the male patrons sat gazing at chic women from behind three-hundred-dollar sunglasses, their elbows resting meaningfully on the Formica tabletops. They didn't have to worry about soiling their lightweight blazers, either. The sleeves had been pushed up to the mandatory shoulder level.

Broskey didn't fit in.

Mayer came strolling through the pastel people and, placing a limp hand on one thigh, waved through the air with the other. "Yooo-hooo. Marcel. Marcel? Is that you? My goodness. You certainly look butch."

Broskey's faced reddened. He was already sweating from the midday heat, but now he was on fire. He tried to stifle his laughter, his drink making its way up to his nose. (Some drink. A pink concoction that tasted like Cold Duck mixed with Kool-Aid.)

Mayer continued to swish forward. "My goodness! I was wondering what you were doing these days. I heard your contract-killer biz went under. Right after Ollie North was taken out of action. Gave me chills to think about that, after all the blood, sweat, and tears you put into it. Mostly blood. Oooooh."

"Will you knock it off," Broskey muttered, running his left palm over his dripping forehead. "Some of these people know me."

Jake slid into the seat opposite him and dropped the Aunt Mable routine. People were still staring. "I doubt it," he said with a shrug. "I don't think any of these people have ever *seen* the inside of a bowling alley."

"I don't bowl."

"It's a state of mind. I heard about the new girl."

"Yeah. I think we have a situation here."

"So? What do we do?"

Broskey shook his head slowly. "Well, what I'm probably going to do is something really stupid that will cost me my job."

"That's where I come in, huh?"

"More than likely. It usually works out that way."

"You're still mad about the time the wild turkey got loose in the school."

"You were the one who was supposed to be holding it."

"Okay. So I made one, small mistake."

"Well, right now, you can't afford to make even the smallest."

Jake began picking at Broskey's food. "What the hell is this?"

"Some sort of quiche, I think. It was supposed to be spinach."

"Either it has mushrooms or warts," Jake commented, playing with the food with a fork. "So what's the plan?"

"I want you to hold off for a day or so. Don't write anything about the killings."

"Oh, come on. Writing is my *job.*"

"I know. I know. But you were talking about a book, right? You didn't want to just sell papers, right?"

"Yeah. But I wasn't talking about putting people to sleep, either, Kev. There has to be a tradeoff."

"There is. You'll be in on every step of the police work, on the QT, of course."

"Of course. And what do I have to do to *earn* this honorary spot in the investigators' hall of fame?"

"Write a series of articles."

"But I thought you just said . . ."

"Not *those* kind of articles. I don't want any Son of Sam open letters *or* recollections of the Hillside Strangler *or* comparisons to Ted Bundy or any other pen pal you can think of. Nothing inflammatory. Nothing sensational."

"Go on, I'm fascinated. By the way, your quiche is so bad the flies are avoiding it."

"I don't have this serial stuff hashed out yet. I'm not even sure if we have one, single perp. I want a day or two to go over everything we've got. But if we do find out we're looking for one oddball, I want to talk to someone on the LAPD's Violent Crime Task Force. A psychologist."

"Ah, dancing shrink to shrink."

"Well, maybe I can use some of the old training, Jake. It might work."

"It's doubtful. You were always bad with big words. You'd call people screwballs. Bad for a psychologist."

"The deal is, with most serial killers, like the few we've had out here, the tendency of the police is to play everything close to the vest. The newspapers are frustrated by a lack of hard facts, so they speculate. They scare people, and then the cops blame the newspapers for scaring them. Plus, the newspapers get a bad rep for encouraging the killer with their blazing headlines. I want to try something different this time, but I'm not sure I can."

"I don't get it, Mr. Holmes," Jake said.

"I want to play this guy, push him around. If he *is* a real sick puppy, he's going to kill again, no matter what we do. Maybe if we play him a tune in harmony, we can get him to kill less."

"Rattle his cage a little?"

"Rattle it enough to register on the Richter scale at Cal Tech."

"About my articles?" Jake asked.

"If we *do* have someone in the grips of co-ed fever in town," Broskey continued, "I want you to interview everyone and anyone about public safety. About the most common mistakes people can make in taking care of themselves."

"Windows left open at night, doors unlocked, hitchhiking, that kind of stuff?"

"Yup."

"No offense, Kev, but that *shit* is boring."

"Uh-uh," Broskey replied. "Because we're going to tie everything in with real-life cases. The present ones and recent ones. I'll give you access to the homicide files for the last six months. Half of them could have been prevented if the victims had exercised just a little more caution, I think. Pull the files, do the interviews. Don't play it up like *the Enquirer*. Do it up Jack Webb style. Don't frighten the audience. Let the audience frighten themselves."

"Just the facts, ma'am," Jake said, grinning. "I like it. I *like* that. It'll be great research material for the book."

"Plus, you'll get all your research done free, by the force."

Jake ate a forkful of quiche. "You know, this isn't half bad."

"It grows on you . . . unfortunately." Broskey grinned. "There's a piece trying to shimmy down your lower lip."

Mayer brushed it aside. "Mushroom?"

"I don't know, but it was moving."

Mayer nearly spat out the food. Broskey laughed. "Caught you looking."

"Okay, wise-ass. One thing I don't understand, though. Why are you taking this case—"

"If it is one case . . ."

"—so *personally?* I mean we're talking Lieutenant Ahab, here."

Broskey drank some of his fizzy drink. It looked like a medical test he had taken once. "I've been trying to figure that out myself. Remember when we first moved to New York, and I refused to look for a teaching job?"

"Don't I ever. I was paying the bills."

"Well, that half a year I spent working for the city's social services? I found myself dealing with the dregs, every day. Wife beaters. Bag ladies. Flashers. Druggies. Drunks. You name it. But I found myself making a big mistake; I was beginning to deal with these people as *people,* getting involved more than I should."

"If I remember correctly, you almost lost your nose over one guy."

"Yeah. Bobby the biter. So I stepped back a bit and then found out that *everyone* coming into contact with these people was an expert on their mental disorders. I mean, even the janitors felt like they could psychoanalyze these folks. They had some of the damnedest theories you'd ever heard and they'd blurt them right into the people's faces. I mean, some poor sonofabitch who was sucking on a wine bottle in SoHo was told he possessed about a dozen different mental disorders a day.

"So I stepped back just a little further and looked at the whole system."

"And . . ."

"And I figured everything was nuts. Not just people. Our

values. The way we dealt with life on every single level was out of whack."

"Do they sell straight alcohol here?" Jake blinked.

"No."

"Just checking. Go on."

"I came out here and became a cop. It seemed like a simpler way to deal with the world. There were victims and there were perps. The victims were innocent. The perps were guilty. I got pretty good at the game. It was like putting together a puzzle. Most of the time, all the pieces were there, you just had to rearrange them. Or if there were a couple of pieces missing, go out and find them.

"It was a matter of personal pride to me that I put all the puzzles thrown my way together. I got a sense of accomplishment out of it. On some days, I actually felt that I was contributing something to, well, society. You know, I was keeping the system from crumbling. I was a *good* guy. I had a marriage. I wanted to be a father."

"Aha, now we're getting to it. You felt chivalrous, right? Making the world a better place for your family. Protecting the realm."

Broskey laughed. "Well, you've got to believe in *something*. Besides, it's better than watching *Ishtar* on cable TV. Then, when my marriage fell apart and things started getting really hairy on the streets, I started to lose it. I mean, how can you deal with a guy who kills three people because he's seen a vision of Mr. Potato Head floating in the sky? I started to just go through the motions. But, I don't know. The last couple of days, I've been getting mad. It's like I've taken enough.

"Those girls couldn't fight back. They didn't have the wherewithal. Maybe if I had fought a little harder, maybe if every person like me had fought a little harder the last couple of years, things wouldn't be so squirrely now."

Jake flashed a curious look at Broskey. "So, what you're telling me is that you either want to catch this guy really badly because one, it's a matter of personal pride; two, you feel it's time to play Superman; three, it's your job; four, you hate cable TV."

Broskey laughed out loud. "Something like that."

He grew serious for a minute. "Maybe you can add number five. I'm sick of Morlocks snuffing out the lives of those who still are capable of being trusting. I'm sick of these scumbags thinking they can get away with taking a human life. I think it's about time *one* of those jerks had his ass kicked but good."

"Spoken like a true egghead," Jake said, applauding.

"I'm just a cop, remember?" Broskey said.

Jake got to his feet, took one last scoop of pulverized quiche, and patted his old friend on the shoulder. "Later, Sherlock. Give me a call when you want old Scoop Mayer to ride into the jaws of death with you."

"As long as I drive." Broskey smiled into his drink. He was gazing into the cutesy pink swamp for a moment when he became aware of a familiar pair of female legs standing next to his table.

"Had lunch yet, Andy?"

Sergeant Andrea Fine took a seat across from Broskey. "I'm on a diet. Maybe I'll hit a ratburger place on the way home."

"There are a lot of calories in ratburgers."

"I doubt that. There's no real food in them. Cardboard doesn't have calories." She smirked. "I waited until the hack had gone before I showed you these."

"You don't like Mr. Mayer?"

"It's not that I don't like him. I don't trust him. He'd sell his mother for a story."

Broskey nodded. "Yeah. But he'd make enough to buy two mothers back. What's up?"

"Remember the name of the guy who produced the slasher film Patricia Sharone starred in?"

"Yeah. Some marina rat. Anson Rhodes?"

"Bravo," Fine answered. "Some say the memory improves with age."

"That's about all that does."

"Well, that stuff you picked up from the Noland apartment. The flyer from the Ace Modeling Salon? You'll never guess who owns it."

"Seargeant," Broskey said, rising. "The world is indeed a mysterious yet disgustingly predictable place. Would you care to join me in a jaunt over to the meddy old marina?"

"I'd be delighted," Sergeant Fine said with a small bow.

The two had just left the wallet-bleeding cafeteria when they heard a commotion across the street.

"Aww, Jeez," Broskey exclaimed, spying an elderly couple fending off the fists of a very young boy in gang colors. The boy had one arm wrapped through the woman's purse strap. The elderly man was trying to swing his cane at the child while still maintaining some sort of equilibrium.

Broskey trotted across the street, dodging a few off-road vehicles filled with bronzed bodies and equally fried brain matter.

He leaped into the park, sneaking up behind the boy, and lifted him up by his collar.

"Okay, Moochie, the scavenger hunt's over."

"Hey, lemme down, Broskey, or I'll pop ya one."

Broskey held the kid aloft while showing his badge to the elderly couple. By this time, the man had collapsed on the bench and his wife was cradling her purse as if it were made of porcelain.

"It's okay, folks. Police."

"Pig! Pig!" the black-haired boy began to shriek. "I got my rights."

"Your rights tended to fritter away when you snatched that lady's purse, Mooch."

"My name ain't Mooch. It's El Roacho. You know that, Broskey. You know I'm a Corpse, too. Watchit."

"I know you're a pain in the butt."

The kid got tired of squirming and let his body go limp. The elderly couple looked at the boy sympathetically. Broskey already knew the ending of this scenario. It was bad enough to be a TV sit-com.

"I didn't mean nothin'," the boy said, sticking his lower lip out to diving-board proportions.

"Yeah. Yeah. I know," Broskey said. "You were jogging while pretending you were a bird and your arm just kind of got caught in this nice lady's purse, and before you knew it, they had mistaken you for a thief and you panicked and your arm was stuck and you couldn't get away."

El Roacho thought this over for a moment. "Yeah. Sumpin like that."

"Right. Come on, squirt."

"Excuse me, Officer," the elderly woman asked. "Where will you take him?"

"Juvenile Hall."

"Oh, my goodness. Is that like a jail?"

"In miniature," Broskey replied. "Come on, Antsy."

"El Roacho."

Broskey stared, first at the kid, who couldn't have been more than four-feet-six-inches tall and about ten years old, and then at the elderly couple. The couple was exchanging guilty looks.

"Jonathan," she said. "Remember all the mischief Billy used to get into when he was that age?"

"Do I ever." The old man chuckled. "Remember when he left his bike out behind the old Plymouth and I ran right over it?"

The old couple laughed.

Broskey wanted to point out that being a sloppy widdle kid is a tad different from being a purse-snatching member of a street gang, but knew it would do no good. And as the elderly couple gazed at El Roacho, the kid pulled out his trump card, his old-people-pulverizing escape plan to end all escape plans.

He cried.

No, he *wailed*.

Broskey found himself holding up a sobbing ten-year-old. Tears spurted from his eyes with enough force to bypass the kid's cheeks. He began to whimper. Then whine. Before long, the kid was sucking in breath like a sump pump, reducing his voice to a high-pitched series of squeaks.

"I-I'm sss-ss-sor-reeee," El Roacho whined. "I d-d-dint mean to do nothing baa-yaad. Waaaaahhhh."

Broskey sighed. He'd witnessed this performance time and time again. El Roacho was an actor of Oscar propor-tions. The kid cranked up the waterworks. The old couple crumbled. "Well, Officer," the elderly woman said. "If the young man says he won't do it again, I don't see any reason for putting him away, do you?"

"You won't press charges?" Broskey asked.

"No," the man and woman said simultaneously.

The old man leaned into El Roacho's face. "You go home to your mommy and daddy now, young fella. They must be missing you."

And the purse he was supposed to return with, Broskey thought to himself. Broskey shrugged and let El Roacho go. The kid gave each of the olders an affectionate hug. "Oh, thank you. Thank you so much. My family is so grateful."

Broskey stood by the bench as El Roacho skipped away, looking very much like an ordinary ten-year-old but for the spray-painted rotting skull on the back of his denim jacket and a series of colorful tattoos on his right arm. As he skipped by Broskey he hissed in the cop's direction. "You're a dead man, Broskey."

"Kids." The elderly woman chuckled. "They never change. One big bundle of energy."

"Yeah," Broskey said, flashing a false smile. And a few rounds of ammo.

At that point a foot patrolman strolled by. "Any problems, Lieutenant?"

"Guess not," Broskey said.

He crossed the street to a public parking structure where Sergeant Fine stood, arms crossed, smirking. "Nice going. You're a regular Michael Landon type when it comes to dealing with kids."

A moment later, Broskey and Fine had pulled out of the lot and were heading up Main Street, toward the marina a few miles away. Broskey heard a familiar scream. He glanced into the Palisades Park.

El Roacho was running madly along the walkway.

He had stolen the old man's cane.

"Should we stop him?" Fine asked.

"Fuggit." Broskey sighed. "Let the foot cop get in his jogging for the day."

Six

Anson Rhodes's apartment was an ultra-modern duplex, sort of a bronze and chrome tinker-toy affair that resembled two shoe boxes stacked on their sides. What it did have going for it were large windows that overlooked Marina Del Rey.

From his tenth/eleventh floor digs, Anson could probably get a good view of every nubile young thing who decided to sunbathe with the top halves of her bathing suit undone for miles around. He could probably also see the potbellied, baby-oiled, badly toupeed would-be Lotharios that waddled around on the prowl as well.

Broskey noted the large telescope next to the window as Wendee, Rhodes's assistant, watched Sergeant Fine's ratburger come precariously close to permanently ruining Rhodes's white rug.

"Gee, I'm sorry," she droned, barely containing herself in her mini-swath of white cloth. "Mr. Rhodes is out for lunch."

"You wouldn't know where, would you?" Broskey asked, eyeing the massive yachts floating in the harbor, tributes to former President Reagan's trickle-down theory that benefited only the ones who owned large buckets.

"Well . . ." Wendee said, shaking her fiery red hair onto her breasts.

"No problem," Sergeant Fine replied, sitting on a pristine white sofa, burger hemorrhaging. "We'll wait."

Wendee suddenly reached a decision. "He's probably down at Polynesia Pete's. He has lunch there every day. He's with a client, though."

"Thanks," Broskey said, eyeing a large black desk covered with eight-by-tens of young girls who could barely hide their enthusiasm.

"Yeah, thanks," Sergeant Fine said, carrying her hamburger with her as they both left the apartment.

Broskey and Fine waited in front of the elevator. "Did you see that place?" Broskey muttered. "Why is it that people with money have absolutely no taste whatsoever?"

"I don't know. I've never had to worry about that." Fine shrugged.

"That was a nice bit of work in there." Broskey grinned. "Getting Wendee to tell us where Rhodes was."

The sergeant held up her hamburger. "I owe it all to the special sauce."

The two left the building and strolled for five minutes along a walkway littered with boats, oblong high rises, bicyclists, and joggers. They stopped when they reached Polynesia Pete's, a Brobdingnagian tiki hut with valet parking.

They were stopped at the front entrance by a young Mexican boy with Rudolph Valentino hair and an outfit left over from the film *Hawaii*.

"Sorry," he said, pointing to Fine's lunch à gogo, "you can't bring food in here."

"That's an editorial judgment," Broskey said.

"No problem," Fine replied, shoving the almost-eaten burger into the boy's hands. "I was done anyway. Enjoy."

The twosome left the blazing sunlight and entered the feral world of Polynesia Pete's. Plastic Japanese lanterns were strung across the ceiling, hovering high above lava-lamp-type plastic torches.

The young and the depressed clung to the large wooden bar, clutching their drinks and nachos.

They strode by a very confused hostess, almost dressed in a sarong.

"Can I help you?" she asked.

Broskey flashed his badge. "Anson Rhodes's table, please."

"W-was he expecting you?"

"Do I look like one of his usual lunch dates?"

"No."

"Then, let's just make this a little surprise, okay?"

The woman nodded and led the pair past a bevy of Tinkerbell-outfitted waitresses. Broskey figured that half of the fun the businessmen had in this place was watching the waitresses bend over to take their orders. The other half came in ordering the drinks, which all had names reminiscent of French hookers. A barely audible, refried disco beat permeated the air.

Broskey and Fine were led to a table where a dyed-blond, middle-aged man with his shirt at half mast sat talking to a buxom, raven-haired woman.

"You understand, there would be some nudity involved," he was saying.

"What's important to me is my *career*," she replied in a voice known only to Disney animators.

He looked up when he saw the intruders.

"Something I can do for you?"

Broskey flashed his badge. "I hope so."

The man seemed to pale under the type of tan usually applied with a brush. "Excuse me, Muffin," he said to the girl. "A couple of old friends have shown up. I'll keep the photos and be in touch."

The young girl squirmed out of her seat, allowing her skirt to ride up past the boundaries of imagination. "I hope so, Mr. Rhodes. *Soon*. You have my number?"

"Uh-huh. That and your astrological sign."

The girl bent over the table and the two kissy-kissed each other on the cheek. Rhodes's upper lip was a rip tide of sweat. The girl bounced away. Broskey and Fine slid into the booth, sitting opposite a very agitated Anson Rhodes. He glared at the hostess, sending her scurrying off. His voice was hoarse, a bare whisper.

"What's the matter with you guys? You can't leave an honest man alone? I told you last week, all my clients are over the age of eighteen. If they're not, then they've given me phony ID."

Broskey nodded, making note of Rhodes's Achilles' groin. "No sir, Mr. Rhodes. We're here investigating two homicides."

"Homicides?"

Broskey smiled. "You know. People who were once alive winding up being anything but?"

"Shit."

"Yeah. That's another word for it," Broskey said. "Two of your clients, Patricia Sharone and Debi Noland, were killed within the last three days."

"I never heard of them."

"Well, maybe we could all go back to your apartment and go through your files. That might refresh your memory. I bet Wendee could help us go through your files. She *does* know how to read, doesn't she?"

Rhodes gulped. "You've been up to my pad?"

"Uh-huh," Broskey said with a smile.

"Let me get you a drink."

"Nothing for me, thanks," Broskey replied. "I'm on the wagon."

He was as surprised to hear himself say that as Fine was. He caught the startled look on her face. "I have to take off a few pounds," he added.

Rhodes pulled in his massive gut. "Of course. I understand. Let's see . . . Sharone, Noland. Yeah. Yeah. I remember them now. Nice girls. Very nice. They were out to make a few bucks. College kids, I seem to recall."

"Go on."

"First off," Rhodes said, wheezing, "I want you to know I run a very respectable organization. All my modeling jobs are strictly on the up and up. No hardcore porn."

"No penetration," Fine deadpanned.

"Hell, no, that's against federal law. Remember all that shit that came down with Meese? I'm no fool. It's all titillation. Nudity. Yeah. But nothing with men, animals, or children."

"A regular Sir Galahad." Broskey smirked at Fine.

"Hey, it's a living," Rhodes replied. "The Sharone girl called herself Missy. She did a flick for me. Low-budget. I think it was called *The Great American Bikini Factory*. Frontal nudity. Kept her pants on. A hard R rating."

"What about the Noland kid?" Broskey countered.

"She wasn't crazy about nudity, as I recall, which made her less marketable. A lot of bending-over shots. Some calendar work. Tease photos. Couple walk-ons, or bend-ons, in one or two sword and sorcery films that were made in Mexico. *The Fighting Sorceress* and *Shivs of Steel*, if I recall correctly. No big deal. Made enough to cover her tuition."

Rhodes finished. No one spoke. The producer/ entrepreneur grew uneasy. "They were really offed?"

"Very much so." Broskey nodded.

"Jeezus," Anson Rhodes exhaled. "Crazy world we live in, huh? I mean, who'd want to do them in?"

"Maybe someone who saw your films," Fine said, smiling sweetly.

"No!" Rhodes exclaimed. "Hell no. Look, Officers. I run a respectable shop. Honest to God. I'm not into any snuff kinda shit. Most of the movies I'm connected with are trash, I know that, but they make a couple of bucks in theatrical, and then, if the packaging is right, a small fortune in video rentals. None of the actors get rich. I get by. It's the producers that make the money. I've made a couple of them myself, so I'm not going hungry, but I definitely don't deal with the kinky trade."

"You married?" Broskey asked.

A smile played across Rhodes's face. "Hell no. Why should I tie myself down? I mean, look at the kids I deal with. They're young. Full of life. I mean, in this town, every waitress can be a star if she doesn't mind letting them out to air during a flick. Catch my drift."

"Uh-huh," Broskey nearly hummed.

"I have the best of all possible worlds going. I mean, I'm surrounded by young honeys who think I'm a big wheel. Sure, in a year or so, they'll know better, but by that time, they'll have made a few bucks, I'll have made a few more, and we'll all have gotten the chance to get to know each other better." He gazed at Broskey. "I mean, the younger the meat, the sweeter the treat, right?"

"I'm a vegetarian, myself," Broskey replied.

"Ever think about AIDS?" Fine asked casually.

"Hell no. That's for queers. I'm no fairy. Ask any of my clients," Rhodes fumed.

"Now, about that underage stuff you're so worried about," Broskey offered.

"Swear to Christ. I've *never* employed anyone under the age of eighteen. College kids only, or the equivalent thereof."

Broskey smiled, munching a stale peanut from a half-coconut shell of alleged snacks. "Yeah. I know. That's what all the folks who employed Traci Lords thought, too."

Rhodes drank his hooker drink down in one swallow. "W-was one of those girls who was offed . . . was one, you know . . ."

"Jailbait?" Fine smiled sweetly.

"Yeah. Yeah. That's it," Rhodes said, drumming his fingers on the wooden tabletop like Gene Krupa in heat.

"Not to our knowledge." Broskey shrugged. "But we're investigating every angle."

"Hey!" Rhodes exclaimed. "I didn't force those girls to come to me. I didn't send them to me."

Broskey stared hard at the sweating man's face. "Who did?"

Rhodes bit his lower lip. His luau shirt was beginning to look like a sponge. "Well . . ."

"Come on, Rhodes," Broskey said. "We're going to find out anyway. Who knows? If you help us out and we *do* find out that some of your models were underage . . ."

"Okay, okay," Rhodes said, readying his song. "Most of the girls, not all, but most, are turned on to me by Cheryl Williams."

Broskey blinked. "Cheryl Williams?"

"Yeah. She needs cash. I give her a finder's fee."

"I thought she was a best-selling author," Broskey replied.

"She's also the queen of alimony," Rhodes said. "When she was an actress, she married half of the Hollywood phone directory. Beat the crap out of most of them. She's gone beyond that now. Now she's a seer."

Broskey nodded. Cheryl Williams was a former chorus girl turned actress who made a big splash in a couple of small celluloid ponds: *French Boogie* and *Happy Feet*. She was an okay dancer with Cinemascope legs and sequined costumes. After her film career faded, she went into TV, starring in a well-received sit-com about—what else?—an ex-hoofer who didn't wear long skirts a lot.

During the past five years, however, she had made a small fortune in the touchy-feely world of celebrity channeling. During a professional bout with the dreaded "don't call us, we'll call you" syndrome, she suddenly discovered she was a very spiritual person. On a chauffeured trip through Tibet, she found herself in touch with a five-thousand-year-old spirit named Eeyore, who allegedly showed her the way to spiritual enlightenment and big bucks via a host of Eeyore books and smattering of in-person celebrity channeling fests.

Broskey could never figure that one out. For one thing, Eeyore, at age five thousand, would have to be a Cro-Magnon man. To his knowledge, there weren't many Cro-Magnons in history noted for their wit or wisdom.

Plus, Eeyore was also the name of the melancholy donkey in the Winnie the Pooh books.

Broskey stopped blinking after a few seconds. "I don't get the connection."

"Well," Rhodes continued. "Bay City College is pretty artsy-fartsy, you know. I mean, they don't just teach readin', writin', and 'rithmetic. They have alternative education courses."

"Crazy shit," Broskey injected.

"Yeah. That's what they call alternative education. Anyhow, when she's not out stumping whatever latest book she has out, Cheryl teaches a couple of courses there. Acting, meditation, channeling, God knows what else."

"And she meets these aspiring actresses," Fine theorized.

"And the ones she thinks have potential"—Rhodes beamed—"she sends to me."

"Probably the work of Eeyore," Broskey said.

"Huh?" Rhodes asked, slack-jawed. "That her partner?"

"In a manner of speaking," Broskey said, nudging Fine. They both got up.

"Is that it?" Rhodes asked. "That's all I have to tell ya?"

"For the time being," Broskey said. "But I'm sure that as soon as you get back to your office, you will, quick as a bunny, dig up those files and let us know any information you couldn't remember here over lunch. Right?"

"Sure. Sure," Rhodes readily agreed, mentally exhaling.

Fine began to walk out of Polynesia Pete's. Broskey leaned over Rhodes's table for one last second. Rhodes was worried. "What's the matter? What are you thinking?"

Broskey stared at the potbellied, slack-jawed, baby-oiled, Hawaiian-shirt-encased slug, visions of the Brothers Warner, L. B. Mayer, and Walt Disney dancing in his head.

"Gosh." He sighed. "They just don't make movies like they used to."

"You can say that again," Rhodes said, flashing a capped grin and waving over someone who looked like Tinkerbell.

Broskey watched Tink ooze over to the table, her tray held at midbreast level.

"I do believe in fairies, I do, I do," Broskey muttered, leaving the murk of Polynesia Pete's and stepping out into the blazing sun of reality.

Seven

Police Chief Donald Medega didn't smoke cigars, he ate them: popped them into his mouth and devoured them like jelly beans. Now, he sat at the desk in the station's conference room surrounded by a smorgasbord of stubby slabs of tobacco in various lengths and state of mulch.

"I think you're crazy," he said to Broskey, lighting another stogey.

"Well, at least we should talk to the man. Hear him out," Broskey replied.

"One: The idea itself is crazy, okay? No, let me add to that. It's criminally insane. All your pal's articles would do is panic the populace. The populace of Bay City. A city, may I remind you, that prides itself in being *better,* in being *more civilized* than L.A. That's why people pay lotsa bucks to buy homes here. That's why they pay so much taxes. That's why our salaries are slightly higher than your average cop's."

"I understand—"

"Two: I don't understand why we have to consult with some *shrink,* pardon the expression, from Los Angeles' department!"

"Because maybe it'll help." Broskey sighed.

"I hate it when you're logical," Medega groused. "Which is most of the goddamn time!" He reached inside his blazer and came up with a handful of Mylanta pills. Popping them, he began to chew furiously. "Have you talked with this L.A. cop yet?"

"No," Broskey said, "but in a general way, he's been informed of our situation and what we intend to do—"

"What situation? We're not even sure if this is the work of one perp or not?"

"If there's a situation, he's aware of what type of situation it might be and what we might do if it turns out that it *is* a situation."

Medega stopped, midchew, and gaped at Broskey. "Say that again."

Broskey shrugged. "I couldn't."

Medega continued chewing. "All right, send the guy in."

Broskey picked up a phone. "Sergeant? Send in our guest."

Medega and Broskey turned as a fiftyish man walked into the room. He wore a suit much too large for his tall frame. He had a gray crew cut and steel-gray eyes, a square jaw on his heavily lined face. He was the kind of cop Broskey had seen in countless Richard Widmark movies when he was a kid. The man's face showed a lot of age, a lot of experience, a lot of tenacity and, Broskey surmised, bad X-rays. Cancer, Broskey figured. This was definitely a Camel's man.

"Chief Medega, Lieutenant Broskey," the man said in a coarse voice. "I'm Detective David Orwell, LAPD Violent Crime."

Even Medega was impressed by the man's granitelike appearance. A round of handshaking done with, Detective Orwell sat down, tossing a file folder on the table.

"Gentlemen, I've read your reports. It's my opinion that you have a lone perp. A very sick one. A very dangerous one."

"Well . . ." Medega began to interrupt.

"I know. There's no conclusive proof yet." Orwell smiled, as if he had heard the Medegas of the force interrupt countless times before. "That's part of the nightmare."

"Nightmare," Broskey echoed.

"The nightmare with a serial boy," Orwell said, "is that

you're going to lose one way or another. You can catch the guy and you'll still lose. He will have already killed—what? —four girls if you had him in a cell right now.

"Maybe by the time you *do* catch up with him, he will have killed six, seven, eight. He'll go to trial. Maybe cop an insanity plea. Even he doesn't, it's doubtful he'll get the death penalty. We'll pay for his lifetime incarceration out of our taxes. Nothing we do will resurrect his victims."

Broskey liked Orwell.

Medega chomped on a new cigar. Orwell eyed the cigars hungrily. "Want one?" Medega offered.

"No, thank you," Orwell demurred. "Doctor's orders."

Orwell produced a small, well-worn notepad from his trouser pocket. "If you do have a serial killer loose in scenic Bay City," he said, glancing at his book, "you're up against the ultimate mindfuck. Not too many law enforcement agents will acknowledge the fact that there is an epidemic of serial killing in this country." He looked up at Medega and smiled. "I've never been too popular."

Medega laughed, lighting a cigar. "I figured."

"Prior to 1950, serial killing wasn't too much in evidence in the States," Orwell continued. "It was mostly mass murderers, perps who got their victims all at once. Right now, the Justice Department figures there are thirty-five or forty serial killers loose from coast to coast. Most law enforcement officers who have studied the phenomenon, however, think that figure is *waaay* below the actual number. Could be three hundred and up."

"Why don't we hear more about it?" Broskey asked. "I mean, we're brother officers, right?"

"Fair question." Orwell shrugged. "The deal is this. The reason most serial killers succeed in their sprees is that they're invisible."

"I don't get it," Broskey replied.

"They do more than just blend in with a crowd," Orwell continued. "Very often, they *are* the crowd. They're the good neighbor next door. For the most part, to the common citizen, they look and act just like you and me. Some are good husbands, model sons, darling daughters, whatever.

They're usually above suspicion. Outwardly they are up-standing American citizens in every manner.

"But underneath? There's something perking. We can't see it, but it's there. When they kill, it's usually without any apparent motive. It's just something they *do.*"

"Kicks?" Medega said. "That's old hat."

"Sure, but it's more than just kicks, in the old-fashioned sense. It's recreational killing. The way you and I might go see a movie or two a month, these folks kill. And if they get away with the first few, they kill more and more. It's their passion. It's like drugs or alcohol. To a lot of people, a little isn't enough.

"They're often very cocky about the murders, as well. The bodies are usually not concealed. The MO is usually quite apparent. The serial killer usually knows he won't be caught. And do you know why?"

"Why?" Broskey asked, confused.

"Because they have *mobility* on their side and mobility cannot be tackled by the police. Let's say you have a guy in Bay City. Let's say he kills a dozen women in this town. The public outcry is tremendous. The police beef up their patrols. He figures, hell, it's getting too hot for me here. I'll split.

"So he gets in his car and drives for two days. That's all. Where does he wind up? Arizona. He starts doing co-eds in Arizona. By the time the Arizona police make any connection with their slayings and the ones in Bay City, this guy could be in Illinois. If he has a car and half a brain, he'll be three steps ahead of most cops."

"So there's nothing we can do?" Broskey asked.

"Only your best," Orwell replied.

"Well, some of these guys are caught, right?" Medega said. "Gacy, Bundy, DeSalvo. They were caught."

"Right," Orwell replied. "Mistakes. Everyone makes mistakes. That's all we can hope for. After a while, they like to think that they're God at what they do and they'll never, ever get caught. They rely on that cloak of invisibility to avoid detection, to slip by the law. But, as they kill more and more, that cloak begins to slip.

"You see, when they're consumed by that passion to kill, they slip into a different reality, their own reality. Very different from ours. The longer they dwell in their own world, the easier it is for us to spot them.

"Personality chinks appear. The good and kindly next-door neighbor gets a bit more cranky, more secretive. The good husband gets short-tempered, maybe begins solitary drives at night. The darling daughter hits the bottle, talks to shadows. Stuff like that.

"Then you have the ego problems. If a guy is a successful killer and the papers are writing about him, the police are looking for him, he's the toast of the town. It's very difficult not to claim to be a star. Christ, we had one guy upstate who actually bragged about being the perp in a bar, in front of twenty people. Only *one* of those people in the bar had the good sense to follow the guy out of the bar and take down his license-plate number. He phoned it into the cops. The cops tracked the guy down. He had killed six young girls and was living at home with what was left of his mother. He actually carried around her head when he went out on the prowl."

"Jesus," Medega whispered.

Orwell nodded. "Jesus squared. And the *real* kicker is that his arresting officers really *liked* the guy. They said he was the politest prisoner they ever took custody of. A regular Eagle Scout. Go figure."

Broskey frowned. "Well, what can we do to catch our boy?"

"He can't be stopped unless you have wall-to-wall police," Orwell said. "The beauty, if that's the word in all this, is that he can kill at random, for no apparent motive, and you guys will all be standing around with your thumbs up your ass. In essence, he has *you* by the balls, not the other way around. He jerks the chain, guys, you do the dancing."

"But what makes these guys tick?" Broskey asked.

"The really unsettling aspect of this phenomenon is that there is no *one* reason for it. Were there hundreds of serial killers back before the 1950s who just weren't detected? Don't know. And if there weren't, why have they surfaced now? Don't know that, either.

"What we *do* know is that there is always a motive for the killings. We usually don't find it out until we catch the guy, though. For instance, the asshole up north who decapitated his mom? Turns out he was overly dependent on his mother. Sounds simple, huh?

"Here's the way it came down. She kicked out his boozing father. Hated men. Became the driving force of the family. Cold, alcoholic type. Basically she ran the show. This kid grew up very dependent on Mom, and since she was such a snide gorgon, he couldn't even voice his frustrations. So in order to vent his rage, he turned to other women. Sounds simple. But it's the kind of simplicity that eludes detection.

"All you can do, gentlemen, is try to be as creative in your police work as the killer is in his killing. We're putting together something called VICAP, now. The Violent Criminal Apprehension Program. It'll be a computerized national system that will detail crime scenes, forensics reports, ballistics, from any crime in America on a federal, state, and local level. Eventually they should make the job a lot easier.

"Usually the whole scenario is laid out right before you."

"But you just don't recognize it." Broskey nodded. "All the puzzle pieces are there."

Detective Orwell grinned at Broskey. "Kid, you have a future in law enforcement."

Broskey smiled at the old detective. "A newspaper friend of mine is going to publish some public safety articles."

"Could help." Orwell shrugged. He stared at Medega. "Or it could blow up in your face."

Medega lit a third cigar. He was surrounded by R. J. Reynolds incense now. "How do you mean?"

"Well, the newspaper articles, the heightened sense of public awareness, could make the guy crack," Orwell acknowledged. "Could trip him up. Could make him more easily spotted. You realize you'll get a lot of crank calls during this period. Still, it's a good shot that if he keeps his work up, he'll be spotted if every citizen in town is rattled."

"What's the down side?" Medega asked.

"The down side is that once the bastard figures everyone's on the make for him, he'll blow town, possibly the state, and set up shop somewhere else where there aren't cops as smart, as quick, as anyone here in this room." Orwell glanced at Medega's cigars. "I think I will have one of those. No, don't get me a new one. I like 'em broken in."

Orwell extended a calloused hand and took one of Medega's burning stogies. He then flashed a genuine smile and stuck it in his mouth, inhaling deeply. His lungs sounded like bagpipes.

"Fuck medicine," he said cheerfully.

"Well, what's your opinion?" Broskey queried. "What do you think we should do."

"Officially?" Orwell asked.

"Officially," Medega said.

"Don't have an opinion officially," Orwell said, puffing. "I didn't come down here officially. Frankly, if my boss knew I was mingling with the Bay City wonders, I'd get canned. As it is now, they keep me on because they feel sorry for me. Yeah, I'm good, but they think I'm obsessed and dying. They're right on both counts."

"Then why did you come?" Broskey asked.

"Like I said, I'm obsessed. When your sergeant described what you had going on out here and how you were planning to deal with it, I figured you had that obsession, too. You do, you know. I can see it in your eyes. I feel good about that, boy. I really do. It's nice to know that when one old iron horse goes, there's a younger one to take his place. It's a pity you're stuck in Bay City, though. Too many people wearing shirts with alligators over their tits."

Medega was growing angry. His pockmarks were glowing. "Well, what's your *unofficial* opinion then?"

Orwell collected his files and got up from the table. "I figure my time's about up here. Unofficially, give it a shot. You can't do any worse playing it crazy than playing it straight. Besides, you have one ace in the hole here."

"What's that?" Medega asked.

Orwell nodded toward Broskey. "This son-of-a-bitch. He's a born cop. Gentlemen, there are panhandlers awaiting my rousting them on skid row. I bid you farewell."

Broskey flashed Medega a "sorry about that, Chief" look as he got up from the table and escorted Orwell to the door.

He turned and faced Donald Medega. Medega was picking scabs on his knuckles that had arisen from his odd habit of rapping them on his desk whenever he was upset. Which was often.

"Well." Broskey sighed. "What do you think?"

"I stopped thinking ten minutes ago, dammit," Medega said, raising his left fist above the conference-room table.

Broskey slipped out the door, easing it closed behind him.

Eight

Kevin Broskey sat in his living room, staring at a three-week-old copy of *TV Guide,* eating frozen Twinkies, and ignoring a poured shot of vodka. Every fiber of his body ached. He eased himself back into the gray-brown sofa and sighed.

It was late.

He rested his head on one of the couch's threadbare pillows and stared at the water-stained ceiling.

Was he obsessed, like Orwell had said?

He supposed he was. He just couldn't figure out why this case was so important to him. Perhaps it *was* ego. Perhaps it was the challenge.

He didn't know what kind of man that made him.

All he knew was that he couldn't be anything but a cop.

He was pretty much a washout as a contempo human being.

He smoked. He loved liquor. He froze around women in anything else but a police-interview situation. He always slept on the couch, because the bed was too lonely. He hadn't changed the sheets since Janet left and he hadn't seen a first-run television program since "The Man from U.N.C.L.E." vanished from the airwaves.

He loved old movies, hated *Beverly Hills Cop,* thought Sylvester Stallone was obnoxious, and found the most interesting portion of the TV news shows the weather.

He tried to close his eyes but, from somewhere on the block, came the shimmering strains of the last Los Lobos album at brontosaurus volume. Plus, there were shrieks to Jesus coming from a female voice in the house next door.

"Alla time I ax you, Jesus. Why you peek me to suffer so? I gotta no good son who suck onde bottle allatime and no profide for heez family. Jeeezus. I see you. I hunnerstand."

Broskey would have shut the windows in the living room but the heat would have killed him.

The Santa Ana winds were blowing tonight—hot, dry gusts that seared the soul as much as they did the crops. When the Santa Anas blew for more than a few days, people grew irritable. Crime rose. Life stank.

It was as if a touch of death was creeping in from the barren deserts of Southern California, howling banshees, bringing their rot to the land under deceptively blue, sunny skies.

Already, sweat was trickling down his forehead.

He gazed out the window at the pathetic garden in his rented backyard. He felt like he was like sitting in a microwave, but with better scenery.

Broskey slithered off the couch and turned on his black-and-white TV. The picture tube sputtered to life. Broskey smacked the side of the TV with his elbow and beheld the image of Hoss Cartwright lumbering across the prefabricated plains of the Ponderosa.

Hoss was falling in love with a doe-eyed girl as he did twice every season. For any Virginia City gal, that was the kiss of death. Hoss was doomed to be a perpetual bachelor. By the end of each of those lovey-dovey episodes, his bride-to-be would be squooshed to death under either a wagon, a rock, or a horse. Sometimes, for the hell of it, the writers had them shot or burned alive, but most of the time, it was those dad-gummed freak accidents that robbed Hoss of the hubba-hubba factor.

Broskey liked television life.

All problems were resolved within either thirty or sixty minutes.

"But, Paw," Broskey heard someone say, "I'm ahankerin' to git hitched."

He sat in front of the TV set, dazed, wanting and dreading sleep. When he slept, he dreamed. And most of his dreams were real beauts, sort of *Friday the 13th* scenarios but without the panache.

He munched on another petrified Twinkie, wishing they were Devil Dogs. They didn't stock Devil Dogs on the West Coast, lovely finger-shaped devil's-food cakes containing rich, creamy vanilla filling that were to die for when refrigerated and eaten with a glass of cold milk.

For a fleeting second, he tried to focus on the day.

Chief Medega hadn't decided what to do about Broskey's plan. He said he'd try to decide by the morning.

By morning, the decision would be made for him.

Laurel Callen didn't like walking to her car after class at Bay City College. She was smart enough to know that anytime after sundown, it was dangerous for a woman to go anywhere alone. She hated the fact that society had forced women into a vulnerable position. But she was savvy enough to realize that she didn't have to play into any macho geek's idea of a hot time, the woman-as-toy riff. Caution was the answer.

Usually, she had a fellow student drive her to her car, which was usually parked on a side street a few blocks from the campus. The college lot was small and usually packed by the time she arrived for the first of her night classes.

Tonight, however, her buddy hadn't shown up and she found herself without a ride.

She began walking across the crowded parking lot as the night students filed out of the main lecture hall.

She dreaded the walk to her car and quickened her pace.

That's when he pulled up.

He asked her if she needed a ride.

She replied no. She was polite, but firm.

He understood, he said. Made a joke about it. It put her at ease. He smiled at her. It was an easy, relaxed smile. He didn't seem so bad. He wasn't exactly the kind of person she'd normally gravitate to but he seemed all right.

She supposed it would be okay for him to drive her to her car. It was only four blocks away. She got into his auto, thinking that she had the guy pegged for someone safe.

Laurel Callen could not have been more mistaken.

Nine

Broskey stood in the hallway outside of his office. He leaned against the wall, wanting a cigarette, and talked to the short, red-faced Sergeant Grady McGlory.

"Mac, how long have I known you?"

"Six years, Kevin, my boy."

"Is it possible that your brogue gets stronger as you get older?"

"Might be genetic."

"Where were you born?"

"Malibu."

"And your parents?"

"Philadelphia, P of A," McGlory said proudly.

"Then how is it, being a second-generation Irish-American, that you manage to out—Barry Fitzgerald the mayor of Dublin when it comes to speech?"

McGlory chuckled. "I'm Irish."

"Right."

McGlory pulled Broskey aside. "Ireland isn't a place. It's a state of mind."

Broskey smelled the liquor on McGlory's breath as the red-faced man began, "No latitude or longitude can bound the Emerald Isle. You'll find it off in Timbuktu or down along the Nile. Wherever mothers stoop to smooth a baby's tousled hair and croon an Irish lullaby, Ireland is there. Wherever men are brave and true and quick to take a stand, and proud to fight, if fight they must, there is Ireland! Wherever lad and lassie meet a merry dance to share, O, echoes of the Blarney Stone, Ireland is there!"

Broskey nodded. "I'll try to remember that."

"You do that, Kevin," McGlory said. "In every good cop, there's an Irishman trying to get out. And you're a *great* cop."

"I must have twins, then."

Everyone knew that McGlory hit the bottle hard, but he was a tenacious little man. He came back from Korea with a Purple Heart, became a cop, watched his wife die, and had two kids get pan-fried in Vietnam. Still, he stayed on the force. He got the job done and then some. Broskey would trust him with his life. He was a good man to have on your side.

Sergeant Andrea Fine rushed down the hallway toward the two policemen. "Lieutenant?" she said, out of breath. "Better get down to Marigold Street, North. The chief is on his way, now."

Within minutes Broskey was at the crime scene. It looked like a Who's Who of the Bay City Police Department. Not only was Medega there, staring glumly at a 1975 Toyota Celica, but the three other gold shields in the department seemed to be conferring about something ominous. They looked like the witches in *Macbeth*.

"By the pricking of my thumbs," Broskey muttered, getting out of his car, "something shitty this way comes."

He strolled past the roped-off section of the street and walked up to Medega. In the background, Bluth and McDonald hovered like frightened cherubs.

"Chief?"

"This does it," Medega said. "This does it!"

Goldstein of forensics sidled up to Broskey as Broskey gazed at what was in the car. It was a nude woman. "It looks like our boy," Goldstein said, "but he's getting a bit creative."

"Shall I try mind reading or you want to explain that?" Broskey said, grinding his teeth, Spanish-dancer style.

"Can't give you the gory details yet, but from a casual examination, it looks like she was smacked in the base of the skull. The blow probably just knocked her out. She was taken somewhere else and done in. Stripped. Then the guy had the balls to bring her back to her car. Unlock it. Place her inside. Return all her personal belongings—purse, driver's license—"

"Student ID," Broskey muttered.

"Dead on, Lieutenant. All her credit cards are in the glove compartment. I mean, the guy was meticulous. He *wanted* us to know who she was—"

"And where she went to school," Broskey said.

Medega began to shudder almost imperceptibly. His wiry body tingled beneath his suit. He grabbed Broskey by the elbow and led him away from the gaggle of cops. In the distance, Broskey could hear the reporters squawking at the police barricades. The story was going to break big this afternoon, bigger by tomorrow morning.

"Broskey," Medega whispered, "how much do you know about me?"

"Not a lot, sir," Broskey answered, confused.

Medega took a deep breath and virtually hissed out a torrent of words. "I was born in south-central L.A. A punk. A pachuko. Nobody ever thought I'd amount to anything, you know? We had gangs back then and I was a member. But I got out of that somehow. I started at the bottom in the police force. The pits. I worked. I worked my tail off for every fucking promotion.

"I *like* being a cop. I *like* being the good guy. I *like* being in Bay City. It makes me feel good to feel like we're a little more law-abiding than the rest of L.A. But I don't know what's happening, Broskey. I just don't know. We're getting as bad, *worse,* than the rest of the city. The rest of the county. Maybe it's because we're so near the beach, you know. When the very rich and the very poor meet, you're in for trouble.

"But *this,*" he said, motioning to the car, *"this* is pissing me off in a big way, Broskey. This is butchery, and it's got to stop!"

"I know that, sir," Broskey said. "The killer is taunting us now."

"He's doing a damn good job."

"He's daring us to catch him."

"Broskey," Medega said, his pockmarks seeming iridescent in the late-morning sun. "You're in charge of this case. You're the best shield in the department. Maybe it's 'cause you're such a weird son-of-a-bitch. You're smart. You're screwed up. I don't know. You *think.*"

"Thanks, sir," Broskey replied, not sure whether he'd been complimented or insulted.

"We're in deep shit, Broskey. We've never had anything like this in Bay City. When that Night Stalker shit happened in L.A., two counties were tripping over each other, not sure what the other was doing. Not comparing information. The guy ran free for at least one month too many because of bureaucratic bullshit.

"Son of Sam in New York? The different boroughs were working *against* each other to nail the guy. I don't want that to happen here. We're a small city. We have a nice dialogue within the department. Use it. Bottom line, Broskey: I want you to catch this bastard. I want you to nail his hide against my office wall. I don't care how you do it. I don't care how unorthodox your methods."

"Yes sir."

"And if you're going to do something really off-the-wall, please, whatever you do, don't tell me about it. I want to cover my ass in the mayor's office."

"Understood, sir."

Medega frowned. "Oh, and by the way, because of the pecking order, I had to assign McDonald to your task force. Keep him busy with red herrings, okay?"

"Yes sir."

Medega glanced at the reporters over his shoulder. He straightened himself up and took one, two, three, four deep breaths. Broskey watched the police chief's face pale, assuming a more humanoid appearance.

"And, now," Medega said. "I will meet the media and lie my ass off. As far as I'm concerned, this is a routine homicide investigation until you and your hack friend Mayer deem it otherwise."

"Thank you, sir."

"Oh." Medega smiled sweetly. "One more thing, Broskey."

"Yes sir?"

"Don't fuck up. If you do, it'll be the last time you do on this department. Like I said, I like you, but I like me better."

Medega turned and strode toward the herd of media representatives, who were smashing into each other at the edge of the barricades like fish in a feeding frenzy.

Broskey watched Medega slick his hair back with the palms of his hands and, affixing a phony smile to his face, wade into the school of snapping, salivating press people.

Broskey took one last look at the body in the car before walking over to Goldstein.

"What more can you tell me?"

"I got a name, an address, and everything that could be found on a driver's license."

"Give it to me. I guess it's time I paid our late lady's home a call."

"Her name was Laurel—like in the canyon—Callen."

"Nice name."

"I'm sure she was a nice girl."

"Me, too," Broskey said, taking a slice of note paper from Goldstein and heading for his car.

He'd make sure her name would remain nice in the newspapers.

Once more, he'd make the perp who did her pay.

He eased himself into the car. His stomach felt like a bag of gerbils.

He cranked the car into gear, burped, and tasted the remains of last night's Twinkies.

He wondered if he could import Devil Dogs.

Ten

J ake Mayer sat like an eager schoolboy in the hamburger joint on Hollywood Boulevard. Broskey chewed his burger in silence, not quite comfortable staring out a window that gave a good view of tourists examining dead stars' names emblazoned on sidewalks, spit-spouting transients, teenage hookers in Spandex, and ashen-faced boys looking for a quick fifty dollars as a tradeoff for any kind of action. The food tasted like papier-mâché.

"You're kidding me!" Mayer said. "Your chief actually went for the idea?"

"In a matter of speaking," Broskey acknowledged, trying to drown out the taste of the burger with an ocean of catsup. "He was pretty upset by this morning's victim."

"Right." Mayer nodded vigorously. "I can understand that. Did you tell him *every*thing? You know, my being in on all the developments?"

"Let's just say I gave him the *Reader's Digest* version of our deal," Broskey said, stabbing a pregnant french fry with his fork.

"We should have a drink to toast this. You know? A real, honest-to-God drink. Waitress? Miss? *Garçonette?*"

A bleach-blond waitress who looked a little like James Arness in drag walked over to the table. "Yeah?"

"Let me have two fingers of Scotch, and for my friend . . . ?"

"Iced coffee," Broskey muttered.

Jake shot Broskey a startled look. "What's this? I invite you to a swank dive on my side of town and you turn into a priss?"

"I'm on duty," Broskey said.

"That's never stopped you before."

"Call me crazy, but seeing five corpses in one morning sort of puts a damper on my usually festive nature."

The waitress gaped at Broskey. Mayer shrugged. "My buddy here is the sensitive type. Why he went into the mortuary business is beyond me. Did you know that most men are buried without pants?"

The waitress continued to gape.

"Honest to God," Mayer continued. "You see, with most funerals and wakes, when they have an open coffin you only see the top half, right?"

The waitress nodded.

"Well, what the mortuaries do is, they just dress up the top half. The bottom half they just hang the old birthday suit on. That way, they make a profit when they charge the bereaved for a whole monkey suit. Amazing, isn't it?"

The waitress nodded again.

"Sometimes I think I should call 'Action News,' you know? That 'hit back' investigative guy. I mean, this is a fraudulent practice. But, every time I think that, I figure, now how could they prove that on TV? I mean, they'd have to send a camera crew into a funeral home, right? And can you imagine what you'd see on TV? Christ! Wouldn't that ruin anyone's appetite right after the six o'clock news?"

The waitress began to slowly back away from the table. Mayer grinned. "Scotch for me and iced coffee for my squeamish pal here."

The waitress turned and sprinted away from the table. Broskey stared outside the window. He shut his eyes. He had a headache. He figured he'd have it for days.

"Earth to Kev, Earth to Kev," Mayer said.

"Huh? Oh, sorry," Broskey said, turning his attention back to the bleeding burger in his hand.

"So, what do we do now?"

Broskey thought a moment. "I suppose you get cracking on your research and get the first article in shape. Have you talked to your editor?"

"Uh-huh. He's about as excited as your chief."

"Didn't tell him about the book angle, huh?"

"Nope. I have this allergic reaction to bodily harm."

"Well, if you want to follow me back to Bay City, we can stop at the campus and say hi to Cheryl Williams."

"That airhead? What's she doing these days, chatting up dolphins?"

"Nope. She's sending young girls off to meet sleazoid producers."

"Ooooh. Very, very bad karma."

Eleven

*W*illiams's class wasn't in session that evening, so two hours later, Broskey and Mayer found themselves in the Malibu home of ex-hoofer turned seer Cheryl Williams. The fifty-two-year-old actress sat, miniskirted, in front of a picture window overlooking the churning Pacific. Her lion's mane of black hair cascaded down over a tanktop that left little to the imagination.

She puffed a cigarette as she spoke. "It's my only vice." She smiled at the pair. "I hope you don't mind."

"Not at all," Broskey said. "I smoke myself."

"I bugger sheep." Mayer shrugged. "That way, when you break up, at least you know you get a sweater out of the deal."

Williams laughed. "Well, there has to be a reason for your visit. I don't have to be psychic to know that."

"We need a little help," Broskey ventured.

"You don't look like the spiritual type." The seer smiled.

"I almost was an altar boy once," Broskey said. "But I was kicked out for messing around with the incense."

Mayer shrugged. "Don't look at me. I'm one of Jesse Jackson's Hymies."

"But it's not that kind of help we need," Broskey continued.

Williams glanced at Broskey's forehead. "Well, someone has already given you a message? What's left?"

"Police business."

"Oh," the long-limbed woman replied.

Williams looked at Broskey. "You, I believe, are a cop. But *this guy?* He has *Enquirer* written all over him."

Broskey chuckled. "You're close. Actually, we're using Mr. Mayer as a consultant. He actually has more experience dealing with this type of case than anyone on the force does."

"What kind of case?" Williams asked.

"That's what we're trying to figure out," Mayer volunteered.

Broskey cleared his throat. "Exactly what kind of course do you teach at Bay City?"

"Actually, I teach two courses," Williams replied, tugging on a Camel. "Acting 101, which is basically an introductory course to stage and an introduction to channeling."

"Channeling," Broskey repeated.

"Oh, yes," Williams said. "The spiritual contact with those who have gone before us."

"Like talking to someone's dead mother?" Broskey asked.

"It's a little deeper than that," Williams replied. "I had a revolutionary spiritual experience a few years back that simply changed my life."

"I bet," Mayer muttered.

"I actually made contact with a being that was five thousand years old. He spoke to me. He communicated to me."

"Like Edgar Bergen and Charlie McCarthy?" Broskey ventured.

Williams laughed again. "Morlock. No, I'm serious about all this. My world, you see, revolves around the super-consciousness of a person, a person's one, eternal, unlimited soul. The soul that is the real you. We are basically and fundamentally spiritual beings. We are not physical beings, we are not mental beings. What I try to do through my channeling classes is to get every student to meditate. To picture themselves in a garden with a stream running through it. Ethereal music plays through a sound system I have hooked up in the classroom or auditorium.

"I ask all those present to visualize a white light in their garden. They walk toward that light. The figure that emerges from that light is the higher self. All I ask of my audience is to greet that self.

"It is that soul that connects us with the God force. We are that God force. We are perfect. The key to spiritual realization and happiness is to move into alignment with that God force.

"For me, my belief in reincarnation and the connection I have with the spiritual world has led me to the realization that, in past lives, I was an orphan living among a herd of rhinos. I was known as the queen of the rhinos and I could communicate with rhinos continents away."

"Yeah." Broskey nodded. "I was married once. I always know when my ex wants more alimony."

"Not quite, Lieutenant." Williams smiled. "You see, I believe that there are thousands of *us*'es floating through time. In my way of thinking time is not linear, everything is happening all at once. The soul encompasses both the past and the future as well as the present. You're focusing on this life because lessons need to be learned.

"Life is a dream. An illusion. Each of us is living our own dream. We are writing it, casting it, acting it. This life, the life that you believe you are living now, is merely a play. You're playing yourself when, at the same time, you realize that you've been playing this role in various existences throughout time."

"Right." Broskey nodded.

"When I was a little girl," Williams explained, "I had this dream. I was always being chased around by a large bear. Finally, the bear chased me to the height of a large mountain. There was no place I could go but down. I hesitated. I clung to the edge of the precipice. Finally I turned around and faced the bear. 'Now what do I do?' I asked the bear.

"'Don't ask me,' the bear replied. 'It's your dream.' Don't you see? Life is but a dream."

Broskey rubbed his forehead. "I appreciate your beliefs,

Ms. Williams, but I have some very real problems to talk to you about, plus I have a fierce headache."

"Poor baby," Williams cooed, crossing her miniskirted legs widely and letting Broskey know that she didn't believe in undergarments. "But I'm afraid we'll have to postpone our talk about your real problems until after my channeling session."

"Say what?" Broskey asked.

"I have a private group gathered in the den for an eight o'clock meeting with Eeyore. I'd love it if you could attend."

"Well . . ." Broskey began.

"We'd be delighted to," Mayer finished. "We really haven't had any experience with channels since HBO started scrambling their satellite signals."

Williams flashed Mayer a "drop dead" smile. She turned to Broskey. "I hope you'll enjoy the session. Why don't you wait up here for a few minutes? I'll have Duretha, my maid, show you into the study when I'm ready."

"Fine, okay," Broskey said, trying not to stare at the woman's taut legs as she exited the room.

Williams sauntered from the room, pausing at the door. "Lieutenant?"

"Yes, ma'am?"

"You haven't understood one word I've said, have you?"

Broskey blushed. "Frankly, no."

"I *do* have great legs, though, don't I? For an old gal?"

"Well, *no*. I mean, *yes*. But you're not old. I mean . . ." Broskey found his face burning. He could hear Mayer chuckling.

"Are you single at the moment, Lieutenant?" Cheryl Williams smiled.

"Yes."

"Good." She heaved a deep, hearty sigh, proving to Broskey that her aversion to undergarments extended to the area above as well as below the waist. Broskey didn't know where to focus his attention.

He found himself staring at the Pacific Ocean.

He heard the door behind them close as Williams left the room. He gazed at the roaring sea.

"What was it that Nathanael West said about Los Angeles?" Mayer muttered. "It was a crazy city because most of the people who lived here moved out from Kansas to see the ocean. Then they saw it. After you've seen one wave you've seen them all. What else can you do but go nuts?"

Broskey stared at the ocean. It occurred to him that Cheryl Williams had, indeed, been born in Kansas.

Mayer seemed to be honing in on Broskey's thoughts. "Hey, so she's a flake. So what? At least she's a *pretty* flake. And those legs? They probably go all the way up to her neck."

"Knock it off, Jake."

"She has a crush on you, Kev. She was giving off this odor, you know?"

"Knock it off, Jake."

"You're blushing, Kev. Didn't I tell you that you needed a gal from Atlantis or someplace in that vicinity?"

"Jake!"

"Okay, so she's a little older. But think about it. If the romance doesn't work out, she can take out adoption papers on you and make it all legal."

"Drop dead."

Mayer clutched his chest, uttered an abysmal scream, and fell onto the floor just as Cheryl Williams's maid walked into the room.

"Miss Williams would like you both to come downstairs now."

Jake stared at the maid from the floor. The woman had legs like a baby grand. "Don't mind me. I died."

The rubbery-faced maid stared at Jake. "That don't surprise me. There ain't nothin' I haven't seen in this old house."

Twelve

Cheryl Williams's study was the size of most people's homes. A massive room that occupied nearly one floor of the sprawling house, with a glass wall overlooking the ocean, the study looked like a geological display at New York's Museum of Natural History. There were slabs of crystal everywhere.

Nearly one hundred people sat, cross-legged, in the room. Cheryl was seated in a plush chair before them, clad in a gossamer-thin golden robe.

The maid led Broskey and Mayer to a spot in the back of the room. Broskey stared at the floor. He hoped Cheryl wasn't long-winded. Sitting cross-legged on a wooden floor in a damp, drafty house would probably do wonders for his back.

The two men sat, bewildered, as the assembled began chanting. If Broskey didn't know better, he would have sworn that the room had chosen the words "scoobie-doobie-doobie" as its collective mantra.

"Is it me, or does that sound like a Frank Sinatra song?" Mayer asked.

"Shhhh," a pretty young girl next to them said.

"Sorry," Broskey said. "This is our first session. We're guests of Cheryl's."

The woman immediately perked up. "Isn't she *wonderful?*"

"Totally bitchin'," Mayer muttered.

The girl ignored Jake and concentrated on Broskey. "And she's such a bargain, too."

"I don't get it."

"Each session only costs three hundred dollars."

"Three hundred bucks?" Broskey blinked.

"It's pretty cheap when you consider it. A hundred for the body. A hundred for the soul. A hundred for the mind."

Broskey nodded as the girl lapsed back into her scoobie-doobie chant.

Mayer leaned toward Broskey. "I think I've found a new career. If I can hook up with a ventriloquist, I can make a mint."

Broskey nudged Mayer. They both gazed across the room. The study was littered with TV and film stars. Sheila Renfew from the late-night soap *Houston*. Bunny Bedella from *Woman Cop*. Burt Slade from the wide-screen *Big Car Rally* series of films.

"Jesus," Broskey said. "This looks like a Who's Who in Hollywood."

"Or a what's what." Mayer sneered.

"TV Guide doesn't have this many names in any of its issues."

"Plus, we have your normal rich folk here, too."

Broskey nodded. There were twenty or so denizens of the den who were show-biz nobodies, at least no one Broskey recognized. Bleached-blond women with pinched faces. Balding, tan men, in five-hundred-dollar casual outfits. A few blue-haired old ladies. A guy with a walker.

What surprised Broskey most was the fact that there were at least three dozen young, perky women in attendance.

"There are a lot of kids here, too," Broskey said.

"Probably some of her students," Mayer whispered back.

"Where would students get three hundred bucks a pop to attend a soirée like this?"

They both exchanged glances and whispered simultaneously, "Anson Rhodes?"

The chanting stopped and Cheryl stood at the head of the class. "Now that we have cleansed ourselves of our earthly ties, let me begin. For those of you who are newcomers, I'm sure you're here because you've read one of my books or have purchased one of my records."

The crowd made a guttural noise of agreement.

"But for the unitiated, let me recap. Life is but a dream. And since your life is your dream, you have the power to change it. Once you achieve God power, once you *are* God, you can control not only what you do but also what happens to you. That's the reason, I believe, that I have not had a single bad thing happen to me in the past five years. I went through a short period when, although I knew about my dream life, I rejected it, tested it. I was robbed six times. Once I surrendered to the fact that *I* was in total control, that *I* could relax my perceptions to allow other spiritual beings, such as Eeyore, to assist me, my luck changed completely.

"Basically, it is in all of you to control *everything* in your world."

Broskey grunted. "Guess that makes my job obsolete."

"Now." Cheryl smiled. "Before I introduce Eeyore. Are there any questions you have to ask me?"

One blond-haired woman with connect-the-dots makeup raised her hand. "Yes?" Cheryl asked.

"I was wondering. I'm new to all this. I read your last book and found it interesting. But what I want to know is, is there any way I could use your New Age spiritualism to help a family of my friend Michael's? Michael was shot to death last week. They're having trouble dealing with that."

"First," Cheryl replied, "you have to ask yourself why you created that in your reality."

The woman was stunned. "Created what?"

"Michael's death."

"I didn't create that. Some little wetback kid with a Saturday-night special did that for me."

"I'm sensing a real sense of hostility here."

"Of course I'm hostile. Michael was a thirty-five-year-old writer. He had everything going for him!"

"Then why did you allow him to die?" Cheryl asked sweetly.

The woman was rigid with anger. "I wasn't even in town when it happened! I was in Spain. At a Club Med!"

Cheryl waved her arms. Three of her followers surrounding the woman extended their hands and calmed the woman down.

"Perhaps, in order to understand better what I mean by the dream we call life, I should bring forth Eeyore."

"Eeyore," the crowd chanted.

"Remind you of anything?" Mayer whispered.

"Yeah," Broskey replied. "Jim Jones in a prom gown."

Cheryl Williams eased herself deep into the chair. Her head pitched back. Her eyes fluttered. The crowd grew silent. Her body convulsed ever so slightly, as if it were the recipient of a paranormal version of Magic Fingers.

Suddenly her back arched.

Eyes still rolled back beneath their lids, Cheryl's face began to twitch.

She opened her mouth. A strange, singsongish voice emerged; part Irish, part Pakistani, all ham.

"I am Eeyore, am I not? Yes, I be. That I am. Eeyore, 'tis I. Veddy good."

"Christ," Broskey muttered. "She sounds like Peter Sellers in *The Party.*"

"Or a head-on collision between Sabu and Barry Fitzgerald," Mayer replied.

"I am here for you, am I not? That I be. So, you are strange to me, thou art."

Cheryl/Eeyore leaned forward in her/his seat and sniffed the air. She tilted toward a TV star in the front of the room. "What is this smell? Who is this Estée Lauder?"

The crowd chuckled. "It's a perfume." The star giggled through her caps.

"Aha," Eeyore said. "This is a new thing for me, is it not. Five thousand years old be I. Old be all of you. We have met, all thou and I, many, many times in time."

An actor who usually played killers wearing hockey masks raised his hand. "Eeyore?"

"Yes . . . Lancelot?"

The man tilted his head, awestruck. "You know, I've always felt that I was a knight in some past existence."

"Oh, that you were and more so," Eeyore chirped. "You were once king of a far-off place I know not of, called France. Regal, you were. Crowns, wore you."

"Gosh," the man theorized.

"A question for me, you have, have you not?"

"Well, actually. I was thinking of changing my agents. You see, ICM would like to have me but I'm already signed with APA. I think ICM would be a great career move but yet I don't want to hurt the folks at APA. I mean, they've been really nice to me. It's just that I want to have *more.*"

"More you shall have," Eeyore sang out. "Everyone should have more. Take. Accumulate. This world is your world, is it not? Have what makes you happy. Surround yourself with happy things. Smiley things. That is your destiny. To be happy."

"Christ," Broskey muttered. "She's just given the go-ahead for everyone in the room to turn Republican."

"I take back what I said about you needing a girl from Atlantis," Mayer muttered. "I don't care how good her legs are."

The actor smiled and settled back down. "Thanks, Eeyore."

"Thanks be to thee," Eeyore said. "Your happiness is my happiness."

Rhoda Barnett, a Hollywood gossip columnist with a hairdo that made most Cadillac grillework look flexible and a face that formed a perpetual pucker was next. "Oh, Eeyore, my television show has been canceled. Is there nothing I can do?"

Eeyore frowned momentarily. "Doubt, you express. Expressing doubt is not a happy thing. A sad thing, that. Trust in yourself. Riches you have earned. More riches will come. What is this thing, this synd-eee-cay-shun?"

"Syndication!" Rhoda exclaimed. "Of course! I could be bigger than 'Entertainment Tonight'!"

"Big ye are and bigger ye shall be, isn't that so? Did you ever that doubt? Fiddlesticks, says I."

Broskey was shaking his head from side to side. "I've never encountered a Cro-Magnon that sounded like fucking Yoda before."

"I dunno." Mayer shrugged. "It's all kind of fun, in a perverted, sick, and self-absorbed sorta way."

"Let's see how much fun I can have," Broskey whispered.

He stood up straight. "Oh, Eeyore?" he called.

Eeyore tilted his head from side to side. "Ah, a new voice. A new presence, senses I. Veddy strong. Veddy masculine. You are a knight, are you not?"

"Nope."

"Aha, a prince perhaps. Royalty for sure."

"A lieutenant. Bay City Homicide."

"Ah, but in lives before, you were royalty."

"That's swell to know," Broskey said. "Eeyore, I have this problem."

"Eeyore can help, maybe?"

"Maybe."

"This problem, it concerns others, does it not?"

"It does," Broskey acknowledged. "I'm not sure how many others. But it really troubles me."

"Then, Eeyore shall hear your troubles, and advise, shall I not?"

"I hope so," Broskey said. "You see . . . someone out there, in this time, in this world, is going around and butchering young girls."

Broskey heard the crowd gasp. He watched Eeyore stiffen.

Broskey smiled and continued. "This is a bad thing, is it not?"

Eeyore nodded vigorously. "Beddybad. Beddybad."

"And the only connection we have is that all the girls were students at Bay City College."

Eeyore's eyes were fluttering like hummingbird's wings now. Broskey figured he got the channeler working at 78 r.p.m.'s. "And it seems that most of the girls had a couple of things in common. One: They all took classes from a woman named Cheryl Williams. Two: Ms. Williams turned them on to a moviemaker named Anson Rhodes."

Eeyore's lips moved. A small word, something along the lines of "eeeep," emerged.

Broskey plowed on. "Rhodes either sucked the girls into modeling or softcore films. Now, I'll be darned if I can get any further on this angle. Do you think you can help me out?"

Most of the young girls in attendance seemed to go into a confused, trancelike state, glancing nervously from Eeyore to Broskey. Eeyore began to sway. "Eeyore is confused, he is. Eeyore is not a modern denizen, is he? He is from the past. He is from the future. Knows not, does he, of the baser instincts of some of the present world's populace."

"So you can't help?"

"Eeyore, alas, is confused. Eeyore, alas, knows not of what you speak."

"Just thought I'd check," Broskey said, getting to his feet. He pulled Jake up after him. The two men left the room.

"What are we leaving for?" Mayer asked. "This is just getting good."

"We have just chipped the tip of the New Age iceberg, have we not?" Broskey smiled.

He glanced over his shoulder. He couldn't be sure, but he thought Eeyore lapsed into a short mantra.

It sounded suspiciously like "son-of-a-bitch."

Thirteen

I can't believe you." Mayer cackled. "You acted like a real prick tonight and you seem to be proud of it!"

Broskey massaged his forehead, watching the scenery on the Pacific Coast Highway rush by. "Just thought I'd stir things up a bit."

"How's your head?"

"A lot better, thanks."

Broskey stared at the barely standing cliff faces that bordered the highway. It had been a dry season in Southern California. Too dry. It was fire weather. Earthquake weather. Landslide weather.

Large metal nets stood next to the road, a vain attempt by Los Angeles County to keep the boulders from sliding off the hillside and onto the road. Boulder tag was a sport that everyone accepted in Southern California. When there was no rain, boulders toppled off mountaintops and squashed even the most prestigious of cars and homes.

When it rained, the hills turned to mud and didn't show too much class distinction in whom or what they engulfed.

Weather was like that in Southern California.

Deceptively placid, but murderously extreme.

Mayer turned off the PCH and headed toward Broskey's rented flat. "Okay, bossman, what's the plan?"

"Can you have your first article in the paper the day after next?"

"I suppose. Why the rush?"

"I just have this feeling that it's time to start applying pressure."

"To who?"

"Whom."

"Okay, to whom?"

"To whoever is going to react to the pressure the most," Broskey replied. "It's time to really start shaking the tree."

"You could get more fallout than you expected."

"Comes with the turf," Broskey said as Mayer pulled up in front of his paint-flaked bungalow.

"Okay, bossman, this is it," Mayer chirped.

"Thanks, Jake." Broskey smiled. "I appreciate the help, the company, and the friendship."

Jake grinned. "Hey, I'm going to be a star because of this. And stop smiling so much. It makes me nervous."

"I feel good, Jake. For the first time in quite a while, I feel good."

Jake nodded. "Naaah. You feel *useful*. There's a difference."

"Maybe," Broskey said, getting out of the car. He watched Jake pull away. He reached inside his pocket for his house keys. He couldn't find them. No matter. His door was probably unlocked anyway. He began to whistle.

He hadn't whistled since Janet left.

He kept on whistling until he reached his front door.

There was a dead cat hanging from the doorknob.

On his white, front door, in blood red, the words DEAD PIG, CORPSES RULE were spray-painted.

Broskey carefully unlooped the noose from the cat's neck and carried it to the curb, where he deposited the pop-eyed animal in a trash can.

Feeling one hundred years older, he opened the front door and entered his house.

He needed a drink.

He needed a smoke.

He wanted to feel that he could die at any minute and be prepared for it.

Cheryl Williams sat in a massive, marble bathtub/Jacuzzi and, motor whirring, bubbles swirling all about her taut body, barked into a squawk box hanging from the side of the glistening pit.

"Anson, why didn't you tell me the cops visited you?" she barked.

A tense voice burped from the speaker phone. "I—I didn't want to upset you, babe."

"Upset me? How do you think I feel, now? That bastard showed up at one of my channeling sessions and spooked the whole fucking crowd! It was like a stampede. As soon as the asshole left, the whole bunch of them headed for the doors. Not even Eeyore could get them to calm down."

"Any permanent damage?" Anson inquired.

"How the hell should I know?" Cheryl sputtered, avoiding a large bubble rising from her tub. "I'll give everyone a week or two to chill out. Then I'll resume my schedule."

"I'm sorry."

"You're sorry? I'm going on a national book tour in three weeks. If word of this leaks out, I'm up shit creek! You should have leveled with me, Anson. You should have let me know. I come through for you, don't I?"

"And I come through for you," Anson interrupted. "You get your ten percent."

"I know, I know. And I appreciate it," Cheryl said, dropping into a soothing tone. "But, darling, we're in this together. I wasn't aware of the killings."

"Me, neither."

"Good. Then we have nothing to worry about."

"The cop," Anson began.

"Broskey," Cheryl muttered.

"What do you think of him?"

"I'm not sure," Cheryl replied. "I took him for a rube when he showed up. He was with this little jerk. I figured the jerk for a slimeball, but the cop? He seemed to me like a pushover. He couldn't take his eyes off my legs or my tits.

Blushed like crazy when I made eyes at him. But later? The guy is smart. Smarter than he looks."

"Jim Rockford." Anson gasped.

"What?"

"Don't you remember 'The Rockford Files'?" Anson replied. "Great TV show?"

"I only watch PBS and MTV," Cheryl replied, grabbing a nearby vibrator and clicking it into action.

"Yeah, right. What are you doing? Shaving?"

"Exactly." Cheryl beamed over the hum.

"Well," Anson continued, "James Garner played this PI named Rockford who looked like an all-around swell guy. Country bumpkin. But when the chips were down, when the odds were stacked against him, he turned into a real Sherlock Holmes."

"What's the point?"

"Be careful of this Broskey guy."

"I hope I never see him again," Cheryl cooed, the humming growing more intense.

"Oh, you will. This guy has the eyes of a bulldog. I've seen eyes like that before. IRS guys have eyes like that: totally obsessed."

"Fine." Cheryl giggled.

"Can you fuck him?"

"What?"

"Can you get him on your side?"

"Who cares?"

"You might . . . soon."

The humming grew louder. "I'll talk to you later, Anson. I have business to attend to."

Cheryl clicked off the speaker phone, turned on the Jacuzzi jets up to full, and concentrated on her rubber friend.

She began to warble a mantra.

Fourteen

Los Angeles treats its whitebread well. Whitebread people live in whitebread neighborhoods, usually picture-perfect burbs where a major crime is considered losing one's radio from an expensive sports car during the night (something that, in New York, is considered more along the lines of brushing one's teeth every day).

It's not that Los Angeles is prejudiced, exactly. It's just that it makes more sense to protect the citizens that pay more taxes and have more influence. In campus campy Westwood, for instance, a fleet of cops will descend on the village when one innocent bystander is killed in a gang shooting. The city was worried that weekenders would start avoiding the trendy restaurants, cafés, and first-run theaters that make up the bulk of the village.

In the less affluent south-central area of town six to ten people are shot a day in gang-related pop-offs. It wasn't until the shootings in south central began to take on Al Capone proportions that the city acted, and that was only because the whitebread populace raised a ruckus. They were afraid those punks would start driving through whitebread neighborhoods.

There are no such things as foot patrols in most of run-down L.A., yet the affluent beach communities have dashing young cops in khaki-colored shorts pedaling lei-surely along the walkways on their shiny new ten-speeds.

Los Angeles makes it clear that it wants to protect its whitebread. Whitebread people don't cause trouble. They usually are on the receiving end. They aren't too street-smart, but they know how to elect officials.

Bay City, being surrounded by L.A., had inherited this great tradition. The city tried not to be as overt about it (it couldn't help but be more subtle; after all, it was a *lot* smaller than L.A., a mere postage stamp on the geographical envelope of Lotus Land). Still, Bay City had its insidious little ways of showing who counted and who didn't.

Take street cleaning. Upwardly mobile and old-money-encrusted streets got cleaned twice a week, like clockwork. Either Monday and Wednesday or Tuesday and Thursday. Streets like the one that Broskey lived on usually received one good cleaning annually and relied, for the most part, on local residents with bad bladders to keep the curbs moist.

While Broskey lay sleeping, his forehead pounding dully, his street longing for a scrub in the early-morning light, across town, a perky traffic patrol cop was making her upscale rounds, preceding the street cleaner, in her traffic cart. The routine was simple. Anyone whose car was parked curbside on a designated hose-down day was ticketed. Bay City prided itself on the amount of parking tickets it gave out. Its cops watched their myriad of meters like anxious mothers, waiting to charge in and ticket the offending auto as soon as it insulted the metallic pole via a dramatic lack of cents.

The traffic cop guided her cart to a sputtering stop alongside a late-model Mercedes, parked along one of the more old-moneyed streets in Bay City.

The sun was shining.

It was after eight A.M.

There was clearly a traffic sign next to the car reading: NO PARKING, 8 AM TO 10 AM, TUESDAYS AND THURSDAYS. Yet here the car was, shimmering defiantly under the recently washed sign.

Producing her ticket book, she strolled over to the rich

car. The traffic cop would probably never own a Mercedes. She relished the thought of this ticket. Life had so few real pleasures.

She gazed inside the car, through the windshield. There was a man inside, head tilted back in the driver's seat. He seemed to be asleep.

He was wearing a maroon shirt made of some shiny material. So, she mused, even the rich tie one on every so often. Even the fat cats, and this guy was pretty fat, had to sleep it off.

She knocked on the driver's window.

No response.

"Hey, mister. Wake up, now. Come on, time to go home."

She backed up from the car, noting the license plate. BG STAR.

She walked back to the driver's door and rapped on the window with her knuckles. The guy didn't move. He must be in a big sleep. She noticed that the driver door was slightly ajar. She opened it slowly.

She leaned her head inside the car.

It was then that she noticed that the man wasn't asleep.

It was then that she noticed that his shirt wasn't really maroon.

And the material wasn't shiny; it was wet.

She backed up to her parking cart, picked up her microphone, and screamed so loud that the street-cleaning guy a block away heard her above the din of his machine. He pulled the machine to a stop. He thought he had blown a bearing. When he heard the high-pitched sound a second time, he picked up a crowbar from his cab, leaped from his machine, and ran down the street toward the Mercedes.

By now, the perky traffic patroller was white and shaking.

And the hood of the blue Mercedes was covered with phlegm.

Broskey was already dressed when he got the call. Since he had fallen asleep with his clothes on, that wasn't such a big deal. He opened his front door, attempting to shake his head clear. Bud was already reading the sports section. He had

Broskey's takeout coffee ready. Broskey blinked. His front door was a clean white.

"I figured you had a pretty bad night, Lieutenant." Bud smiled, handing Broskey the java. "I took the liberty of painting your door."

Broskey was genuinely moved.

Bud shook his head. "It's a shame the element that's creeping into the neighborhood. By the way, the people from four doors down took the cat. I think they're planning a barbecue."

Broskey winced. Bud was smiling, as happy as if he were in his right mind. "I already read the sports section," he said, carefully refolding the paper and thrusting it in Broskey's direction.

"Keep the whole thing," Broskey said, fishing in his pocket for a ten spot. "I don't have time for it this morning."

Bud was ecstatic. "Gee, thanks, Lieutenant. I love the paper. Especially the funnies. I love Calvin and Hobbes."

Broskey handed the tenner to Bud. "Here, Bud. You've more than earned it this morning."

This time, it was Bud who was moved. "You're a prince, Lieutenant. In Calvin's eyes, you'd probably be king of a solar system."

"Calvin?"

"The kid in the comic strip. He hangs out with his stuffed tiger. When the world gets too crazy for him, things too tough, he daydreams his troubles away. The tiger comes alive and the little kid can go anywhere and do anything. His life is a dream, Lieutenant. He controls everything. Wouldn't it be great if life was really like that?"

"Out here it sometimes is," Broskey said, taking a sip of coffee. "You sound like someone I met last night."

"Another bum?"

"Nope. A movie star turned guru."

Bud was puzzled. "I don't get it."

"She's like Calvin, only she makes a fortune out of making up daydreams for people too lazy to do it on their own."

"She does?"

"Uh-huh. She communicates with a ghost, her tiger. She calls her tiger Eeyore."

"I thought Eeyore was a donkey in a kid's book." Bud blinked, retrieving a piece of knowledge from his preshattered past.

"And the people she deals with are asses." Broskey grinned. "But rich ones."

"Do a lot of people do guru-ing?" Bud asked.

"Uh-huh. We have tigers named Eeyore, Mafu, Ramtha. . . ."

"World's a screwy place." Bud shrugged.

"Bud, I bet you'd make a good guru." Broskey smiled.

Bud laughed. "You think so?"

"Sure. Just tell the people what they want to hear, blink your eyes a lot, and speak in voices."

"I can do a great James Cagney," Bud said, lapsing into the movie star's voice. " 'You dirty rat.' "

Broskey took another sip of coffee. Bud continued. "How about W. C. Fields? 'Ah, yes, my little begonia. 'Twas a woman who led me to drink . . . and I never had the courtesy to thank her.' "

"I think you have the hang of it, Bud. Voices are no trouble for ya. Now you need a tiger, your very own Ramtha."

Bud cackled. "How about Wotha. Maybe his full name could be Wotha Hey. Sound spiritual enough?"

Broskey walked toward his car. "You've got the hang of it, Bud. You're on your way to a fortune. Now, don't go spending the whole ten on Night Train, okay?"

Bud nodded, switching into a Rochester voice. " 'Don' worry, boss. I'ze on my way to a higher plane of existence.' "

Broskey glanced at the smiling derelict sitting in front of his shiny, new white door. For a few moments, he felt like he actually liked people.

That feeling frittered away as he pulled his car behind the Mercedes. Goldstein and the forensics men pulled in behind him. He had beaten them to the scene. Unfortunately, McDonald and Bluth, their clothes newly pressed, were already present. The perky meter maid was sitting on the curb. The two cops were consoling her. A lot.

McDonald was giving her a neck massage.

Bluth was working on her ankles, staring at her well-tanned legs.

A uniformed officer was interviewing the street cleaner.

Broskey walked past the Mercedes. It reeked of blood, death, and vomit. He stared at the Hardy Boys giving the pert patroller the equivalent of a New Age feel-up. "All right," he said, "you can stop petting her. She's not a cocker spaniel. What have we got?"

McDonald flipped through his notebook. "Guy's name is Anson Rhodes. Ring a bell?"

I'd like to ring your fucking chimes, Broskey thought to himself.

McDonald grinned like a half-wit, an action he seemed to feel comfortable with. "Looks like a suicide."

Broskey turned his back on them. "Go back to your rubdown."

He approached the car and gazed inside. It was indeed Anson Rhodes, his bronzed face contorted to the point where it resembled Bela Lugosi's. Most of the blood had drained from the face, giving it a ghoulish look. Small patches of blood were spattered everywhere. A gun lay on the driver's side.

"Suicide?" he heard Goldstein say.

"I don't think so," Broskey replied.

"Me, neither," Goldstein said. "There's not enough blood in the car around the guy's feet and the guy has lost quite a bit."

"So, we have a gun and we have a suicide victim," Broskey muttered. "Got a pencil?"

Broskey held out an outstretched hand. Goldstein smacked a pencil into it. It had a picture of Mickey Mouse on it. Goldstein blushed. "I took the kids to Disneyland last week."

"Nice place." Broskey nodded. "Reminds me of city hall."

Taking the pencil, he eased open Rhodes's shirt. There was a hole there the size of a fist. "That's an exit wound, not an entrance wound," he commented, Goldstein taking furious notes.

"So," Goldstein concluded, "unless our victim here had arms like an octopus, it is very doubtful he could have reached behind the back of his seat and shot himself through the spine."

"The guy *was* an octopus," Broskey said, "but not in the aquatic sense."

He stared at the front passenger's seat. There was a large puddle of blood there, too. Whoever did in Rhodes was nice enough to chauffeur him to this street, with Rhodes propped up in the passenger's seat. No way the blood would have dripped there from a body sitting behind the wheel.

Broskey gingerly opened the back door on the driver's side and examined the rear of the driver's seat. "No hole here, Watson," Broskey said in a bad British accent. He stared at the dashboard. "No sign of a bullet there, either." He got out of the car and, squatting down next to Rhodes's blood-soaked legs, probed around the floor of the car with the pencil. "Got a plastic bag?"

Goldstein handed him a small pouch. Using the pencil, he picked up a small piece of bloodied notepaper. Carefully bloodied around the edge but leaving an address crystal-clear in the center. He placed it in the plastic bag.

"Suicide note?"

"Nope. An address. Here, you can hold it."

"Oh, thank you, sir."

Broskey reached into his pocket for a cigarette. He produced an empty packet. Goldstein pulled out a half-smoked pack and offered Broskey one. Goldstein explained the package away. "Hey, who wants to be *too* healthy?"

Broskey stared at the car. "So, what do we call this?"

"It would seem that we have ourselves a murder that was committed by someone very stupid who wanted us to think it's a suicide."

Broskey nodded. "Or, we have a murder committed by someone very smart who wants to irritate the hell out of us by making it seem that he's very stupid by leaving us his calling card."

"The address?"

"Uh-huh." Broskey took a deep drag of the unfiltered cigarette. The nicotine rush nearly caused his eyes to sail out of his skull. He stifled a series of death-rattling coughs. "Goldstein, leave a couple of men here at the scene to finish up. I want you with me."

"Yes sir."

Broskey faced the Hardy Boys. They were still massaging the perky woman, who seemed quite over her shock and/or nausea. "You two stay here and rub down Bambi a little while longer."

The girl blinked and stared at Broskey. "Sheri," the girl corrected. "Sheri."

"My mistake." Broskey smiled thinly, walking toward his car, Goldstein in tow.

Goldstein called to the girl, "Two r's and one i?"

The girl shook her head in the negative. "One of each."

Goldstein shrugged. "What's going on with our children? My kids are named Ira and Mary."

He walked after Broskey.

"What do you think we'll find at the apartment, Lieutenant?"

"I *know* what we're going to find," Broskey muttered. "And I don't like it." He slid into the front seat of his auto. "We're going to need another body bag and a lot of self-control."

Fifteen

*B*y nine-thirty in the morning, the Santa Anas were blowing full tilt: hot and dry. It was already eighty degrees near the beach, which meant, in the Valley, it was probably over ninety; smog was everywhere, and the air quality was poor.

This was the time when Broskey was thankful he had moved to an ocean community, although living in the Valley probably would have curtailed his smoking. All you had to do was step outside your home and breathe in.

He sat in the car with Goldstein for a moment, in front of a nondescript stucco apartment with the same address that was on the plastic-bagged piece of evidence on the dashboard. The pair watched the palm fronds crash down to the street from the sway-palm trees.

"Gonna be a hell of a day," he muttered.

The two left the car. The Wave Crest was one of those apartment complexes built in the late 1960s when someone, suddenly, discovered that if there was more housing more people would move to Bay City. More people meant more shops and more taxes.

Broskey gazed up at the stucco edifice. There was an orange concrete wave built onto the front of the building.

More apartments also meant less 1920 bungalows. They had to be torn down, you see, to put up these cheese boxes. Broskey supposed the Wave Crest wasn't all that ugly; it could have been worse. It could have been one of the buildings built during this decade. Prefabricated boxes hauled to a site by beer-bellied teamsters, assembled in a big pit already dug, and then fronted by some kind of squirrely piece of architecture that was supposed to let you know that this wasn't just an ordinary group of connected boxes.

Naaah. It was a bunch of boxes with a phony front.

Accordingly, Bay City now sported some of the ugliest apartment buildings in existence this side of West Los Angeles. Gulag à gogo joints designed to resemble the Alamo, pagodas, southwestern adobe homes, Aztec pyramids, and northeastern barns.

A hot gust of wind caused Broskey to sweat.

"Gonna be a hot one today," Goldstein said, lighting up a cigarette and gagging. He offered one to Broskey. Broskey shook his head no. He could still taste the last one in the pit of his stomach. Neither man wanted to go inside.

"It's *already* a hot one," Broskey replied.

"It'll be hotter, just wait," said Goldstein, his armpits rapidly reaching high tide.

"I know that."

"Just thought I'd point it out," Goldstein replied.

The two men stood there in silence.

"It's earthquake weather, too," Goldstein said.

"That's a lot of crap."

"That's only what the people at Cal Tech say," Goldstein answered. "Whenever we have an earthquake out here, it's always after we have a few days of Santa Ana winds. It's a fact."

"Hasn't been proven."

"A lot of facts haven't been proven. When you're my age you don't try to prove facts. You just accept them at face value."

Broskey sighed and began walking up the small flight of concrete steps leading to the front mailbox and buzzer system. He checked the ten names on the buzzers. "Manning," he began to read. "Band. Klinger. Peterson. Svenson. Edwards."

"No first names?"

"Not even a first initial."

"I suppose we should just start pressing all the buzzers, then."

"Half of the people are probably at work by now."

"No super?"

"Nope. Guess we'll have to buzz en masse."

Broskey started pressing buzzers. No response. The two men stood there, helpless, in front of the locked entranceway door. An old man with an older dog walked up to them. "Can I help you with something?"

"Yes," Broskey said, producing his shield. "We're police officers. We're trying to get inside."

"Well, I can help you there." The well-tanned man smiled, the hot wind blowing through his blond hair. He pulled a key out of his pocket and opened the front door.

There is a God, Broskey sighed.

"Any trouble?" the old man said, extending a hand. "Ike Svenson."

"Have you lived here long, Mr. Svenson?" Broskey asked.

"Since this place went up. Back in sixty-five."

"Do you have any neighbors here who are young women?"

"Sure." The old man chuckled. "Got lots of them. That's why I stay." He winked at the two policemen. "The pool is right outside my window. I got binoculars."

"We're looking for a girl," Broskey began.

"I gave that up years ago." Svenson cackled, emitting a hissing sound.

"No. A *young* girl. College-student type?"

Svenson screwed his face up into a parody of concentration. "Well, they all look young to me, but I figure you mean Marie Sessa. Is she in trouble or something?"

"Or something," Broskey found himself repeating. "Which apartment?"

"Well, she just moved in a few months ago, so she got the one out back. That's the one people leave the fastest. No view. You look down on an AM–PM Minimarket parking lot. You get a lot of fumes. A lot of drunks singing in Spanish late at night. It's not the best apartment in the place. I've got the best apartment. It's right next to the pool."

"Thanks, Mr. Svenson," Broskey said. "Apartment number?"

"That'll be Two-E."

The two policemen walked up a narrow stairway leading to the second floor of the complex. The sunlight that drenched the outside of the building was curiously missing on the second tier. The building's large roof effectively banished light from the exterior hallway.

Broskey and Goldstein paused before the door to 2E. "How will we get in?" Goldstein asked. "We don't have a key."

Broskey fished into his pocket for a handkerchief. He found a paper napkin from a happy-hour joint he had stopped in a month ago. It was time to have his slacks dry-cleaned, he figured.

"I don't think we're going to need one, Goldstein," he said, carefully placing the napkin on the doorknob so as not to obliterate any fingerprints in his heart he knew weren't there. He gave the doorknob a slow turn.

Click.

He glanced at Goldstein. "I can smell it from here."

The burly forensics man nodded his head. He knew what Broskey meant. It wasn't a smell your nose picked up. It was an odor that went right to the soul and stuck there like an arrow. Broskey swung the door open.

The apartment was small and dingy. Exhaust fumes from the parking lot outside hung in the air. A small foyer was neat and well kept. A picture of a winking Jesus was framed on a wall next to the door.

Jesus blinked as the intruders proceeded to the living room.

Sparsely, but neatly furnished. The best of Sears. Little

107

Hummel statues dotted the coffee table. A huge statue of the Blessed Virgin crushing the head of the snake Satan was perched atop the TV.

Another statue, this one of the Infant of Prague, stood on a bookshelf.

A Bible was clearly in view.

Broskey shook his head sadly.

In the kitchen, nothing amiss. Plaster birds sang mutely from atop the kitchen cabinets.

"Miss Sessa?" Broskey called, his voice breaking, his heart breaking, too.

"Just the bedroom left," Goldstein said, pushing open an immaculate bathroom door.

Broskey walked to the only remaining door. It was ajar. Using the toe of his left shoe, he nudged it open. Sessa must have collected teddy bears. Lots of them.

The ransacked room was covered with teddy-bear parts, ripped open at the seams, the stuffing hanging from them.

In the middle of the room was Marie Sessa, in a similar condition.

Broskey didn't enter.

He stood in the archway. This was the most violent death yet. The killer was growing bolder. Getting cockier. The killer knew the police were on to him. That fact didn't faze him. In fact, it seemed to encourage him, heighten the thrill element of it all.

Tears were welling up in Broskey's eyes.

"Let's call in my boys." Goldstein sighed, placing a pawlike hand on Broskey's sagging shoulder. "Come on, Lieutenant, let's go."

The two men walked silently to the car. Goldstein entered and got on the radio. Broskey stared at the orange-colored wave frozen midbreak on the building.

This shouldn't be happening, he thought. He shouldn't be here. All he ever wanted to do was to help people. Ever since he was a kid. He grew up in a rotten little factory town named Lindfern, New Jersey. He watched people get buffeted about all his young life.

His parents squirmed under the thumb of bank loans and

layoffs. Oil-refinery fires from across the highway would turn workers into burgers within seconds. Race riots found friends killing friends. Even when he was a kid, he wanted to do something that would help change all that, to help people gain control of their lives.

At first, he thought he might want to be president. His grandmother, Nanny, however, in the late 1950s, clued him in. He could never be president. He was a Catholic. Being the pope, she assured him, was the answer. The thought had frightened young Kevin. Who wanted to go through life in a dress? Plus, he was just starting to notice girls. He didn't know what it was about girls yet, he was only eight or nine, but he knew that priests weren't affected by it.

When John Kennedy was elected, Broskey was off the hook with Nanny. He could still be commander in chief. Then, when Kennedy was assassinated, Nanny felt vindicated. "See? That's what they do to good Catholic boys in Washington."

Fortunately, Nanny died of some sort of seizure just when Broskey reached puberty. The threat of the Vatican disappeared. He decided that he'd be a teacher. Help people when they were young. Later, he fancied himself a counselor.

Now, he was pretending to be the upholder of law and order.

He stared at the concrete wave before him, his suit of armor clanking down around his ankles.

"They're on their way, Lieutenant," Goldstein said quietly.

Broskey still couldn't get the picture of Marie Sessa out of his mind's eye. A human rag doll, used and discarded, tossed down among the other broken toys.

He was aware of an ashen-faced man staring at him. It was Svenson. Tears running down his face. "I—I went inside looking for you," he sobbed. "I saw what they did to her. God, how could anyone do that?"

It occurred to Broskey that Svenson had probably put his hands on the door and God knows what else. He just didn't have the heart to yell at him.

"How could anyone do that?" Svenson shrieked. "Animals. That's what we're living with. Packs of animals!"

"There go our prints." Goldstein sighed.

"Just alert your boys to the fact that Svenson's prints will be there and they probably don't mean much. Have them look for latent ones on the body. I'm sure Mr. Svenson didn't actually go into the room," he whispered quickly.

He turned toward Mr. Svenson. "Come on, Mr. Svenson, why don't we get you back into your apartment?"

He put an arm around the sobbing tenant and led the man back to his flat. It was a small, fern-filled room. The old man collapsed, sobbing, on the couch. His blond wig slipped, revealing a dome of very white skin. From a distance it looked like he was wearing a white beanie.

"May I use your phone, Mr. Svenson?" Broskey asked.

The old man nodded, choking back little-boy spasms of tears and shock.

His elderly mutt, a part-terrier critter with one ear up and one ear down, cocked its head and looked at its master. Then, Broskey would have sworn, the dog stared at the ceiling in the direction of Marie's apartment. It howled. It howled like a banshee, sending chills up and down Broskey's shaking frame.

He dialed the phone. "Jake? It's Broskey. How's the first column coming? Almost done? Great. Look. Put it aside for an hour or so, will you? I'm going to tell you a story that your paper might like. A story about an actress, a film producer, and some lovely girls who are not so lovely anymore. No direct quotes. Draw your own conclusions."

When Broskey was done a few minutes later, he turned and faced Mr. Svenson. Mr. Svenson was petting his dog with one hand, his wig with the other.

"I'm leaving now, Mr. Svenson. A patrolman will be in to question you in a few minutes."

The man nodded mutely.

Broskey stepped out into the heat. A deserted swimming pool stood before him, sparkling in the sunlight.

He probably shouldn't have made that phone call. When the story hit, a lot of feathers would be ruffled.

But he was mad. He had to shake things up a bit. Someone out there was killing innocent people. Someone out there was taunting him. Anyone, everyone connected with that slime should know what it meant to feel heat. Real heat.

The victims, after all, wouldn't be feeling anything anymore.

"Lieutenant?"

Broskey turned. It was Goldstein, a concerned look on his face. "Why don't you go home and take a shower or something? Take lunch early. It looks like you've had a rough time."

Broskey caught a glimpse of himself in the pool. His clothes looked like crumpled Saran wrap. "Thanks, Goldstein. I'll do that." He walked to the entrance of the building. "Thanks," he muttered a second time as Goldstein watched him get into his car and drive off.

When Broskey arrived home, Bud was still on the steps, reading the paper.

Bud knew from the expression on Broskey's face that the lieutenant wasn't up for a quick impersonation of Bogart or Lorre. In his richest, Shakespearean voice, Bud intoned, "These are the times that try men's souls."

Broskey was almost shaken out of his skin. Bud's voice sounded like a funeral shroud.

He stepped inside his overhot bungalow and stripped off his clothes. He needed a shower, all right. He needed to wash the sweat off. The stench off. The years off.

He shambled toward the bathroom, stepping over small piles of dirty clothing.

It was only eleven o'clock. Already he had walked into two homicides.

He turned on the leaking shower spigot. Lukewarm water dribbled out. Tiny drops dripped down his naked body.

Sixteen

*B*roskey sat slumped in his chair, all calls on hold. He had a small mountain range of file folders in front of him and none of what he read gave him an uplifting, Southern Californian experience.

Two files were from forensics.

Marie Sessa had been extensively tortured before she died. Not major stuff. Something along the lines of the medieval practice of a thousand small cuts. Cigarette burns around the nipples. Penetration with foreign objects. Bite marks galore. Battery, slaps mostly, pinches, fingernails.

He tried not to picture the woman in his mind, but he couldn't shut her out.

Unfortunately, his mind had clearer reception than his TV.

As for Anson Rhodes? It was pretty much as Broskey had figured. The sleazeball had been murdered somewhere else and then nicely placed in his car and driven to a more distinctive site.

He closed the files rubbing his head.

The Santa Anas were howling outside his window, spewing their hot breath inside his office. Stirring papers. Causing him to sweat.

Today, Los Angeles was the type of inferno that not even Dante would buy a ticket to visit.

Sergeant Fine entered his office, carrying a stack of files that made the Encyclopedia Britannica look like a short story.

"This came for you, from the L.A. Gang Task Force."

"Thanks, Sergeant." Broskey nodded as the blond woman gently placed the file folders on the edge of his desk.

"You want your messages?"

"All I want now, is to die in my sleep."

The sergeant smiled. "Coward. Your wife—"

"Ex-wife."

"—called three times. Cheryl Williams called, pretty angry, I think, ten times. I think that's a record for you."

"Alert the media."

"Speaking of the media, your buddy Jake called. He said thanks, and that he'd call you tomorrow morning."

"Thanks, Sergeant."

"And Chief Medega would like to see you."

"Oh, joy. Oh, rapture."

Broskey tilted his Naugahyde chair back slightly and stared at the ceiling. He began to count tiles.

"You have plans for tonight?" the sergeant asked.

"You just brought them in," Broskey said, nodding toward the L.A. files.

"What will you do for dinner?"

"Probably scrounge something up at home. Maybe stop at a ratburger stand on the way home."

The sergeant stood before Broskey. She had applied a new layer of lip gloss before entering his office. "Well, *I* have dinner plans," she announced. "But if you need someone to bend an elbow with, I could always . . ."

Fifty-one. Fifty-two, Broskey counted. "Huh? Oh, thanks, Andy. I think it's going to be a really late one."

"Broskey?" the sergeant asked.

"What?"

"Are you in trouble?"

"Emotionally? Physically? Professionally?" He tilted his

chair down, the Naugahyde clinging to his sweating body. "I don't know, Andy. I think the chief probably will be able to spell it out for me."

He got up and walked out of his office. "Let me take a rain check on that elbow bending, okay?"

"Whatever you say, sir," the sergeant said.

Broskey took the ancient staircase of the Bay City police station up to the third floor where the chief had his office. It was the only office with air conditioning. Medega didn't ask for many privileges, but the guy had had his lungs scrambled in Nam and, as a result, was highly sensitive to pollution of any kind. Bad air. Pollen. Just about anything that stank, except for cigars. They were, he said, the perfect antidote to Agent Orange.

Medega had a secretary, Bernice, who had been with the Bay City police force forever. Some wags insisted that she got to this tract of land first and the city fathers were forced to build the station *around* her, thus the longevity of her tenure.

She had served twenty-two police chiefs. Medega was her favorite. "My bastard son," she called him.

Broskey struggled with the stairs, willing his heart to pump enough blood to his brain to avoid a stroke.

He entered Bernice's lair. The woman sat behind her desk, waving a small Japanese fan to cool off her massive face. To say Bernice was large would not do justice to her imposing figure. She looked like Herman Melville's wet dream.

She liked Broskey.

Broskey, being a big "Gentle Ben" fan as a kid, also had a soft spot in his heart for Bernice.

"Bad day, huh, Kevin?" she said, the sweat on her brow resembling Niagara Falls.

"You could say that." Broskey nodded.

"You deaf? I just did." She smiled, exposing her newly purchased teeth. Apparently, her dentist had also worked on Trigger at one time. The teeth were big and clicked. When Bernice talked, she sounded like two Spanish dancers. "Go on in, he's waiting for you."

"Anything I should know about?"

"And spoil the surprise?" Bernice cackled. "Suffice to say that the chief has just spent a very rewarding hour with Mayor Roberts."

"Shhhit," Broskey muttered. Bay City had one doozy of a Mayor. Gina Roberts was a quasi-newcomer to politics, but in the oh-so-chic-modern Bay City realm, she was a real princess. A thirty-five-year-old firebrand who had earned her stripes as a radical-feminist lesbian, she managed to bowl over the entire community by wearing pink prom gowns during her campaign and vowing to help the elderly and beef up the city's rent-control system.

To her credit, she had done both.

On the down side, she was the kind of woman St. George probably would have lost two out of three falls to.

Broskey cleared his throat and opened the chief's office door.

Medega sat behind his desk, white knuckling the afternoon edition of the *Trib*.

"Come in, Lieutenant," he said softly.

Broskey eased the door closed behind him and quietly slid into the chair before the chief's desk. When Medega was mad, he shouted. When he was very, very mad, he whispered.

"How was your day?" Medega said, almost inaudibly.

Broskey was sweating in spite of the air conditioning. "I've had better."

"So have I." Medega smiled thinly. He put the newspaper down. His pockmarked face seemed to have a life of its own. Broskey would have sworn Medega's head was being animated by Disney dropouts on speed. "Have you seen the afternoon paper?" Medega said, his grin frozen.

"I'm afraid I haven't, sir." Broskey coughed.

"A fascinating piece on the front page. All about the co-ed killings. A suicide that may have been a murder. An actress turned crystal-ball gazer named Cheryl Williams. It's fascinating, Broskey. A real eye-opener. Your friend Jake wrote it, in fact."

"Like I said . . ."

Medega was grinning now, like a death's head. "I know. I know. You haven't had a chance to peruse the newspaper as of yet. I understand. You were on the scene for two rather grisly homicides today."

"Yes sir."

"So I just *know* you didn't have the time to call your friend Mayer. Which is why I just *know* you're not the unidentified police source who is quoted for about half of this goddamned article."

Broskey gulped. Medega went on. "So I'll just chalk it up to McDonald, shall I?"

"Whatever you see fit, sir," Broskey said. He had never seen Medega in such an icy state before.

Mayor Roberts must have given birth before his eyes.

Medega pulled out a cigar. He lit it. Inhaled. Coughed up smoke. Inhaled again. "The mayor and I had quite an interesting chat this afternoon."

"Really?"

"Yes. And, in fact, your name came up quite often."

"I'm flattered."

Medega leaned back in his chair. "Lieutenant, let's stop playing the mindfuck games, shall we? You're a good cop. I know that. You know that. I'm a good cop, too. We have that in common. But when things get screwed up, my ass gets chewed up before yours does. Privilege of rank. Right now, I am sitting on a buffet, courtesy of the mayor."

"I'm sorry, sir."

"Good. You may well be quite soon. Here's the deal in a nutshell. Cheryl Williams is threatening to sue both your friend Jake and his newspaper for slander. We are definitely going to be involved in that suit. As a matter of fact, she is considering suing Bay City unless we can substantiate the allegations made about her in the article."

"Everything that was in that article—"

"—which you haven't read—"

"—which I haven't read"—Broskey gulped—"is true."

"Good. Then come down on her hard. Call up Jake. Call up Walter Winchell. I don't care. Give hard, cold facts. Blow her and her lawyers out of the water."

116

"I will, sir," Broskey said, rising.

"Not yet, Lieutenant," Medega said. "Please. Relax. Consider yourself my guest for a few eternities more."

Medega took a long drag on his cigar. "As to the little matter of Bay City looking like Dodge City . . ."

"Sir?"

"The mayor is understandably upset that we have people getting murdered in their bedrooms and their cars. She is even more upset about what that might do to the city's tourism."

"Well . . ."

"She is upset that if we let these murders continue, other people with twisted minds may figure us to be soft, may consider our citizenry easy pickings, may gravitate to our little town and make it the frou-frou equivalent of a shooting gallery. And as much as I dislike Mayor Roberts, I must agree with her assessment of the situation. So, this is why I called you here, Lieutenant."

"Sir?"

"Get the bastard."

"Well, we *are* trying, sir."

"Use any means necessary. You have your buddy at the paper putting pressure on the killer. Fine. I don't care whether you drive him out of Bay City. I want the killings to stop. Let him be someone else's problem. I can live with that."

"There is the problem of the gangs, Chief," Broskey said nervously.

"Roust them. Fry them. I don't care. If it means clubbing them, trussing them up, and hiring a limo to send them back to scenic Los Angeles, do it."

"They won't stay in L.A. long, sir, with the TV cameras and the publicity street sweeps."

"Then toss them in jail, Lieutenant. Find them. Arrest them. Jaywalking. Littering. Drinking in public. Sleeping in a park. I don't give a good goddamn. Make their life a living hell. I promise you we'll ream them in court. Everyone here is pissed off about this shit. Even the Public Defender's

117

Office. I want you to be an emissary of sorts. I want you to let those darlings know that they are dead meat in this city.

"We are smaller than L.A. We have less red tape. We know our citizens better."

"I'll try, sir." Broskey nodded.

"You'll *do*, Lieutenant," Medega said, "because you know what will happen if you don't? I'll be hung out to dry. The mayor likes me as much as I like her but she can't fire me because I do a good job. Once that woman sees a chance to dump on me, she will. Before that happens, however, I will dump on you in a major, major way."

Medega sighed and took a deep drag on his cigar. "Nothing personal, Broskey."

"I know, sir. I'll work on it."

"Okay. That's it."

Broskey slowly got to his feet. "Thanks for the pep talk, sir."

Medega flashed a lopsided grin. "Hey, what are friends for?"

Seventeen

*T*he complaint call from the president of Bay City College, one double-strength Hefty bag of wind named Bryce Walton, came early in the morning.

Now, as Jake Mayer and Kevin Broskey walked across the suburban college campus, Broskey was growing flustered. The next article by Mayer had appeared that day and, all in all, it was great.

Not only did it contain many of the tips Broskey had requested (after dark, check that all sliding doors are closed tightly; if not, have them braced in a half-open, yet locked position, etc.) but it was sprinkled liberally with quotes from some of the dead girls' families and friends.

Prominently quoted in the article were the two co-editors of the *Bay City College Lion,* Melanie Melnick and Stan Webster.

A female voice wafted over the concrete hills of the campus. "Jake?"

Jake turned around and smiled. Two students, one male and one female, were walking toward them. "Hey, guys."

Broskey shot Mayer a startled look. "Hey, I pick up extra money lecturing on campuses all over the state. It's good for another six or seven grand a month. I'm on a first-name basis with *all* the star students." Jake grinned.

"A legend in your own mind," Broskey replied.

"Nah," Jake replied. "It's just that I love money almost as much as I love myself."

"Which is a lot." Broskey smirked.

"I take the fifth on that," Mayer said, watching the students approach them.

The boy, a tall, lanky kid with straw-blond hair, ice-blue eyes, and a lopsided smile, extended a hand.

Jake made the introductions. "Lieutenant Kevin Broskey, this is Stan Webster, English-education major and co-editor of the *Lion.*"

Broskey took the thin hand and shook it. The boy had an amazingly strong grip. "Pleased to meet you, Lieutenant," Stan said. "I hope you catch this creep."

"Me, too," Broskey admitted.

"And," Jake continued, "this is Stan's better half. Melanie Melnick, library-science major and all around firebrand."

"Cut it out, Jake." The girl laughed. Broskey found himself staring at her. She wasn't pretty, in the California sense of the word. She had short black hair. Wide and wild brown eyes. Her skin was too white. She was a little too short, even for her wiry frame. But every inch of her body seemed to radiate energy.

Broskey swallowed hard. No. This couldn't be the feeling he thought it was. He was either entranced by her or he had his ulcer back.

He was hoping for the ulcer.

"Lieutenant Broskey?" Melanie asked, tilting her pixie face inquisitively. "Are you all right?"

"Sure. Sure," Broskey replied. "It's just that I'm a little preoccupied."

"He's a *lot* preoccupied," Jake enthused. "Did you know that some street gang tried to off him last night?"

The girl's face paled. "No."

"Yes," Jake said, nodding quickly. "A shotgun to the old cabeza in a parking lot. But Kev, here, he hit the dirt. Bullets spraying all around him. The only one injured was his beloved car. A loaner from the force."

"No shit!" Stan exclaimed.

"Yes, shit," Jake said. "This guy's a regular supercop, except that he's a wuss with a gun. Brainpower plus, though. A good one to have on your side in this thing."

"Well, I'm glad you're on our side, then, Lieutenant." Melanie beamed.

Broskey shook her hand, his heart melting. This was ridiculous. He was old enough to be her uncle or something.

"The prez is probably getting more pissed off as we speak," Melanie bubbled. "Shall we go into the lion's den?"

The foursome walked across the concrete and steel expanse that passed for Bay City College.

A few moments later, they were seated in front of a steely-eyed fellow in his forties, who did not seem too pleased to see them. In fact, pleasure didn't seem to enter into the life of Bryce Walton a lot.

A former lawyer and union negotiator, he had been appointed to the presidency by a fluke. His brother had become dean of the school. The preceding president, Wilfred King, had had the bad luck to have a heart attack during a basketball game. Walton's brother, Kirby, lobbied hard to have his brother named president. It worked.

Shortly thereafter, Kirby had the worse luck of being caught with his pants down with a home-economics major in a Kama Sutra position that required a blotter, a Xerox machine, and several waves of white-out.

Walton was forced to dismiss his brother.

Clearly, Bryce Walton was not a happy man by nature. He held up the morning edition of the *Trib.* "Excuse my profanity," he said, his light-bulb-shaped head oozing sweat. "But what do you call this crap?"

"It's a newspaper," Melanie replied.

"Sir," Stan added.

"The *Trib,* to be exact." Jake smiled.

Broskey's insides moaned. This was going to be a beaut of a meeting.

"I don't know if you understand what you've done here, but this article is highly inflammatory. It could ruin our school. You see, gentlemen and lady, we rely heavily on contributions from our alumni just to survive. With this school placed, in public, in such a scandalous light, I am *positive* those contributions will slow to a trickle.

"This . . . this . . . *article* is based on supposition, linking coincidence with coincidence. There are no facts. There is no hard evidence. Several women have been killed. They were all students at this college. Mere coincidence. Bay City is a small town. Those women could have worked in a dozen different department stores, yet the stores wouldn't be named in a story of this . . . *ilk.*"

"But, sir," Melanie ventured, "they *didn't* work in stores. They were all students here."

"And *you,* young lady," the president went on, "have a lot to account for. Your quotes here rival the Brothers Grimm when it comes to sheer fantasy. 'Lax security.' 'Unrealistic attitudes towards sex.' 'A virtual cornucopia of rape victims.'"

The prez was working himself up to a high boil. "And I quote, 'The administration has chosen to ignore the high incidence of date rapes on and off campus involving Bay City students. Why shouldn't someone feel bold enough to go a step further when everyone on campus seems to be looking the other way? Why should a killer fear the outside authorities when he practically can operate unnoticed on the grounds of the college?'"

"Sir," Melanie began.

"I'd like to say something about that," Stan interrupted.

"I don't want to hear it," Walton fumed.

"Maybe I can shed some light on the events leading up to the story," Jake began.

"I read the goddamn newspapers," the president exploded. "I know what's going on."

Broskey felt his fist pound into the side of his chair. He found himself rising, red-faced. "Do you?" he roared. "Do you *really?*"

Melanie and Stan shrank down in their chairs. Jake popped a wide smile. The president was startled. Broskey leaned over the light-bulb-headed man's desk.

"Have you seen these kids? Have you seen what they look

like after your 'fantasy' killer does them? Do you see their dead eyes? See how they've been tortured, mutilated? See their blood splashed against a wall, clotted on letters from home or record albums they loved or teddy bears they collected?"

"Well," the president began.

"No. Because you don't *have* to. I *do*. You sit here behind a desk in the middle of this bright and shiny college campus. You're fine. You're safe. You have nothing to fear. You're not young, female, alone, attractive, and very, very vulnerable. If someone came up to you and demanded your wallet, maybe you'd fight them. Maybe, even a guy in as rotten shape as you could get a punch across. Maybe you could frighten the guy away.

"Or maybe you can hand the wallet over, knowing that the guy would probably be satisfied and not blow your brains out. But a twenty-year-old woman? She knows she's in for trouble as soon as she's accosted. Women aren't the weaker sex, President Walton, but they sure are the more victimized. Every day. Every hour. Almost every minute, a woman is assaulted. In Los Angeles, seven out of ten women will be raped during their lifetime. But when the attacks get rougher, then we get murder.

"Murder victims aren't very nice to look at. Maybe I can convince you about the severity of the situation by taking you to the next crime scene with me. And make no mistake about it, there will be a next crime scene. And why?

"Because sometimes people, young people, are too trusting. Sometimes they aren't aware of the facts. They don't know that if they leave a door or a window unlocked, someone may walk into their home who's not a nice person. They don't know that if they hitchhike from this campus to a parked car, the person that picks them up may not be a Boy Scout.

"Mr. Mayer here tried to inform your students, your potential victims, of those facts. These students you're threatening were *brave* enough to cooperate. We live in a passive society, Mr. Walton. Passivity breeds victimization. These students you're breathing fire on had the guts to say something. If anything, I would think you would be proud of them."

Broskey took a deep breath. "I know *I* would be. Maybe if there were students like this around when I got my degree, I'd be sitting where you are now *praising* these students for trying to save *your* campus."

The president blinked. Melanie and Stan were astonished. Mayer was laughing uncontrollably.

"You are worried about the school losing money," Broskey said, his face flushed. " *I* am worried about this college losing students. Bright students. *People* you can never replace. People who are part of your community, your *family*.

"What Mr. Mayer's article tried to do, what these *kids* are trying to do, is alert this city, this campus, to the fact that when one of your students gets killed, we *all* should grieve. We've lost one of our own. One of the innocents. One of the good guys. The article wasn't sensationalized, Mr. Walton. If anything, it was tasteful. I'll bring you photos of the victims, if you like, and show you just *how* tasteful it was."

He heaved a deep breath. "Murder, Mr. Walton, is anything but neat and clean."

The president sat there, looking as if he'd been kicked in the groin by a large creature long thought extinct.

"What should I do?" he gasped. "What can I do?"

"Cooperate," Broskey said, sliding back in his chair. "With the police. With Mr. Mayer. With the school newspapers. Let them do interviews. Let them report the facts. Sure, it may scare a lot of people. But better you have a campus filled with frightened, cautious people than a campus filled with dead ones."

Broskey poked his forefinger into the side of the wooden chair. "Imagine what *that* would do to your contributors."

"Yes, yes, I see." Walton nodded.

"I was sure you would." Broskey smiled. He caught Melanie Melnick grinning slyly at him.

"Well, as you say, Lieutenant." The president sighed. "It *is* a serious problem, and now that I've been alerted to just how serious it is, I can assure you I will cooperate as much as I can."

He extended a hand. Broskey gripped it. It felt like a pound of halibut steak.

"Thank you, President Walton."

The president nodded. The truants were dismissed.

Outside, in the sunlight, the two students were still awestruck. Mayer was cackling. "You should have seen Kevin in the debating society in high school. He was a killer. Other kids would get up there and logically set up their points. Kev would get to the podium and bellow, work the people into a frenzy. He was ahead of his time, a regular Jesse Jackson."

"You *were* pretty hot in there." Melanie smiled.

"Sorry," Broskey apologized. "I guess I lost control."

"I've never seen the president piss in his pants before." Stan emitted a laugh that sounded like a bloodhound.

"It was beautiful," Mayer said. "So, where do I go from here?"

"My files are your files." Broskey shrugged.

"Great, let's get at them," Mayer replied.

The two men faced the two students. "I'll see you guys tomorrow." Mayer smiled. "I'll be a regular on campus for a while."

"Great," Stan said enthusiastically. "We can have lunch."

"If you like cafeteria food," Melanie added.

"We'll try to line up support on campus," Stan said.

"The frats, the sororities, the student council," Melanie added. "They'll all cooperate, Jake. I know it."

"Great. Maybe I'll get a varsity sweater out of the deal."

"Well, we gotta go," Broskey said.

"I hope we'll see you again, Lieutenant." Melanie smiled.

Broskey's heart skipped a beat. "I'd *like* that," he said, meaning it.

The two men marched toward Jake's car. "Nice kids," Jake said.

"Yeah. It's nice to see normal kids every once in a while."

"Want me to take you back to the station?"

"How about driving by my place on the way back? I want to check something out."

"Your security guard?"

"Yeah."

En route to the station, Jake dutifully guided his car past Broskey's rented bungalow.

Broskey clenched his fists.

Bud wasn't there.

"Bad sign?" Jake asked.

"Could be." Broskey sighed. He nodded in the direction of the station. "Take me home, Jake."

Eighteen

Broskey walked slowly toward his office door. He could hear the yelling of female voices going on inside. He winced. He wasn't up for this, he really wasn't.

"You have no right to just barge in here, lady," Sergeant Andrea Fine was bellowing. "I can have you thrown out right now."

"Try it," the other voice taunted. "You'll be up to your neck in legal papers. I know some of the biggest lawyers in Hollywood. I've *fucked* some of the biggest lawyers in Hollywood."

Broskey eased open his door and saw a fuming Cheryl Williams in his office. "Good morning, Miss Williams." He smiled.

"You . . . you . . ."

"Policeman," Broskey supplied, feeling as if he were making a living out of finishing other people's sentences.

She held up a newspaper. "Yesterday's story was slander-ous enough, but *today's?* How dare you connect me with this Anson Rhodes fellow! I'll sue you! I'll sue the newspaper!"

Broskey nodded to Sergeant Fine. She walked out of the office, leaving the door open behind her.

He walked by Williams, pointedly ignoring her, and went to a small Mr. Coffee machine, still holding yesterday's cold brew. In fact, he couldn't remember when the coffee was made. He seemed to recollect that the machine broke around Christmas time. He swirled the coffee around in the pot slowly, allowing Williams to percolate. He placed the pot down and eased himself into his chair.

"All right, Miss Williams. You want to play word games? I'm in the right mood for it today. Before you go around suing anybody, let me clue you in. We went through Rhodes's office.

"Have your lawyers call us. We'll tell them about your name on his Rollodex. The appointments with you we found on his calendar, written down in his own handwriting. The photos we found of the dead young women tagged 'Referred by Cheryl Williams.' We'll tell your lawyers about pulling his phone bills from the phone company records and the amount of phone calls he made to your home and to your office on campus.

"In fact"—Broskey smiled—"we'll prove that you and Rhodes have been working a sweet hustle for a good many years. How's that?"

"You bastard," Cheryl Williams seethed, her long hair almost writhing.

"Ouch. Sounds like a slanderous remark to me," Broskey said, feigning anger and offering her his patented Cheshire-cat grin. He wanted her to know he had her.

He also didn't want her to realize that everything he had just said was bullshit.

Rhodes had been very successful at being secretive. All they had found in his office were office supplies and a three-year collection of *Penthouse* magazines.

He continued to grin. Cheryl Williams looked like she had just had her forehead massaged by a brick.

She was obviously turning all this over in her mind. Abruptly, she dropped the lawsuit angle. She tried putting on a plaintive expression, but she was too angry to pull it off successfully.

"Do you know what this is doing to me?" she whispered.

"Haven't the vaguest."

"I've been suspended from the campus. The president is looking into my dealings with Rhodes. He may sue."

"There seems to be a lot of that going around these days."

"My clients are backing off. I don't have enough people booked for my next three channeling sessions to make them worth holding. And my publishing company canceled my publicity tour! They may not even go into an automatic second printing on my new book. They're taking a wait-and-see attitude. Do you know what that means?"

"They're going to wait and see?" Broskey blinked.

Williams clenched her hands at each side. She was shaking now. It had nothing to do with her spirituality.

"This is all your fault! I hold you personally responsible."

"I'll get over it. Now, if you're through . . ."

"I am anything but through, mister. I'll see you behind bars for this. Either that or I'll see you dead."

"And I'll see you to the door. Good-bye, Miss Williams."

Broskey quickly rose from behind his desk and, firmly grabbing the twitching actress/guru by the elbow, escorted her to his door and into the hallway.

"Good-bye, Miss Williams," he repeated.

"Just remember, you son-of-a-bitch, I'll get you, one way or the other."

"Fine. Fine."

"I'm *serious!*"

"The exit door is that way, Miss Williams." Broskey smiled. "I suggest you use it, and, oh, by the way: have a nice day."

The woman spun around and marched toward the exit. Sergeant Fine walked up to Broskey. "Fulfill your bullshit quota for the day yet?"

"I'm getting there."

Fine smiled at him. "Did you have a good evening last night?"

"Compared to December seventh, 1941, it was great."

"A lot of paperwork?"

"Uh-huh. That reminds me. I have some more to tackle."

The blond sergeant with the sad eyes seemed to grow

agitated. Traces of pink appeared on her white skin. "You didn't ask me about my evening."

"Huh?"

"You didn't ask me about my evening. You *never* ask me about my evenings."

"Okay. I knew you had a date. I didn't know if you wanted to talk about it. Okay, how was your evening?"

"It *sucked*," Fine said. "It was a date from hell. A podiatrist. He talked about feet all night. I know more about Dr. Scholl's products than any person living west of the Mississippi who does not have a tootsie fetish."

Broskey blinked. "Gee, I'm sorry, Sergeant."

"Are you?" Fine asked. "We've been working together two years and you've shown absolutely no interest in my personal life. You don't know where I live. You don't know how I spend my free time. I, however, always make it a point to find out how you are, what you've done off duty, how things are going. Have you ever wondered why?"

Broskey's mouth was slowly opening, forming a very large *O*.

"No, I bet you've never even wondered once," Fine said. "Well, let me give you a clue. It isn't because I think your off-duty drinking and passing out is the most fascinating stuff I can hear about, okay?"

Broskey's mouth was locked in an oval.

"Lieutenant," Fine said. "I am a single, attractive woman. I have a great body. I'm smart. I am *not* just a sergeant. Okay?"

"Uh-huh."

"Well, okay then. Just treat me like a human every once in a while."

Andrea Fine turned and strode away, leaving Broskey standing stunned at his door. He was covered with sweat. He walked over to the window in his office and opened it. The room actually got hotter.

"It's the Santa Anas," he said. "It has to be."

A few more days of this and the whole town would be going crazy.

Broskey stared at the file folders on his desk. He didn't know how things could get any crazier.

His phone rang. It was Goldstein.

"I'll be right up," Broskey said, jogging out of his office. He ran up the flight of stairs leading to where the forensics lab was located.

"I just thought you should know about this, Lieutenant," Goldstein said, taking a pair of wire-rimmed glasses off the tip of his nose. The glasses were high-powered things. When Goldstein wore them, he looked like a linebacker auditioning for a Mr. Magoo film.

Goldstein pointed to several small plastic bags on his desk. "This is stuff we collected from the homes of the dead girls," he said in a monotone. "Most of the stuff we found at the crime sight was easily identifiable. Larger items. Envelopes, stamps, that kind of stuff. Small things. Hair, pieces of fingernail, clothing fibers."

Broskey peered at the envelopes. Each contained what looked like a single piece of confetti, either black or silver.

"But we couldn't figure out what we had here. At the first crime scene, we didn't think anything of it. Just a small sliver of silver paper. But we bagged it. Second crime scene, we found a black sliver. Not an eyebrow raiser by any means, but we bagged it as well."

Broskey knew that Goldstein was slowly getting to the point, something he was very proud of.

"The girl in the car," Goldstein went on. "Now *that* was interesting. Next to her clothes? In the trunk? Another piece of paper. Couldn't figure it at all. Then, in the Sessa girl's bedroom we got lucky. We got a bigger piece."

He held up a bag. Indeed, the piece of paper in that bag was slightly bigger. "See? A little bit of black, a little bit of silver, and a little bit of green. If you look really closely, you'll see a black outline."

Broskey squinted his eye. He couldn't see it.

Goldstein led him over to an eight-by-ten. "We made a blowup. What does that look like to you, Lieutenant?"

Broskey gazed at the black-and-white photo. A round,

curved line appeared at the lower portion of the picture. "You've got me, Goldstein. To me, it looks like a drawing of a fingertip or something."

Goldstein beamed. "Go to the head of the class, Lieutenant. You may have a second career in this lab."

"I may consider it." Broskey smirked.

Goldstein walked over to a desk. "So, we examined the papers again. A bit of black. A bit of glossy green. A bit of silver. A silver portrait with a black finger. Paper, foil, flat black cardboard stock. What's the source of all three?"

Broskey was stumped, as Goldstein knew he would be. The burly man reached into a desk drawer and tossed a small package on the desk.

"Here's another personality quirk of the killer we have to consider," he announced.

The packet skidded across the desk. Broskey caught it, his chest tightening.

Polaroid 600 film.

"Our boy's a shutterbug, Lieutenant." Goldstein sighed. "Not only does he want to kill these kids, but he wants a trophy as well."

"Oh, Jesus," Broskey exhaled. "Are you sure?"

Goldstein nodded, gingerly taking the packet away from Broskey. He opened it. Inside the cardboard flap was a protective silver seal, not to be pulled off until the film was ready to be inserted into the camera. On the seal were line drawings of hands showing the proper way to load the film.

Broskey tore open the seal.

Inside was the film.

Goldstein produced a camera. "Here."

Broskey took the camera. He looked at the film cartridge. It was topped by a bright, shiny green tab. He popped the cartridge inside the camera. The camera whirred. It spat out a protective cardboard sheet, the size of a Polaroid picture. The construction-paper-like rectangle was white, green, and black.

"I rest my case," Goldstein said.

Broskey put the camera down. "Do you think he deliberately left these behind?"

"I doubt it," Goldstein said. "This isn't the kind of stuff a sicko usually leaves as a calling card. My guess is that he left the fragments behind by changing the film quickly."

"Huh?"

"Well, these cartridges are sold in two- and three-packs. If our boy was taking step-by-step photos of his work, he could go through two or three packs easy."

"And if he got into it, if he got off on the photos," Broskey continued, "he'd be concentrating more on the speed of the reloading than the care involved in doing it. He'd tear the paper off. Toss the unused cartridge somewhere. Stick in the new one. One. Two. Three. Later, he'd gather the spent cartridges and be on his way."

"Uh-huh. Tells us a couple of things about the fellow," Goldstein acknowledged. "He's probably impatient. A regular camera, let's say a thirty-five millimeter, can do a lot better job of taking photos. You get a lot more photos to the roll as well. But you have to *wait* to have them developed. A spastic spaniel can work a Polaroid and have the pictures appear within a minute."

"Double the pleasure," Broskey said. "The guy has his victim in front of him, as well as on the end table in a series of still lifes."

"We also know that our boy probably isn't a professional photographer," Goldstein said. "A proper photographer would one, not be using anything as cheesy as a Polaroid, and two, could get high-quality prints of whatever awful stuff he wanted to shoot and develop them himself in his own darkroom, thus avoiding the risk of some squeamish guy in a one-hour photo joint calling the police."

Broskey gazed at the ceiling in the forensics lab. New tiles to conquer. "Or," Broskey said, "we could have an impatient photographer who wants instant gratification."

"I never thought of that," Goldstein muttered.

"No matter," Broskey said. "You're probably right. Let's keep this between ourselves for the time being, Goldstein."

"You've got it."

"The way I figure it, in another day or so, with Mayer's stories breaking, we're going to be deluged with whackos.

They'll be confessing to everything from our killings to the murder of the Lindbergh baby."

"I thought they caught the guy who did that," Goldstein replied.

"His widow said it was a frame-up."

"Aren't they all?"

Broskey smiled slightly. The California prison system was bursting at the seams with people whose wives said they were innocent.

He walked over to the windows in the lab. They were bigger than the ones in his office. All the windows were open as much as they could be. Hot air was billowing in.

Devil winds.

Made people crazy.

You could see the ocean from Goldstein's lab. It was blue and pristine, in spite of the shit and sewage that was pumped into it every day.

"So," Broskey said. "How about this weather we're having?"

"Yeah," Goldstein said, fingering the camera. "Shitty, isn't it?"

Broskey stared at the ocean. "Ever notice how quickly the Pacific can turn brown?" he asked no one in particular.

Nineteen

*B*roskey sat sweating in his office, surrounded by an avalanche of file folders. Night had fallen. The devil wind still howled outside.

He didn't notice Captain Medega's figure in his doorway. "You look like shit," Medega whispered.

"You sound like my ex-wife."

"What do you have for me on the killings?"

"Which one?" Broskey sighed, leaning back in his chair.

"What about the girls? Rhodes? Do you think this batty actress is connected with all this?"

Broskey shook his head slowly. "Probably not, but when you don't have a weapon with a high degree of accuracy on your side, you better load up with birdshot. Spray the area. See who falls."

"You have anything factual for me?"

"Nope. You saw my reports."

"They read like an exercise in fiction. We know our boy's a shutterbug. We know he's making us look like assholes. What else do we know?"

"He probably offed Rhodes as well," Broskey said. "Just to make us nuts. The guy's daring. He also is on the inside track as far as leads are concerned."

"Theory or fact?"

"Makes sense to me. Rhodes was killed before we really had a case on him. His name was mentioned in the paper, of course, but I find it really squirrely that the killer got to Rhodes just before we were going to put some real pressure on him."

"You're hinting there's a leak in the department." Medega frowned.

"Could be. Could be McDonald, or maybe we have ourselves a killer who hangs out at cop spots. There was this case in Northern California a few years back; I can't remember the fellow's name, but he was a real sick boy. He found out how the investigation was going by hanging out at a few bars that San Francisco's finest hung out in.

"Played it very low-key. Listened to what the boozing boys in blue had to say. Was very careful what questions he asked and how he asked them. Do you know how he figured out how to pump them for information?"

"No."

"He watched 'Police Story.' He read Joseph Wambaugh. He gleaned every bit of information on the head trips of a cop by watching TV and reading books."

"Think we might be encountering this kind of nut?"

"That's the only answer I can come up with."

"There's another possibility you're not mentioning."

Broskey nodded. "I know. But I don't even want to think about it."

"The killer could be on the force."

Broskey frowned. "Long shot, Captain."

"I hope so."

The captain turned to leave. Broskey, remembering Sergeant Fine's tirade and the face of Melanie Melnick, cleared his throat. "Captain?"

"Yes, Broskey?"

"Do you think I'm a cold man?"

"No colder than most," the captain said, not quite understanding.

"I mean, do you think I'm capable of a relationship?"

The captain frowned. "Broskey, are you serious?"

"Yeah. I mean. My life is my work, you know? I've never

really been able to juggle a personal life and a professional one. *You* do it, though. You have two kids, a loving wife, the whole shmear."

Medega flashed his crooked teeth. "Broskey, I have a wife who claims she doesn't recognize me when I come home from work at a decent hour. I have two kids who call me Uncle Daddy. They're almost college age now and the last time I spent a day with them, I think they were seven years old. I'm a guest in my own house. That's how I juggle things."

"Oh," Broskey muttered. He waited for some great insight.

"You want to have guaranteed affection when you get home from work at night?"

"Yes sir, I think I do," Broskey said.

"Buy a dog."

"Huh?"

"Not a pedigree animal, buy yourself a cheap mutt. They'll be eternally grateful and return your affections manifold. Anything else? I'm due to read Dear Abby in five minutes."

"No sir. Thank you, sir," Broskey muttered.

"Jeez, it's hot in your office," Medega said, wiping his brow.

"Santa Anas."

Medega nodded, stifling a sneeze. "Earthquake weather."

Broskey nodded. "So I've heard."

Broskey watched Medega leave. He stared at the files in front of him one more time, zeroing in on the ridiculousness of the Rhodes murder.

He ran a finger across the file. What kind of life was this, anyhow? He had a money-funneling ex-wife, a missing derelict named Bud, a love-starved sergeant, a snuffed-out sleaze-film producer, a hoofer-turned-seer-turned-lawsuit, a street gang named the Skullers scaring the bejesus out of a gang called the Corpses, a police officer who leaked more than an alky with a bad bladder, and a very nasty serial killer to contend with.

The hot wind blasted him along the spine.

It gave him chills.

The phone rang again. He was loath to answer it. The way things were going, he wouldn't have been surprised if someone told him that Godzilla had surfaced in Venice and was threatening to play wok and roll with the residents.

"Hello?" he almost whispered into the phone.

"Hello? Lieutenant Broskey?" a female voice replied.

"Who's this?"

"It's Melanie Melnick, remember? From the college?"

Broskey heaved a colossal sigh. For the first time all day, he felt vaguely human. "Sure. Sure, I do. What's a nice girl like you doing calling a cop like me?"

He knew he sounded like an asshole as soon as he said that, but before he could react, it was too late. Anyhow, it was better than saying "hubba, hubba" over the phone.

Surprisingly, the woman on the other end of the line laughed. It was a nice airy laugh, like pixie dust. "I just wanted to check to see what a cop does during his off hours."

"Usually I stumble home, try to find something that's not totally green to eat, and then pass out," he said truthfully.

"How would you like an alternative plan tonight?"

Broskey's heart skipped a beat. You're old enough to be her father, he told himself.

"Well, I don't know. What do you have in mind?"

"Well, Stan and I . . ."

Broskey's heart sagged. "Stan?"

"My co-editor, remember?"

"Oh yeah. Stan."

No matter. You're old enough to be her uncle.

"We made some progress today and we'd like to tell you about it."

"I'm a little tired, Miss Melnick. . . ."

"Oh, come on. We really want to work with you on catching this guy. Besides, I'd *like* you to come. . . ."

Broskey found himself grinning. Calm down. You're old enough to be her cousin.

"Really?" he said, astounded.

"Sure. I've never really talked to a cop before, except for

my school crossing guard when I was little. And that doesn't count. He was ancient. Not at all interesting."

Broskey's grin almost caused his jaw to crack. "Where and when?"

"Music Max. Anytime you're ready."

"I can leave now," Broskey said.

"Great. I'm looking forward to it," she said. "'Bye."

"Me, too," he said into the dead receiver. "Me, too."

He got up from his desk, grabbed his coat, and headed out the door whistling.

It was clear that he needed something more than a dog in his life.

He bounded down the hallway and headed for the front door. Calm down, he told himself.

You're old enough to be her brother.

Twenty

"o, Kev! Over here!" Broskey heard a familiar voice call as he entered the smoke-filled cacophony known as Music Max. In the far corner of the bar area sat Melanie, Stan, and Jake Mayer.

"We thought you'd never get here." Mayer smiled. "Get in any shoot-outs lately?"

Broskey smiled, slightly intimidated by Melanie's elfin grin. "Nothing so exciting," he muttered. "Just had a lot of paperwork to get to."

"A likely story," Mayer said pointedly to the students. "He's so modest. Not many people know this but 'The A-Team' was based on Kevin's life story."

"You're kidding." Stan gasped.

"He's kidding," Broskey said.

"True." Jake sighed. "He doesn't even like guns."

"Too loud." Broskey smiled. "So, how goes the fight?"

Stan nodded for Melanie to do the talking. "Well, after the Gettysburg Address you gave to the prez today, he really got on the stick. Campus patrols have doubled. He's put private security guards on overtime.

"In addition, we've gotten the frats and the sororities to institute something along the lines of a Neighborhood Watch program, but on campus. Basically, after dark, students escort other students to their cars on the campus lots."

"A buddy system." Broskey nodded. "That's good. That's excellent."

"I see a 'but' materializing," Mayer said.

"That's as good as you can get on campus," Broskey cautioned, "and it's admirable. But the real problem seems to lie off campus. Your parking lot is small. A lot of students park their cars on side streets, sometimes blocks away. If there's any way, you should extend the buddy system to include those people."

"How about vans?" Stan said.

"Good idea." Broskey nodded. "If you can organize any and all students who have vans to sponsor some sort of shuttle program. A mini-bus type of thing. It'll be inconvenient for a lot of the students. They won't get to their cars as fast having to wait for a ride, but they'll be a hell of a lot safer."

"We may have to pay the drivers," Stan said.

"Can the president supply the dollars?" Broskey asked.

"Not really." Melanie sighed. "It's up to the Student Council and *there* we have a problem."

"How so?"

"The president of the council is Tippy Round," Melanie said.

"What kind of name is Tippy Round?" Broskey blinked.

"An important one," Mayer said. "Do de name Senator Alex Round ring a bell witcha?"

"Oh, Jeez," Broskey said. "Failed Democratic presidential candidate. The only Democrat in California who regularly votes with the Republican governor."

"And a screaming banshee of a wife who advocates the censorship of rock lyrics." Melanie smiled. "Reggie Round."

"Whatever happened to names like Ira and Mary?" Mayer asked.

"I have a friend who has a lock on those," Broskey said. "How much of a problem will Tippy be?"

"A big one," Melanie said. "Basically, if she supports our

efforts, she's going to look like she's acknowledging the fact that there's danger. She'll make the newspapers. Her father is campaigning next year on a 'I've made the city streets safer' routine. So if she supports us, she basically slaps him."

"Is there any way around her?" Broskey muttered, ordering a shot of vodka.

"Hard to say." Melanie sighed. "A lot of kids suck up to her because she's rich and Daddy's richer."

"Great." Broskey sighed.

"She says we're making the school sound like it's under a state of siege," Stan said.

"In a very real sense, it is," Broskey replied. "Look, I don't want to scare you any more than you already are. But it looks like we're up against someone who is totally heartless in the way he kills. You probably heard about that movie producer who was shot?"

The students nodded.

"We have reason to believe," Broskey said, "that he was shot because our killer wanted to taunt the police. The man had a connection to the women, but I don't think he was connected with their deaths. Basically, we have a game player out there. He's not only getting off on the women he's killing, he's getting off on the sport of the chase."

"Welcome to the wonderful world of police work, boys and girls." Mayer smiled.

"You have to deal with this every day?" Melanie asked Broskey.

"Weekends, too," Broskey said.

"That's horrible!" she exclaimed, catching the hurt look on Broskey's face after she had let it go. "Sorry. I mean, that's horrible for you."

"I was thinking of buying a dog," Broskey responded.

Mayer quickly changed the subject. "On the plus side, the prez of the college has allowed me free access to interview anyone I damn so choose, including Flipper—"

"Tippy." Stan laughed.

"Whatever—as well as the friends and acquaintances of the deceased. Tomorrow, the second article appears and I will spend half of my day in your beloved police station doing research for the rest of the series."

"Here's to research." Broskey grinned, downing his drink in a single gulp. "And to the insights it may bring."

"Here, here," Melanie said, flagging down a waitress. "Another drink for Dick Tracy."

"And Hemingway," Mayer added.

Broskey frowned slightly. "You really see me as Dick Tracy?" he asked Melanie.

She laughed softly, realizing she had punctured Broskey's ego. "No. More like Harry O. Remember? The David Janssen show?"

"I thought you'd be too young to remember that." Broskey smiled.

"My baby-sitter let me stay up and watch it." She grinned.

"Ooooh, that hurt." Broskey laughed. "Well, I've got to go. My wheelchair is parked outside next to Ironsides'."

"She let me watch that one, too." Melanie smiled.

"Still, I'd better be going," Broskey said.

"Stay and enjoy the fireworks," Mayer said. "I see a famous face approaching."

Broskey looked up. A frizzy-haired blonde in a miniskirt that showed a lot more woman than style was sauntering toward them. Her tanktop was cut to "see" level, defying several laws of gravity. Broskey was forced to shake his head and smile. The kid obviously had money. What there was of the clothes were not of the off-the-rack variety. Give 'em an inch and they'll soon try wearing it as a dress.

He stared at the swiveling woman. She had the particularly vacuous look on her face known only to the very religious or the very political. What she lacked in spark, however, she made up for in top-heaviness. Broskey figured that if she ever arched her back, people for miles around would die from tanktop fragments.

"Is that Dippy?" Broskey asked.

"Tippy," Melanie barked, her voice carrying more than it should have. She added in a whisper, "Actually, she's both."

"I bet she's pissed about our meeting with the president," Stan said, sweating.

"Well, well, the campus muckrakers, hard at work." The blond girl sneered. Broskey was amazed. For a girl so young, she had a very hard face.

"As it so happens," Melanie said, her voice rising almost as much as her left eyebrow, "we *are* at work. Tippy Round, this is Jake Mayer from the *Trib* and Lieutenant Kevin Broskey of the Bay City Police Department."

Broskey had never heard his name uttered with such reverence before. For a moment, he felt like King Arthur had just knighted him.

Tippy was not impressed. First, she gazed at Jake. "You're the one who did the biased article advocating communism and murderous innuendos in rock lyricism last year," she said. "I have a file on you."

"Actually"—Jake laughed—"I've never considered Twisted Sister either Reds or members of the Manson clan. But maybe if I researched more . . ."

"You're thinking of Motley Crüe," Broskey pointed out. "I believe they were brainwashed by the Chinese in eighty-two and then attended Sirhan Sirhan Prep."

"I stand corrected." Jake bowed.

"And *you*," she said, focusing her attention on Broskey, "you're the one who's stirring up trouble on campus."

He found himself eye to stripes with her tanktop. Please, God, he thought, please don't let them loose. I could lose an eye. "Actually," he said, leaning back enough to gaze up into her eyes, "the trouble *is* on campus. I'm just trying to alert everyone to the fact."

"You're also the one who's making trouble for Cheryl Williams," she said. "She's a friend of my family's. If anything happens to her, my father will make sure that you have a lot of explaining to do."

"Well," Broskey said, bridling. "If Daddy can't figure things out, I'm sure Eeyore can."

Broskey was astonished to see Tippy laugh. "You have rocks, Lieutenant."

"But I draw the line at crystals." Broskey smiled back.

"You're okay for an old guy," Tippy said, suddenly sounding her age. "But I just can't support your effort to

144

panic the school. I mean, we have rules enough already on campus, dealing with education and our social life. It hardly seems fair for us to worry about crimes that go on outside the campus."

"Murder is very seldom fair." Broskey shrugged. "But I respect the way you feel. Maybe I would have felt that way myself when I was your age, but I doubt it."

Tippy studied him. "I'm a business-education major, Lieutenant. What was your major?"

"Educational psychology," Broskey muttered.

"Then you should realize," Tippy said, "that the more you push some people, the more they push back. I don't like being pushed. My father likes being pushed even less."

Broskey placed his drink before him. "I don't enjoy it either, Ms. Round. But think about this: Unless you push some people around, they keep on doing terrible, awful things. My job is to push this killer around. Push him out of your life. Out of the lives of every kid in this room. When you think about it, that doesn't sound so bad, does it?"

Tippy smiled. "Well, you'll have to push without the support of the Student Council."

"I seem to have done okay so far, without that support," Broskey said. "I guess I can live without it. No hard feelings."

Tippy smiled. "If you ever want to lecture on campus, let me know, Lieutenant. I can arrange it."

"Thanks."

Tippy walked away. Stan and Jake were amazed. "I thought she'd kill you," Stan said. "She usually goes right for a guy's balls!"

"Fortunately I left mine in my other slacks," said Mayer.

"I thought it was disgusting," Melanie fumed. "She was flirting with you, Lieutenant!"

"Hardly," Broskey said. "She's a young war-horse. I'm an old, er, older war-horse. She wasn't flirting."

"She practically threw herself on you!" Melanie declared.

"I think that's the way she always stands," Stan pointed out.

"She wasn't flirting. Besides, she's too young." Broskey chuckled.

"She's as old as *I* am," Melanie said, offended.

Broskey winced. His foot was in his mouth up to his knee, now. He glanced nervously at Jake. Both Jake and Stan were grinning.

"So, how about this weather we're having?" Mayer said brightly.

"Yeah," said Broskey, loosening his tie, "earthquake weather."

Melanie Melnick stared hard at Broskey. Her pixie face broke into a grin. "Natives call them shakers, Lieutenant."

Broskey laughed. "Back home, Shakers were a religious group." His laughter stopped short. A high-pitched scream reverberated in his ears.

Dear God, he thought, bolting from his table, his companions staring at him oddly. Broskey was on his feet and nearly out the door a full thirty seconds before the other patrons of the bar registered the sound of the scream.

He skidded to a halt in front of a yelling young woman, in front of the club. "What happened?" he demanded.

"My purse! My purse!" she babbled, trembling. "He took it."

She pointed down the street. Broskey saw a man skidding around a corner.

"Thank God," he muttered as the patrons tumbled out of the bar. He coaxed his feet into running mode and, in spite of a pack-a-day residue, pleaded with his heart to send his body into motion. Before he knew it, he was chugging down the block after the purse snatcher.

Vaguely he heard Mayer calling his name from behind.

Broskey slid around the corner, careening into a trash can, sending a mountain of half-eaten sandwiches, discarded issues of the *Watchtower,* and untold used condoms tumbling out onto the sidewalk.

He chased the purse snatcher down the street, which was no more than an alleyway used by trash pickups. It was a dead end. The purse snatcher, a wild-eyed man with a red crew cut, stared at Broskey. The guy was in his midtwenties, but he had obviously lived a hard life. He looked like the first husband of a widow.

"Okay, son, I'm a police officer. Let's have the purse."

The thief gave Broskey the purse, hurling it with all his might toward the policeman's head. Broskey ducked, avoiding a mild concussion.

He slowly walked toward the man, pulling out his revolver. "Okay. Now, I want you to turn around, face the wall, and spread your arms and legs wide open. Okay?"

"Fuck you," the purse snatcher said. "I know my rights."

Broskey blinked. Apparently the thief's rights included the possession of a knife. He pulled a switchblade out of his hip pocket and flipped it open.

Broskey saw the way the man handled the knife. He wasn't a trained knife fighter. He was a slasher, not a thruster.

"Now, you really don't want to get into any more trouble, do you?"

The red-haired geek screwed his face into a parody of concentration. His lower lip nearly engulfed his nose. Broskey wasn't sure the psychological approach was working.

The thief stared at Broskey, who continued to inch his way forward.

"You really don't want to hurt me with that knife, do you?"

The red-haired man considered that for a second. By God, he *did* want to hurt the cop. He ran forward, screaming, slashing at Broskey wildly. Broskey sucked in his gut (he'd have to watch that drinking), causing the knife to pass harmlessly by his midsection. The knife did, however, pierce his lone, clean blazer, becoming enmeshed in the lining.

"Goddamn," the thief exclaimed, getting stuck in Broskey's coat.

"You little idiot," Broskey said. "Do you know how much this coat cost?"

He raised the gun high and brought the butt down firmly at the base of the thief's skull. The man fell more quickly than "Moonlighting's" ratings. He lay, sprawled, before Broskey's feet as the policeman gingerly tried to remove the knife from its lining. Maybe he wouldn't lose the whole coat after all. Linings could always be patched.

Without warning, the young thief leaped up. Broskey was taken by surprise. A shot rang out and the thief fell. Broskey gaped at his own gun. He hadn't fired it. He *never* fired it.

"Are you all right?" Mayer said from behind.

Broskey stared at the kid. He was bleeding from the knee. Jake stood next to Broskey, holding a small-caliber handgun.

"I got him." Jake smiled. He saw Kevin's ashen expression. "Don't worry. I've got a permit."

"Not to carry, I bet," Broskey muttered.

"Are you going to fink on me?" Jake asked. "I get more death threats than most sports commentators. I've been carrying a gun for years."

"Just don't fire it anymore, okay?"

"I don't have to."

Broskey bent over and cuffed the thief. "Do you realize the amount of paperwork I'm going to do now?"

"I thought I just saved your life," Jake said.

"This kid wouldn't have hurt me . . . much," Broskey muttered. "Now, because he's shot, I have to give a report to forensics. Your gun isn't going to match my gun. I'm going to be dancing for days trying to juggle ballistics."

"Sorry," Jake muttered. "Will I get into any trouble?"

"No." Broskey sighed. "Give me the gun and I'll fudge the reports."

"Are you going to *keep* it?" Jake asked, eyes wide.

"I'll get it back to you in a day. Somehow."

"Thanks, Kev. You're a pal."

"Right. Just don't go around playing Lone Ranger anymore, okay?"

"Hey, I could have shot him in the head," Jake said. "I have the contact lenses for it."

Broskey turned and saw a very shaken Melanie Melnick

and Stan Webster run down the alley. A crowd of bystanders congregated behind them.

"Any of you recognize this entrepreneur?" Broskey said, turning the unconscious man toward the crowd.

"I'm not sure . . ." Melanie began.

"But . . ." Broskey prodded.

"I think he's one of the new security guards the president hired today."

Broskey rolled his eyes heavenward. "Remind me to talk to your president about proper hiring procedures tomorrow."

He picked up the purse and dragged the prisoner out of the alley. "Hot soup, coming through," he barked.

At that point, the purse snatcher began to regain consciousness and wriggled along the ground like some sort of salmon in heat. The guy was tearing Broskey's arm out of its socket. Broskey's first reaction was to give the fellow a quick kick between the legs to calm him down, or at least give him other things to think about, but with so many bystanders, he figured *that* move wouldn't exactly improve police–community relations.

The crowd parted as Broskey headed for the curb. The victim of the purse snatching stood, still shaking, in front of Music Max. "Miss? You'll have to come down to the station to make a statement. We have your purse."

"I don't . . . I don't know . . ." the girl whispered, gazing at the bleeding, semiconscious rent-a-cop.

"I'll take her," Melanie volunteered, putting an arm around the trembling woman. "She's a freshman. She doesn't know what to do. I'll take care of her."

"Are you sure?" Broskey asked.

"What the heck. I've never seen the inside of a police station, except on 'The Mod Squad.'"

Broskey flashed her a startled look. Melanie shrugged. "My babysitter . . ."

"Yeah, yeah." Broskey chuckled as he dumped the thief into the back of his car.

At the curb, Jake Mayer and Stan Webster watched the two cars drive away.

"One thing about hanging around with Kevin Broskey," Jake said admiringly. "Things are never dull." Stan was still shaking. Jake shrugged. "Stupid, often. But dull? Never. Come on, junior, I'll buy you a drink."

"I think I may be sick."

"Well, make up your mind. Why should I waste two-fifty?"

Twenty-one

After a pep talk by Melanie, the young freshman woman agreed to press charges against her assailant. Broskey tossed in an assault-on-a-law-officer charge for good measure. The freshman was sent home in a squad car and, after three hours of paperwork, Broskey heaved a sigh of relief.

"How much time do you think that guy will get?" Melanie asked, perched, her legs crossed, on a chair across from his desk.

"Knowing our judicial system?" Broskey mused. "If he claims he knows information about the assassination of J.F.K., he'll get two weeks and an official apology from the department."

Melanie emitted her elfin laugh. Broskey melted. He stared at the young woman.

"You like me, huh?" she asked bluntly.

Broskey thought hard how to answer that. He came up with a brilliant, "Auhhhhhah."

"Look. Normally, I wouldn't be talking to you this way, but I don't know, I feel sort of weird. It's like tonight, watching the purse snatcher and you catching him and feeling so in the middle of everything, I just feel buzzed.

151

Like I've just jogged five miles or so. It's okay that you like me. I like you, too." She shrugged.

"You do?" Broskey asked, blinking. He felt like he had just been hit by one of Cupid's stray darts, right around the large intestine.

"Don't act so surprised." Melanie laughed. "You're not *that* bad."

"Well, you aren't either," Broskey blurted. "I mean, but we, you and Stan . . ."

"Stan and I are just friends. Don't you have any women friends?"

Broskey thought of Sergeant Fine. "I did. I *do*. Yeah."

Melanie was beaming now. "So, now what?"

"But you date, right?"

Melanie smiled secretively. "I'm dating the pope. Actually, I'm only using him to get to God." She saw a lighter on Broskey's desk. "You got a cigarette?"

Broskey reached into his top drawer and pulled out a package, which shook mysteriously in his hand. He hoped she didn't notice. If she did, she didn't react. She allowed him to light her cigarette and took a deep breath.

"Chivalrous." She grinned. "That's nice. Look, Lieutenant—"

"K-Kevin," Broskey hiccuped.

"Look, Kevin. I'll be honest with you. I don't date anymore. Why? Because, frankly, I'm tired of going out with guys who look like Reeboks ads, have the brains the size of peas, and will never have to worry about sudden inspiration in their lives. I'm tired of feeling *smarter* than everyone I go out with. Oh, I don't believe I'm telling you all this."

"But I'm . . ."

"Older? So what?"

"Sixteen years older," Broskey said, amazed at the thought. "There are millions of entire persons as old as the difference in our ages."

"Doesn't bother me. You like old movies?"

"Yeah."

"Me, too. You like to read?"

"Yeah."

"Me, too. Are you gay?"

"No!" Broskey exclaimed.

"Do you have AIDS, herpes, syph, or any other diseases I should know about?"

Broskey was astonished. This woman had seemed so quiet this afternoon. "Uh-uh. Unless you count the time I lived with those lepers in Vegas." He smirked.

"Well, then I think we should hang out together and see what happens. The worst you can do is stop cooking that green stuff at home. I cook pretty well."

"But I work weird hours," Broskey said defensively. Suddenly he felt as if he didn't have a chance. He didn't know whether he felt threatened or elated. Mylanta wouldn't have hurt, though.

"So do I. I'm a full-time student and a part-time editor."

Broskey was teetering on the edge of the precipice. Melanie Melnick chose that moment to smile. Her bright eyes sparkled. She ran a thin finger through her short, black hair. Broskey toppled. "You'll hate me." He laughed.

"You'll hate me more," she said.

"Tell you what," he said, rising. "Let me take you out for a proper dinner and we'll exchange life stories."

"Résumé night, huh?"

Broskey nodded and led her down the hall. In the lobby, near the booking cage, Bluth and McDonald were munching burritos while watching the TV. "Hey, Lieutenant. Lookit this."

Broskey led Melanie to the squawking boob tube. A very distinguished Cheryl Williams was talking to reporters. "Of course, this has been a big misunderstanding. I have volunteered my assistance to the Bay City Police Department. Anything I can do to help in finding the murderer of that pathetic little man, whom I knew only casually, years ago . . ."

Broskey rolled his eyes. He supposed his threats had worked.

"And what about the rumor that you're considering suing both the *Trib* and the police department?" a reporter asked.

"Oh, my dear boy." Cheryl laughed. "A person as spiritual as myself would never stoop to such a low and degrading act."

Yeah, Broskey smirked. Try to salvage your spook biz, honey. You've already blown it.

"Come on," he said to Melanie. "I know a rotten Italian place."

He led her to the door. "Hey, Lieutenant," McDonald called. "Is that your daughter?"

Broskey winced. Melanie smiled pertly at the officer. "No, junior. I'm his main squeeze."

Broskey laughed aloud, watching McDonald shrivel. Bluth was dumbstruck. Only Melanie remained calm. "I couldn't help myself," she whispered on the way out to the parking lot. "I hate twerps like that."

"We *do* have a lot in common," Broskey admitted, leading her to his car.

Broskey returned home, whistling. Somehow, being with Melanie brought that out in him. Usually he hated whistling almost as much as he hated humming, which registered right up there with accordian playing.

Broskey shuddered, remembering Catholic school, crew-cut accordianist students, and endless renditions of "Lady of Spain" at every school assembly for twelve years. He had always wanted to write a paper somehow connecting Catholicism with the fine art of accordian playing. He just never got around to it.

Melanie had turned out to be an actual native of California. Her parents were from up north, arch-liberals, and she, growing tired of bean sprouts and chatting with dolphins, relocated to the Los Angeles area to wallow in crassness. She hadn't been disappointed. She had a nice, bemused air about her.

She found Broskey entertaining as well. ("I've never seen any man sweat so much around a woman," she marveled.)

Broskey pulled up in front of his house, gun drawn. Following last night's skeet-shooting incident, he felt it best to play it safe.

He walked up to his front door and eased it open. Everything seemed normal.

He flicked on the light switch. He glanced out on the front step. The newspaper was still lying there, untouched. Still no sign of Bud, though.

He let his torn coat fall on the floor and made a move to turn on the TV.

There was no TV.

He glanced around the room.

His stereo was gone.

So was his clock radio.

He sat down on his sofa, flabbergasted. He'd been cleaned out. Who in their right mind would want to fence his stuff? You'd have to be shooting up Sterno or be a certified Laughing Academy member to think Broskey's cache was valuable.

It was then he saw the note under the cold cup of store-bought coffee. He picked it up.

Dear Lieutenant Broskey,

I am truly sorry to have had to borrow your home entertainment center, but I was in dire need of cash. The pep talk you gave me the other day inspired me. I am off in search of a new career and, hopefully, monetary gain. I promise you, I will return your goods as soon as possible. I must thank you for all your kindnesses and, believe me, with the confidence you have given me, I will be able to return your items manifold in the very, very near future.

> *Yours truly,*
> *Benjamin "Bud" Holden*
> *A friend forever.*

Broskey held the note. His first impulse was to go into a tirade. You couldn't trust anyone these days. His anger faded quickly, however, when he realized that Bud was sincere. He *believed* he was going to make it. He *believed* he was going to be able to pay Broskey back soon. What the heck; in a way, Bud was the best friend Broskey had. The guy was always honest. Plus, he knew how to refold a paper so that a second person could read it without the whole thing exploding in your hands.

Broskey began to laugh. He wondered if anyone had as crazy a life as he had.

Twenty-two

*B*roskey again awoke to the sound of the telephone ringing and Mrs. Ramirez next door driving the devil out of her oven. "Hout, Satan," she screamed. "These rolls are for the sainted birds in my yard. Saint Francis, he tell me personally, to bake the rolls just so, so they pop up like on de television. Satan, leave my pilot light alone!"

Broskey eased himself off the couch. The phone had stopped ringing. He knew it would start again in a minute or so, so he took the opportunity to retrieve his newspaper off the front step.

Swinging the door open and being blasted by sunlight and slap of hot air, he bent down and found a manila envelope along with his copy of the *Trib*. He brought both inside and, sitting on the battered couch, placed the envelope on the coffee table.

"bRosKEY" read the label on the envelope. Each letter had been cut out of magazines and pasted together, giving his name a cock-eyed look.

He opened the envelope and slid the contents out onto the tabletop.

Broskey stifled the urge to scream.

They were photographs, very nasty Polaroids: a step-by-step exercise displaying the torture and death of Tippy Round.

He kept his hands off the photographs, moving them around with a swizzle stick left over from two dinners ago. He gazed at the photo until he felt his face redden. At that point, the phone rang.

It was Medega.

"Have you heard the news?" Medega said, his voice deceptively calm.

"No. But I'm looking at what I think you're talking about."

"The senator and his wife are on their way down from Northern California."

"They're not going to like identifying her," Broskey said.

"How do you know?" Medega said. *"I* haven't gotten to the murder scene as yet. Goldstein called me ten minutes ago."

"Because, Captain"—Broskey sighed—"I am looking at a set of photographs hand-delivered to my door, showing the last night that Tippy Round spent on planet Earth."

Medega said nothing, but Broskey could have sworn he felt the phone heat up. Finally, Medega replied. "Twenty-five Sierra Avenue. Meet me there. Bag the photos and bring them."

"I'm on my way."

Broskey and Medega watched Goldstein and his forensics team do their best to put Tippy Round's shattered world together again. As usual, only the bedroom was destroyed, the rest of the opulant apartment, with its thick white carpeting and Art Deco furnishings, was totally unblemished.

Broskey saw Medega stare at some large murals hanging on the wall. "I bet these are originals," he muttered. "They must go for upward of two hundred grand each."

"I think we can assume robbery had nothing to do with this, Chief." Broskey sighed.

"I know, I know," Medega said. "Just thinking out loud. Broskey, this one is going to push us against a wall in a very big way. For one thing, we have our first celebrity victim. Her parents are going to raise hell. Her funeral will be on the front page of every newspaper west of the Mississippi.

"Plus, this is a fairly well-to-do neighborhood, not the usual kind of middle-of-the-road apartment neighborhood that college kids bunk in. The ex-mayor of Bay City lives three doors down. The ex–police chief two blocks. The people here are going to freak out."

"They have a Neighborhood Watch here, right?"

"Right. So, they'll freak even more. In spite of the watch, someone got inside this house and did some nasty things to a very young lady."

Broskey nodded. "I'm on the spot, right?"

Medega nodded. "Center of the frying pan. It's your investigation. You're the one calling the shots. It was your idea to have your newspaper pal stir things up. Prod the killer. Well, you've prodded him all right. He's killing more frequently now."

"Chief," Broskey began, "there's more than that going on here. The photos. How did he know about the photos?"

"I take it you didn't see the eleven o'clock news last night?" Medega smirked.

"Nope. I was out kind of late," Broskey said.

"The photo angle was leaked. It made the broadcast."

"Shit. How the hell are we supposed to stay one step ahead of this guy if he's following our progress better than most of the department?"

"That's a fact we can't change," Medega said grimly. "If—as usual—it's McDonald that's leaking this stuff, there's no way we can catch him. There's no way we can prove it. There's no way we can, legally, discipline him until we actually see or hear him passing on information. I don't think it would do too much for department morale to have his office phone bugged, do you?"

"What would you like me to do?" Broskey said. "What more can I possibly do?"

"Bullshit," Medega said.

"Is that an instruction or an opinion?" Broskey blinked.

"Both. Get back to your office and use your college

education to come up with the most effective statement you can give to the press. I want you to press all the buttons. Make people angry. Make people weep. Make people scared. Do whatever you have to, to make it seem like we're *this* close to finding this guy. I want that statement in an hour. I want to see your face on every noonday TV broadcast. I want to short-circuit whatever salvos Senator and Mrs. Round are going to fire.

"Drag everything into it. We have every available man on this case, we're stretching our resources, we're putting the meager amount of state and county funding we receive into overtime."

"Are we?"

"We are now," Medega replied.

"What about an open letter to the killer?" Broskey asked.

Medega thought about it. "Would you write it?"

"I don't think I should; that would draw too much attention to me, to the investigation, to the department, but I could get Jake involved. Basically, I could do the research, get him to folksy it up, and have him run it in the paper. That way, the paper would also be involved in the hunt."

"That could make the killer cockier," Medega said.

"Chief," Broskey pointed out, "the guy is already sticking it to us in every way possible. Maybe, if the *Trib* gets involved, he'll be flattered by the attention. We run a second and third letter that, perhaps, insinuates he boffed his mother or something. Hit him with some psychological clichés. Maybe he'll start writing to set the record straight. If we can get him to communicate, eventually we might get him to show up for a one-on-one interview with either Jake or myself."

"We don't have until 'eventually,' Broskey," Medega said. "We had until yesterday. As of today, the mayor has put us on notice."

"Our jobs are on the line for real?"

"One week to show results or show the reason why."

"Impatient little dickens, isn't she?" Broskey muttered.

"She already has my replacement picked out." Medega

frowned. "And I imagine, yours, too. I'll try to keep her off your back as long as I can. It might be a matter of hours, it might be a matter of days, before she begins pumping you for information."

Broskey turned his back on the carnage. "Okay. I'll hit the typewriter and get to the press. After that, Jake and I will do up the open letter. I'm sure Jake will love hogging the spotlight."

"Modesty doesn't seem to be one of his virtues," Medega said.

"He's great at punctuation, though," Broskey replied. "I'd like to spend the afternoon roaming around Bay City College, if it's all right with you. There has to be something we can find out there."

"Hunch?"

"Hunch," Broskey replied.

"Take McDonald and Bluth with you," Medega said.

"Chief! They'll just muck things up! McDonald wouldn't know a brainstorm from an early-morning fog!"

"Granted his vocabulary is small, but the turnover is terrific."

"I'd love to introduce him to lockjaw. Chief, please . . ."

"I'd rather have them in the field with you than in the station near any hard evidence forensics gathers. McDonald will have less to broadcast."

Broskey nodded. He couldn't argue logic, much as he would have liked to.

He left Tippy Round's apartment and took the elevator down to the lobby. The building was a modern, double-buzzer structure, with all the latest security devices.

Broskey sighed. This killer was like a will-o'-the-wisp. He seemed everywhere.

He walked past the uniformed men outside and headed for the car. He'd probably find Mayer doing research at the station. Maybe Jake would help him word the bullshit statement as well as the open letter.

He saw Sergeant McGlory and paused. "Sergeant, we have problems."

McGlory nodded. "Indeed we do. Five cars stolen in one day. We think it's the Skullers, but popular opinion has it that it's the Corpses. I think the Corpses will pop soon."

Broskey sighed. "Forget the gang stuff for the time being. We have a serial killer that has us by the"—he remembered McGlory was a rabid Catholic and curbed his tongue—"by the privates. To be honest, I'm backed so far against the wall, the writing is on me. The chief is taking a lot of heat from the mayor. We have to help take it off him."

"Ready, willing, and able, Lieutenant." McGlory smiled. "I'd feel as honored as Saint Patrick tackling the snakes."

"I want you to check the files. Roust every convicted or suspected sex offender in town, using all your legal discretion, of course."

"Of course." McGlory winked. "But we did that after we found the second girl."

"Go back and hit them again, harder. I want them to sweat. I don't care if they're paroled rapists, sheep fondlers, or Peeping Toms. I want them to feel as frazzled as we do. One of them might not be the perp, but maybe, if we send them running, squealing like stuck pigs, onto the streets, they'll make contact with the killer. Let him know the heat is on for real. Maybe, if he gets nervous enough, he'll slip up."

"And when he slips, we'll be there to catch him," McGlory said.

"Or just let him hit the pavement," Broskey said. "At this point, I'd prefer the latter."

"Understood, sir."

Broskey entered his car. "Thanks, Mac."

As he drove toward the station, he passed a large billboard advertising California's Lotto game. YOU TOO CAN BE A WINNER! the board proclaimed.

Broskey sighed to himself. Some folks just weren't designed that way.

Today, he felt like he was giving failure a bad name.

Twenty-three

By the time Broskey reached the college campus that afternoon, he was exhausted. The way he felt, if he smelled flowers, he'd automatically look for a funeral.

He had issued his statement for the media.

It was the usual police pap, but delivered in a fairly heartfelt manner.

Jake's letter to the killer would make the afternoon editions. It read like a plea from Pat O'Brien, playing a priest, to James Cagney, as a killer, from an old "B" movie. As a matter of fact, that was just what Jake was trying for.

The following day, he had plans to run a letter actually written by the archbishop of Los Angeles.

Broskey winced, thinking of all the assorted nuts that would flood the tiny Bay City police station in search of forgiveness for whatever dastardly crimes they thought they had committed.

Another car had been stolen, this one an off-road vehicle. Presumably the Skullers were hard at work. The kids had probably been very good at auto shop in school.

A rash of robberies on Los Angeles' west side was connected with the gang. That worried Broskey. The Corpses were bound to react to the pressure to outdo the Skullers.

Senator Alex Round and his wife, Reggie, had visited the morgue and had emitted cries that shook even Goldstein.

Forensics had shown that Broskey's Polaroids had been clean when delivered to Broskey's house. In fact, the only prints that had shown up were on the envelope. They had been Tippy Round's. The killer had probably forced her to create the envelope herself before the attack began.

Broskey plodded across the campus. His legs felt like lead weights. The Santa Anas singed his skin. He was alternately sweating, shivering, and coming down with one humdinger of a cold.

Mayer shadowed Broskey as they passed featureless building after building. Whoever created the Bay City campus was never introduced to Legos as a child. If he had been, he would have gotten the rectangular motif out of his system.

McDonald and Bluth followed Mayer.

"Excuse me, sir," McDonald said, his voice fraught with irritation. "Just why are we here, anyway?"

"We're here to talk to people, McDonald." Broskey sighed.

"About what?"

Broskey stopped dead in his tracks, almost causing Jake to run up his back and perch on his shoulders. Broskey whirled around. "About the victims," Broskey said, his forehead pounding. "About who they knew, what classes they attended, what their habits were, if they had had any arguments with anyone in the last few months, any encounters with suspicious characters, any crank calls, if there was *anything* in their very short lives that struck *anyone* else here on campus as being the slightest bit odd."

Broskey turned and continued walking down the concrete pathway leading toward the newspaper office. "You guys take the study halls first," he called over his shoulder.

Mayer and Broskey entered the student center. They found the newspaper office. Melanie and Stan were seated, ashen-faced, surrounded by every sorority and frat leader in the school.

Melanie looked up at Broskey. "Kevin . . . this is terrible. We just saw Tippy last night . . ."

"I know, I know," Broskey said. "Our job now is to prevent that from happening again."

She nodded. Stan pointed to a rugged-looking young man, seated, hands folded, in the corner of the paper-strewn office. "This is Chip Brouner," he said. "The acting president of the Student Council."

The kid looked up. His eyes were red from crying. "Lieutenant? You have the entire council's cooperation. Whatever we have to do to catch this shit—whatever it takes—we're with you."

All the students in the room nodded solemnly. Broskey felt his body sag. He was relieved. He was also feverish. "All right," he said. "First we talk about student patrols, about security measures. This campus has to be locked tighter than a steel drum. I also want the frats to keep an eye on all student hangouts. Anything suspicious, call me."

"The football team volunteered," Chip said, "to help in any way, too."

"Fine"—Broskey nodded—"but no rough stuff. Our killer is just that. Someone who takes human lives like we munch peanuts. He wouldn't think twice about knocking a linebacker on his ass permanently. Now, as for the community-relations bit, we have Jake Mayer here to work with you. He'll be your source of information and he'll be a gatherer of information. We want the killer to know that this college is off limits. We want him to know that not only are the police after him, but every single person on this campus, or near this campus, is wise to him. We want to shut him out completely. Is that clear?"

Broskey eased himself into a chair as Jake started his pep talk. Melanie sidled up to him. "You look terrible."

"I feel like I'm wearing a tight hat and tighter shoes."

She placed a small hand on his forehead. "You're burning up."

"Burning out is more like it."

"What you need is some chicken soup."

"I need a vacation more."

"I can only offer you chicken soup," she whispered. "When you're off duty, tonight?"

He nodded feebly. It sounded good. "Total access," Jake was stressing. Melanie subtly massaged Broskey's neck as he leaned back in the chair. He closed his eyes. For a moment, all was peaceful.

But only for a moment.

Twenty-four

*B*roskey led Jake back to his car. "Come on," he said, "I'll drive you back to the station."

Above them, the hot desert winds whistled through the drab, gray power lines surrounding the college campus. Broskey leaned on the car for a minute, his body racked with chills.

"You coming down with something?" Mayer asked.

"Terminal ineptitude," Broskey said, his teeth chattering. He watched a disgusted McDonald lead Bluth to their car and drive off. He knew they hadn't gotten anything substantial from their canvasing the campus. He knew they hadn't tried.

He glanced at a pole bearing a handmade poster: WERE YOU A LEPRECHAUN IN YOUR PAST LIFE? A BEAUTIFUL PRINCESS? A DASHING VIKING? COME SEE THE MOVIE CHANNELER. HEAR THE SPIRITS OF YOUR FAVORITE MOVIE STARS ADVISE YOU OF YOUR PAST, PRESENT, AND FUTURE LIVES. LOCATED AT THE CORNER OF LINCOLN AND PICO DIRECTLY NEXT TO SUSHI HEAVEN.

Broskey shook his head and slid into his car. "I bet Oregon is nice this time of year." He sighed.

"You'd look bad in a lumberjack shirt," Jake pointed out.

Jake stood on the gas and sent the car lurching out of the

campus lot. He misjudged his speed and wound up crunching into the rear fender of a zippy little *pink* sports car.

"Great," Broskey moaned.

"Don't sweat it." Mayer smirked, getting out of the car. "It was probably an Oriental woman or a coked-up preppie. Watch the master at work."

Mayer screwed himself up to his full munchkin size and waddled, John Wayne style, toward the injured vehicle. He saw the driver was a woman. Aha, he smiled, easy prey.

"What's the matter withya?" Jake sizzled. "Yablind or somethin'?"

An attractive woman leaned out of the car. "Are you talking to me?"

Mayer stood on his tiptoes and gazed into the car. The woman was wearing a very short skirt. He turned toward Broskey and winked. Broskey, however, sat, ashen, gazing at the license plates of the *pink* Mercedes in front of him. BAYCITY I.

Jake was still grinning as the woman exited the car. "I suppose this was somehow all my fault."

"I suppose so." Mayer nodded. "We're on official police business."

"You are?"

"Yes, ma'am." Mayer nearly cackled. "Right there, in that car, is Bay City's finest homicide man." He leaned in toward the woman, trying to get a glimpse of her cleavage. "We're on official business. Very top secret. Life-and-death stuff."

Broskey slowly got out of the car. "Jake, I wouldn't if I were you."

"Don't be modest, Kev." Mayer beamed. "I'm sure the insurance will cover the damage and I'm equally sure that this lovely lady would love to hear all about you . . . *us.* Wouldn't you Miss . . . uh . . . Miss . . ."

"Miss Roberts," said the woman in the pink mini-dress. "Gina Roberts. *Mayor* Gina Roberts of Bay City."

She flashed a very wide smile at the two men. Broskey's stomach did a somersault.

Mayer was producing beads of sweat that were leaping

into low orbit at an angle rivaling the best of Dagwood Bumpstead's efforts.

"Now, Mr. . . ."

"Mayer." He gulped.

"You were about to talk about insurance . . ."

"My fault entirely," Mayer muttered.

"As I thought." The mayor grinned. "Now, about this top-secret police business?"

"Nothing special," the short journalist smiled. "The kind of routine police work that happens every day."

Broskey slowly slid back into the car, hearing his career vanish with the flush of a political toilet.

Twenty-five

Two hours later, Broskey collapsed behind his desk. Reaching into his top drawer, he found a half-filled bottle of Advil. He popped six in his hand and chewed on them.

Sergeant Fine walked in. "Heard you had a tough day, Broskey."

"Only in every sense of the phrase."

"While you were gone, your wife—"

"Ex-wife."

"—called six times, Cheryl Williams called, breathing fire, twice, Sergeant McGlory said he'd see you when you got back—I just buzzed him so he should be on his way up—the mayor left some of her phone sunshine, and some Twinkie named Melanie called."

Broskey clenched an Advil between his teeth. "I assume," Fine continued, "it's the little cutie McDonald and Bluth were chortling over this morning. Your 'main squeeze'? The one you were diddling with in your office last night?"

She held up a cigarette, Broskey's brand, with lipstick on it. "Have you taken up working in drag after hours?"

Broskey decided that any response would be useless. Besides, he ached all over.

"I've already seen the mayor. We're having lunch tomorrow."

"I'm impressed." Sergeant Fine smirked. "By the way, don't bother to bring your animal magnetism. She doesn't go for boys."

"You want to take my place?" Broskey smiled thinly. Fine simmered and left the room.

Sergeant McGlory entered, a file folder under his hand. "I heard about your glorious day." He grinned.

"Glorious?"

"You managed to make a very big impression on the mayor, I understand."

"Thanks, Sergeant. The mayor has requested my presence at lunch tomorrow. Do you think we'd make a swell couple?"

"I'll say a prayer for you."

"Better say a rosary."

McGlory raised his eyes heavenward. "'May God grant him many years to life. For sure God must be knowing. The earth has angels all too few, and Heaven is overflowing.'"

"That's very nice, Sergeant."

Broskey sagged in his chair. When McGlory got into Clichés 101, it could take him hours to complete the course. "You have something for me, Mac?"

"Oh, that I do, that I do. When we were running down our Perv Hall of Fame, look who we found, residing at our very own Bay City College campus."

He tossed a file in front of Broskey. "Roger Dante. Age fifty-five. 1960s burnout. Has a long police record arising from the period of love-ins, sit-ins, protests, and drug busts. Branched out in the late sixties. Arrested for beating several girlfriends. Molesting a neighbor's wife. Two counts of attempted rape. Lewd conduct. Got out of most of the sex stuff on technicalities."

Broskey looked at the file. These days Dante taught both creative writing and French literature at the college.

"Good work, Sergeant." Broskey nodded.

"I was wondering, though," McGlory began. "I'm glad we found this boyo and I hope the information will help the investigation, but why is it that no one had picked up on this fella before now? Who's actually working the campus?"

"McDonald and Bluth," Broskey muttered. "I'll have a chat with them in the morning."

"Enough said," McGlory replied. "Tsk. Tsk. The Bluth boy has promise but he's a follower. But that McDonald, he's all flash and no substance. A bit of a dim bulb, too."

"I'll talk to them, Mac."

"Well, see you in the morning, sir."

Broskey stifled a sneeze. "And take something for that cold," McGlory added. "You look like horsepucky, sound worse, and this weather we're having . . ."

"Earthquake weather." Broskey nodded.

"Not a good time to be feeling bad," McGlory said, walking out of the office.

Mayer popped his head in. Broskey felt as if he were on display in some police sideshow. "Have any plans tonight?" Jake asked.

"As a matter of fact, I do," Broskey said, "if I don't die of pneumonia first."

"That's too bad," Mayer said.

"Me dying of pneumonia?"

"Nah, not that. That I could take. I was looking for a drinking partner before I make the long drive back to West Los Angeles."

"It's a ten-minute ride, Jake."

"You have no drama in your soul," Mayer said, shaking his head sadly. "See you tomorrow. Read all about our campus heroes in tomorrow's first edition. And, Kev, thanks for covering up the gun bit last night. I've been thinking about that. You could've gotten into a lot of trouble."

"No problem. I'll get the gun back to you tomorrow. A lot of people in forensics owed me favors."

"Don't bother. Already got it. I did a favor for the head of the unit's sister a year ago."

Broskey was amazed. "Why don't you run my investigations *for* me? You know more people than I do. You'd probably have an easier time of it."

"I need a front man," Mayer said. "Make it legal. And by

the by, if I don't see you before your lunch date, have a *great* time with the mayor tomorrow. I hear she has great legs."

"From who?"

"Some waitress I met downtown."

"Jake?"

"Yeah?"

"Leave me alone."

"Boy, chauffeur a guy around town from the goodness of your heart and they sure get grouchy." Mayer laughed, leaving.

Broskey leaned back in his chair and slowly dialed the phone, savoring every number.

"Hello?" Melanie Melnick said.

"It's me." Broskey smiled. "Your knight in rusted armor."

Broskey leaned against the overstuffed pillow in front of Melanie's fireplace. A low, gas-fed fire, which emitted little if any heat, hissed dully before him. He wrapped the terry-cloth robe tighter.

Melanie returned from the kitchen. "Your clothes are almost dry. I've never seen a man sweat like you do. Are you part meat loaf or something?"

"I'm coming down with a cold. I hope I don't give you any germs."

"Don't worry about it, I'm a vitamin junkie. You do look terrible, you know."

"So people keep telling me."

"Sorry. I know. I know. You had a terrible day. How do you do your job every day without going crazy?"

He gazed into her wide, bright eyes. There was intelligence there, innocence, hidden knowledge. She sat, waiting for him to respond, like Tinkerbell waiting for Peter Pan's next adventure. "I don't know. I try to have pleasant dreams, I guess."

"What do you dream about?"

"Lots of things."

"Do you have one recurring dream?"

"I'd have to think about that."

"*I* have one," she said. "I dream that I turn into a fierce tiger and run through the jungles, taking on anyone who gets in my way. I always win, of course."

Broskey nodded. "Of course. Funny. I hadn't thought about this, but usually the dreams I remember, the ones that aren't connected with work, are all in color. I see this large, bright blue bird, sort of a peacock actually, but different somehow. I'm in this garden, this wonderful garden, and the bird appears, soaring above me.

"It calls to me, in a way, not anything you can hear but a call you can feel. I raise my arms and I float in the air, like a kite. I fly alongside the bird, not like Superman, but like a fish swimming through the air, wriggling, twisting, and turning in the currents. I like that dream. It's very peaceful. Whenever I have it, I wake up feeling good."

He gazed into the fire. "That usually lasts about two minutes. Until the phone rings."

"You know what I think?" Melanie asked.

"What?"

"I think you have the soul of a poet."

"Come on," Broskey said. "It's just a dream."

"Yeah. But look at our dreams. I'm tiny and female and I dream about being powerful, a savage beastie with the power to destroy anyone who tries to bar my path. You're a cop. You're surrounded by grit and blood all day and you dream of escape. But not just escape, of freedom, of flight, of a better world."

"I never thought about it that way . . . and I'm the one with the East Coast shrink training."

She leaned forward and pecked him on the cheek. He shook his head suddenly, like a dog doused with water.

"Did it hurt that much?" Melanie laughed.

"I—I just didn't expect it." He grinned, blushing. "No. It felt fine. Great, even. I'm just not used to dealing with . . ."

"Women?"

"People," Broskey replied quickly. "With dealing with people."

Melanie's smile faded. "That must hurt you a lot, I bet. I

bet you're the kind of person who really wants to care about people, but most of the ones you meet are either crazies, thugs, killers, or victims."

Broskey managed a lopsided smile. She *was* smart. "I think you're on to something there."

Melanie ran a delicate hand over Broskey's stubbly chin. "Can I ask you two things?"

"Sure." Broskey nodded.

"One: Would you stay the night, even if we didn't do anything? I'd feel safer sleeping with someone. And two: Do you think the killer will strike again tonight?"

Broskey's mind went into overdrive. He quickly factored in how many officers were patrolling on regular duty, how many were putting in overtime hours, where they were situated, and how he would feel waking up in someone else's house.

He touched her hand. "The answer to number one is yes. The answer to number two is we're doing all we can to prevent it."

The harsh rhythms of Music Max were making Claire Simmons jittery. "Of course I'm nervous," she told the man at the table. "Everyone is nervous. That's the only reason I'm still here."

"I don't get it," the man replied.

"I'm waiting to see if someone I know walks in so I can find someone to follow me home."

"You're that scared?"

"Of course I am," she said, sipping her umpteenth drink. "This guy just seems to come up out of nowhere; he's like a ghost or something."

"Ooooooooh," the man said, laughing. "Scary stuff. The killer is probably the long-lost cousin, once removed, of Count Dracula!"

Claire laughed. "God, I haven't laughed in a week."

"Feels good, doesn't it?"

She nodded her head, slightly drunk.

"Tell you what," her companion said. "I've always wanted to play Sir Galahad. *I* can follow you home."

"But I hardly know you," she said.

"Oh, come on. *Everyone* here knows me."

Claire thought for a moment. "No hanky-panky, though."

"I'm allergic to hanky-panky. I have a note from my doctor to prove it."

Claire Simmons laughed again. She liked this man with the wide smile and the quick wit and, true, she *did* know him. "All right," she said. "I'm parked in back."

"Sounds like a painful condition," Jake Mayer said, helping the girl to her feet.

Broskey lay on the brass bed, cradling Melanie in his arms. Outside, the Santa Anas were howling.

"What are you thinking?" she asked.

"In all my years out here"—he smiled—"I've never heard the Santa Anas sound so peaceful, so beautiful. I guess it's the company I'm with. You make everything seem new. Everything seems so refreshing."

"I think it's just that you're falling asleep."

Broskey nodded lazily. "Yeah, that, too. You know what would make this night perfect?"

"Is it legal?"

"Sure." Broskey smiled. "Some old rock and roll. Old rhythm and blues. Something like Otis Redding. You have any Otis Redding records?"

Melanie smiled. "Nope. I could write my parents, though. I'm sure they do. They could mail them to us."

"Please . . ." Broskey smirked. "I can feel my arteries hardening."

"The oldest stuff I have is Andy Gibb."

"Jeez."

"That counts! He's dead, too."

Broskey sighed. "I'm either falling asleep or dying of premature senility."

Melanie giggled. "Let's see if we can find out which . . ."

Claire Simmons staggered into her apartment. "Whoopsie." She laughed dizzily.

"Watch that first step, it's a lulu." Mayer closed the door behind them.

"Thanks for walking me upstairs," Claire said. "I feel a lot safer."

She smiled at him. "Well, I'm going to bed."

Mayer laughed. "Now, I know better than to think that's an invitation."

Claire pouted. "You don't mind leaving, do you? I'm really tired."

"Not at all, but do you mind if I have a nightcap first?"

"Nope. There's some beer in the fridge."

He put his satchel down on the table. "What's that?" she asked.

"Huh? Oh, it's a book I'm working on. I don't like to leave the pages in the car. I carry them everywhere."

Claire shot him a suspicious look. He made his eyes cross. "Old writers' superstition."

"You're a scream."

"That I am," he said. "Owwoooooo. Point me to the fridge."

"It's that way," she said, heading for the bedroom. "I'm just going to put my sweats on. I'll be back in a minute."

"You want one, too?"

"Sure," she said, zigzagging around the couch toward the bedroom. "Why not? I'm not driving anymore."

"Nope," Mayer said, smiling, watching the woman close the bedroom door behind her, "you're not."

He walked over to his satchel and quietly removed a Polaroid camera. He still had six shots left. He glanced in the satchel. There were still three rolls of film unopened. Great. That was plenty. He gazed down into his bag of tricks and saw the metallic shape of his revolver.

"Can't forget you." He chuckled.

He slipped his gun into his left jacket pocket and a small, leather-bound blackjack out of the satchel and into his right pocket.

He slowly walked toward the bedroom.

Claire was struggling, half-seated on her bed, trying

drunkenly to get out of her dress when the door flew open. "What?" she gasped.

A flash of light went off, blinding her.

"Say cheese." Mayer cackled.

The earthquake hit just past four A.M. It was centered off the coast of Malibu. Cal Tech, the following morning, would tell reporters that it registered at 4.5 on the Richter scale, a substantial but not overly dire affair.

Broskey felt the bed rock, figured it was just God's magic fingers putting him to sleep, and returned to his flight with the bluebird of happiness.

In his arms, Melanie Melnick assumed it was Broskey cradling her into a deep sleep. She wrapped her right hand around his sweating torso and hugged him.

In West Los Angeles, Jake Mayer sat flipping through his collection of Polaroids, emitting a strange, high-pitched giggle. He felt the room shake and stuck his tongue out at the night sky outside his open window. "Nyah. Nyah. Missed me."

In Bay City, in her bed, Claire Simmons didn't feel a thing.

Twenty-six

Broskey awoke to the sound of rain. He opened his eyes and saw Melanie Melnick, fully clothed, sprawled on the edge of her bed, reading the morning papers.

She looked up at him and smiled as he yawned. "Look who's back in the land of the living."

He sat up in bed, rubbing his head. "I wouldn't push that."

"Did you know that we had an earthquake last night?" she asked.

"I thought it was the result of my cologne. Was it bad?"

"Well, as far as cologne goes . . ."

He tossed a pillow at her. She ducked and he grabbed the front page. The earthquake hadn't done any appreciable damage, just rearranged a few china cabinets and library shelves. He slipped on the terry-cloth robe and padded out of bed, nearly walking into a wall.

"Feeling better?" Melanie asked, taking him by the hand and to a fresh pot of coffee and a toasted bagel.

"Except for a profound loss of equilibrium, yes."

She pointed to the bagel. "I hope you don't mind that there are no green spots on it. I know how you bachelors eat."

179

"I'll try to make do," he said, enjoying the attention, enjoying the company, enjoying just about everything. He glanced at the one-bedroom apartment. It was quite a cheerful place, in the morning light. It's rectangular 1950s design was pretty drab, but Melanie kept it stuffed with flowers and plants, so the whole place seemed unique and alive.

He stepped onto a small balcony overlooking the complex's pool area. Outside there were more plants, more colors, more life. He gazed up into the drab morning sky.

A spring rain was falling.

Rain, in Southern California, is different from rain in any other part of the country. Usually it amounts to the type of moisture manufactured by a group of squirrels spitting between their teeth from a rooftop. A drizzle, at best.

Sun-worshiping Californians, however, treat every drop like a major event. TV newscasters can barely contain their excitement, showing slides of umbrellas and large charts of every cloud formation from Malibu to Japan.

Wary motorists, aware that motor oil will rise from the dry roadways with even the slightest trace of moisture, thus making the streets pretty slick, decide that the best way they can cope with rain is to either drive at incredible speeds or slow down to a crawl, gun the gas when a light turns green or hit the brakes suddenly when a light turns red.

As a result, after even a five-minute sprinkle in the Los Angeles area, there are at least fifty fender benders to report and maybe even a few six-to-ten-car collisions.

Most of the time, Broskey figured that L.A. drivers could save a lot of insurance premiums if, on rainy days, they'd let their pets drive. The animals would probably show a lot more common sense.

"Why are you grinning?" Melanie asked, grinning.

"I don't know," Broskey admitted. "Why are you?"

She leaned her small frame against his. "Same reason."

Suddenly there was a pounding at the door. Broskey turned to Melanie. "Expecting a lynch mob?"

She glanced at her watch. "Nope. Lynch mobs don't get here until ten. It's only eight."

She hurried to the door. Jake Mayer was standing there, frantic. "Kev! Get dressed! Hurry!"

Broskey put the coffee cup down. "What the . . . ? How?"

"They've been trying to reach you at home for the last half hour. They asked me to try to find you. I figured you might be here." He glanced at Melanie. "I checked the student phone directory."

"Trouble?" Broskey said, walking into the bedroom where his newly pressed clothes lay.

"Could be bad, Kev. Really bad. About six Corpses tried to hold up a mini-mart this morning."

"And?"

"One of the clerks hit a silent alarm. Two hotshot cops showed up, guns drawn, siren howling, as the kids were leaving."

"And?"

"The kids didn't leave."

Broskey hopped into his pants. "So, now we have a hostage situation?"

"Ten or eleven people are stuck inside with some very nervous kids armed with some very big guns."

"Great," Broskey said, running into the kitchen and grabbing half a bagel. He faced Melanie. "I'll call you later?"

"You'd better." She smiled. "I don't press all my dates' pants."

He kissed her full on the lips and ran out the front door. "We can take my car," Mayer said, jogging down a flight of stairs. The two leaped into his Honda and fishtailed out into the street.

"The two cops," Broskey muttered, pulling out his revolver and making sure he had a quick reload strapped to his belt. "The hotshots?"

"McDonald and Bluth." Jake nodded.

"Great. 'Romper Room' meets *Dog Day Afternoon*. Great start. Great start."

Mayer slowed the car down as he approached the police barricades two blocks away. McGlory was waiting in a flak jacket, outside the parameter.

His face lit up when he saw Broskey. "Thank God,

Lieutenant," he said. "I was just saying a prayer to the Blessed Virgin that you'd arrive."

"What do we have, Mac?" Broskey said.

McGlory pointed toward a parking lot at the end of the empty street. There were several cars parked in the lot, most of them boasting large, gaping holes. One of the cars was an unmarked police unit. It looked a little like Swiss cheese.

"Officers McDonald and Bluth tried to storm the place, like a couple of cowboys. Now they're pinned down. They've been yelling at us to storm the place, bring in choppers, drop tear-gas bombs onto the roof, etcetera, etcetera, and so forth. About the only thing those dumb bunnies haven't asked for is atomic weapons."

"Christ," Broskey muttered. "I'm glad you held back."

"Well, actually, we didn't have too much of a choice," McGlory said, pointing toward large potholes in the street some twenty yards from the police barricades.

"Jeez," Broskey exclaimed, "those kids did that?"

"They have some pretty heavy weapons, Lieutenant."

"Does the chief know about this?"

"Uh-huh. He said to wait until you got here." He handed Broskey a small, rectangular device.

"What the hell is this?" Broskey asked.

"A beeper," McGlory replied. "The chief said he's been trying to give you one for six years. He said now's the time for you to shut up and take it, beggin' your pardon, Lieutenant."

"Better living through science, huh?"

"There's instructions that come with it. I have them in my car. The chief wants you on call twenty-four hours a day."

"Lucky me. Has anyone tried to establish contact with those kids in there?"

"Phone's dead. I wouldn't trust either one of the fair-haired boys in the parking lot with a bullhorn."

"Good thinking."

"The chief has the LAPD SWAT team on standby."

Broskey nodded. "Let's hope we don't need them or that lot will be filled with hamburger patties wearing Reeboks." He turned to Mayer. "Stay behind the barricades and keep your head down. Mac, what kind of heavy stuff do you have in the van?"

McGlory led Broskey to a police van nearly filled with weapons. Broskey reached inside and grabbed an Armalite AR-180 assault rifle.

"Don't you want a heavy assault rifle, Lieutenant?"

"Nope. This is better for shooting on the run. It's effective for about a hundred and fifty yards. You have a bullhorn?"

McGlory handed Broskey a horn and led him back to the barricades. Broskey clenched his jaw. "It's such a nice day, I think I'll go for a walk."

He slid under the barricade and jogged down half a block. He ducked instinctively when he heard a dull *blapidy-blapidy-blap.* Large hunks of concrete erupted from the deserted storefront next to him. Rolling on the rain-slick street, he waited for the concrete wads to stop showering down on him. He jogged back to the barricades, the street erupting behind him.

"Hey!" he heard McDonald bawl over the radio. "Are we going to take out these punks or not? Sergeant? Sergeant?"

Broskey snatched the radio. "This is Broskey, McDonald. The answer to your question is no. Somebody in there has something very big and very powerful that they're shooting."

"All I saw was a shotgun," McDonald declared.

Broskey cradled the microphone in his hand. "Remind me to give you a lesson in firearms," he growled. "A shotgun doesn't do the damage you're staring at in that parking lot. My guess is they have something like a Heckler and Koch HK-91. It's a heavy assault rifle."

"So what?"

Broskey rolled his eyes. "McDonald, that thing can fire for days on end without jamming. It fires a seven-point-ninety two NATO cartridge. Those little bullets are heavy enough to smash through trees, car bodies, and brick walls."

"Oh shit," he heard a second voice mutter from the parking lot. The voice of sanity: Bluth.

"Come on, Lieutenant," McDonald said. "They're just kids."

"Kids do the darnedest things when they have more firepower than cops," Broskey said. "Just sit tight until I get there."

"Then what?"

"Then I try to set up some sort of dialogue."

Broskey couldn't be sure, but he thought he heard the word "chickenshit" come over the radio. He ended transmission.

"How will you get in there?" McGlory asked.

"I know an apartment building facing the lot."

"That must be the place the old man is at," McGlory replied. "Wouldn't allow himself to be evacuated, the old dear. Said he sunbathed every morning, even in the rain."

Broskey smiled, remembering the well-tanned and wigged Mr. Svenson at the Wave Crest. He muttered a "wish me luck" and jogged down the street, along the police barricades.

McGlory nodded. "A special Irish blessing from the heart of a friend. May good fortune be yours, May your joys never end."

Mayer gaped at the man. "Do you always do that?"

"What's the matter, Mr. Mayer, don't you believe in God?"

He shrugged. "Whenever He believes in me."

Within five minutes, Broskey had zigzagged his way to the front of the Wave Crest apartment complex. Police had left the front door unlatched. Broskey eased his way in.

Outside, sitting in the drizzle under an umbrella, was Mr. Svenson, reading a very damp edition of the *L.A. Trib.*

"Good morning," Broskey said.

"Good morning, Lieutenant." Svenson smiled, his dog cowering beneath his deck chair. "How about that earthquake last night, eh? It was a nice one. Not too rough. Not too mellow. Just right."

He gazed at Broskey's light assault rifle. "On your way to the mini-mart?"

Broskey nodded.

"Well," Svenson said. "Why don't you use my apartment

as a shortcut? I'd walk you through it but things got a little intense inside there a few minutes ago. I thought it would be safer out here."

Broskey smiled. "Why didn't you just leave the building with the other tenants? It's a lot safer."

Svenson shrugged. "The minute you give into crime, Lieutenant, that's when crime gets the upper hand. You should know that."

"You're right," Broskey said, "I should."

"Good luck."

Broskey walked around the pool and into Svenson's apartment. It was perfectly in order but for a two-foot hole blown in the far wall next to the sliding doors. Svenson's apartment didn't face the mini-mart, but it was adjacent to an alley that emptied out into the mart's parking lot.

Broskey eased himself through the sliding doors and padded softly down the alleyway. Large hunks of the concrete block wall separating the alley from the lot had been blown away. When he reached the end of the wall, he peeked around it. Twenty yards away, McDonald and Bluth sat, huddled, next to their unit. Half of the front of the car had been blown away. So far, the gas tank hadn't been touched.

McDonald looked angry.

Bluth looked terrified.

Broskey's heart went out to Bluth. Had they been nearer, his foot would have gone out to McDonald.

Broskey held his breath, tucked his head low, and duck-ran toward the car.

Buddabuddabuddabudda.

He watched the ground explode around his feet.

The two cops were staring at him from beyond the sizzling concrete spray. He tucked his knees up and cannonballed across the remaining section of the ever-changing parking lot.

He rammed into the bottom of the car.

Blat. Blat. Blat.

Large sections of the hood flew up in the air.

185

Then, silence.

Broskey caught his breath. Bluth was smiling at him. "I'm glad to see you, Lieutenant."

McDonald said nothing.

Broskey unslung the rifle from his shoulder and unclamped the bullhorn from his belt. The bell was slightly dinged, a result of his impromptu display of acrobatics, but it seemed to be in working order. "Looks like you two have gotten yourselves into a bit of a pickle."

"And how," Bluth said, sweating.

"Nothing we can't handle," McDonald said, seething.

"You're doing a damned creative job of it so far." Broskey smirked. "How many hostages?"

"Ten at the most," Bluth said. "When we pulled up and the perps ran inside, we saw a handful of people scatter to the back of the store. The perps were raising their guns toward them. Then one or two of them started firing at us."

"Did you return fire?" Broskey asked.

"Of course," McDonald said. "Did you want us to be sitting ducks?"

"You *begged* to be sitting ducks as soon as you went screaming up to that place. I don't suppose, when you were returning fire, that you thought of the hostages as being sitting ducks? You know, innocent, unarmed folks, caught in a cross fire? That sort of silly stuff."

Bluth suddenly found the ground beneath his knees very interesting. McDonald's face was beet red. "Are you reprimanding me, Lieutenant?"

"McDonald," Broskey said, "if I wasn't your superior, I'd offer you in exchange for the hostages. I'd love to see you play piñata. That's the only way some people get sense knocked into them, with very large sticks."

"I can bring you up on charges for that remark," McDonald said.

"Later, hotshot," Broskey said. "First, let's get those people out of there, okay?" He raised the bullhorn to his lips. "Yo! Inside! Moochie, you in there?"

Silence.

"Yo!" Broskey called. "Moochie. Talk to me."

"The name's El Roacho," came a tiny voice.

"You'll always be Moochie to me," Broskey announced.

"That you, dead man?"

"One and the same," Broskey called. "Have you gone for long walks lately, with your new walking stick?"

He heard the kid laugh. "Dead man. What are we gonna do? Nobody's hurt, man. We didn't hurt nobody. We were looking for pocket change. You know how it is."

"Yeah," Broskey called. "I do. Cops don't make much more than checkout baggers."

"I lost my job, too," El Roacho called. "Somebody told the manager I was a killer Corpse. We're gettin' a bad rap, Broskey."

"Bullshit," McDonald muttered, too close to the bullhorn.

"What was that?" El Roacho bellowed.

"One of these geeks here sneezed," Broskey said. "Look, seems to me that a dead man can negotiate some deal with Corpses, right?"

Silence.

"Right?" Broskey repeated.

"Sounds good."

"Okay. Where are the hostages now?"

"In the back, by the kitty litter. We made them bunkers outta them, like in war films, 'cause those crazy cops out there was just shootin' up the place. I mean, Corpses only shoot when they been shot at or when they're trying to make a point, you know that."

Broskey nodded. "Okay, Moochie. So, what do we have here? A robbery that went bad. Okay. We get you for attempted robbery. And I bet you don't have permits for those nasty guns you have."

Laughter from inside. "We borrowed them."

"Okay. So right now, we have you for attempted robbery and possession of illegal firearms. No big deal."

"Will we do time?"

"A little. A good lawyer can probably get you tossed into a juve hall or something. You're young, right?"

"Sorta."

187

"So, we're looking at a paid vacation for you and your buddies for a while. But—and this is important, Moochie, I want you to think about this—if you guys do one of the hostages, you can all go up on a murder rap. You know the governor we have now? The guy thinks he's John Wayne. If he doesn't give you a death sentence, he'll make sure you rot in prison."

"We could take it."

"Yeah, Moochie. But that would be the end of the Corpses, wouldn't it? I mean, all the primo members are inside with you."

Silence.

Finally. "You're okay for a dead man. I swear, Broskey. Once we get out and I get a new gig, you'll always get double bags on your groceries."

"With a promise like that," Broskey called, "I'll write the manager a reference letter myself."

"You'd do that for me?" El Roacho called.

"No," Broskey replied, "for the eggs I buy."

Laughter filtered out from inside the store.

"So," Broskey said, "what were we going to do?"

"We'll come out with our guns and leave the hostages inside?" El Roacho asked.

"Right. Leave the hostages right where they are and come out with your guns. Then, when you come outside, toss all the guns in a pile over by that VW bug. The yellow one. You see it?"

"I see it."

"And then, slowly, raise your hands. When all of you have your hands raised, I'll signal the all-clear and we'll bring you in."

"You on the level, dead man?" El Roacho asked.

"Dead men don't mess with Corpses," Broskey replied.

Silence.

"Sounds fair," El Roacho called. "We're coming out now."

Broskey sighed and slid down behind the car. It looked like everyone would get out of this in one piece.

"You're just going to let them *walk?*" McDonald said angrily.

"No," Broskey said. "We're going to get them to throw down their weapons, cuff them, book them, and then let the judicial system play with their heads."

"But they're *killers!*" McDonald demanded.

"What difference does it make if we shoot at them or arrest them?" Broskey said. "We still get them."

"They *shot* at *us!*" McDonald declared. "They shot at *me."*

Broskey pointed a shaking finger at McDonald. "Don't try to play supercop, McDonald. In spite of what you think, you don't have the haircut for it."

"He's right," Bluth muttered. "It doesn't make any difference."

"It does to me," McDonald said.

Broskey heard the Corpses leave the store. Before he could stop him, Broskey watched McDonald leap out from behind the car and raise his revolver. "Police!" McDonald yelled. "Freeze."

He fired one round.

Broskey pulled Bluth close as the Corpses opened fire. They had shotguns, high-powered rifles and .45s.

McDonald never got off a second round.

The storm of bullets hit his body from every angle imaginable. It lasted but five seconds.

McDonald's body hit the pavement in parts small enough to be loaded into a shopping cart.

Bluth began to cry. Broskey turned to Bluth. "And *that,* my dear young officer, is what you get for watching 'Miami Vice.'"

"You're a dead man, dead man!" El Roacho bellowed from the front of the store.

Broskey sighed and leaped to his feet, catching the gang unaware. They saw him and raised their weapons. They looked like toddlers playing tough guys.

Broskey opened up with his assault rifle. He squeezed the trigger tightly, feeling the weapon buck up against his shoulder. He didn't want to look at the front of the store, but he had to keep the kids in his sights. They were cop-killers now. This was legal. This was justifiable.

This made him feel like shit.

He watched the six young men dance like marionettes with tangled strings.

Blood began spouting in small founts from their torsos.

Around and around they spun, touching each other, colliding with each other, in a slam dance of death.

Finally, the last one on his feet, El Roacho, signaled it was over. He gazed across the parking lot at Broskey, his dead eyes opened inquisitively. "What for?" he seemed to cry. "What happened?"

When El Roacho hit the ground, Broskey slowly lowered the gun. "I'm sorry, Moochie," he whispered.

He helped a sobbing Bluth to his feet and propped him up against the car. Hostages began wandering toward the front of the store. They were school kids mostly, tough guys and mini-molls. They saw the carnage outside and began to cry and vomit. They clung to the arcade games and shrieked like trapped animals.

Broskey walked over to McDonald's pieces. "You asshole," he said, by way of an epitaph. He slowly walked down the deserted block toward the police barricades.

Twenty uniformed officers, led by Sergeant McGlory, ran up to him. "Is everything all right?" McGlory wheezed.

"No," Broskey said, "everything sucks, but the hostages are safe. Call the meat wagon. We have a half a dozen dead kids back there and one cop who went all to pieces."

McGlory blinked. "What shall I tell the chief?"

"Tell him not to worry." Broskey fished into his pocket and pulled out a small wad of metal. "I still have my goddamn beeper." He continued to move toward the barricades. Jake Mayer was waiting for him.

"Kev! Kev! Are you okay?"

"Fine, Jake."

"I was worried about you, buddy," Mayer said, putting an arm around Broskey. "I mean, if anything ever happened to you, it would be like my brother getting hurt. I mean, you're like my twin, you know?"

"Thanks, Jake. Would you do me a favor?"

"Name it."

"Would you drive me home for a minute? I have to get a change of clothes."

Jake stared at Broskey. The policeman's suit was covered with mud, blood, and bits of semisolid matter.

"Sure, Kev. Sure," Mayer said, hugging Broskey, leading him to the car. "What are friends for?"

Twenty-seven

*S*amurai Sushi was one of those places that catered to the trend setters in Bay City. Located near Main Street, it was the home of power breakfasts, power lunches, and power dinners, gatherings where perfectly coiffed people dropped names like anvils and chanted the mantra "three-picture deal" over and over again.

No matter that the site had once been a steak house that catered to local fishermen less than a decade ago. Now it was the home of the Hollywood hangers-on and the musk crowd.

Broskey fiddled with his badly constructed tie as Mayor Gina Roberts sucked on a swizzle stick with little or no effect. "I appreciate your coming here, Lieutenant, especially in light of this morning."

Broskey fiddled with his food. He never considered raw fish a fitting dinner for anyone but a citizen of MarineLand. "Uh-huh," he said, wondering what the green things were in his wad of white mash surrounded by seaweed.

"That was a commendable piece of police work."

"Uh-huh," Broskey said halfheartedly.

"Of course, I'm sorry about that young officer who was slain, but I'm sure he died a hero."

"Oh, yeah," Broskey said.

"You sent a hard-hitting message to the gangs of the Los

Angeles area. Stay out of our turf. Bay City is for law-abiding citizens only. Try any monkey business and the law will come down on you and come down hard."

"I was wondering what message I sent this morning. Would you mind if I ate your salad?"

Mayor Roberts, her face perfectly made up, wiped a wisp of blond hair from her eyes. "You don't like fish?"

"Not really." He shrugged. "I was brought up a Catholic. My mother was Irish. She had this unique ability to take the flavor out of any and all fish. We used to look forward to frozen fish sticks. At least they tasted like cardboard."

"I'm sorry I brought you here then. We can order something else."

"I'm not really hungry."

The mayor put on a consoling expression. "Oh, yes. I understand." She took a swig of her Bloody Mary. "Well, this morning you seemed to put an end to one of my biggest problems: the growing gang presence in Bay City. But I'm afraid I still have a very big problem to deal with."

"Me, too."

"This co-ed killer. I'm afraid that something has to be done."

"We're doing our best, ma'am," Broskey said.

"I'm afraid that isn't enough, Lieutenant. What about Medega? Is he cooperating with your investigation? You can confide in me. I know you two have clashed in the past. Frankly, I wouldn't be sorry to see him go. He's been a thorn in my side since I assumed office. He's very old-fashioned. Bay City has to change with the times, to grow, modernize. To be honest"—she smiled pertly—"I would like to see a younger, more forceful man in the job."

Broskey stopped fiddling with the salad. His stomach was still churning. He was watching McDonald's insides become his outsides. He was feeling the recoil of his rifle as he shot down a half-dozen stupid, half-educated kids who thought having tattoos meant power.

"Someone like me?" he asked.

The mayor smiled by way of response.

"Divide and conquer, huh?" He smirked. "Thanks, but

no thanks. For the record, Medega is a great cop. We don't always agree, but if we did, I'd think there was something wrong. Medega's handling the killings the best he knows how, by going after every small detail we can come up with."

The smile on the mayor's lips faded. "Lieutenant, may I ask you a personal question?"

"Sure, I'm no longer a practicing Catholic."

"Do you like me?"

"I don't know you."

"I mean, you *really* don't like me, do you? I can see that in your eyes. Is it because I'm a woman who prefers the company of other women to men? Is that it?"

Broskey tossed his fork down. "Ma'am, I don't care if you prefer the company of horses to men. Doesn't bother me in the least. What does bother me is that these killings are somehow being pigeonholed as a political matter. They aren't. There are living, breathing young kids out there getting done in. Real-life people being tossed around like rag dolls."

"I understand your feelings, Lieutenant—"

"I don't think you do," Broskey said, sighing. "Half of the time I don't myself. This morning? We didn't have to kill those kids. We could have cuffed them. But one young asshole decided to play supercop.

"I watched him get blown apart. Then, because of that nitwit, I was forced to pick up a rifle and butcher six frightened, confused, shit-upon half-wit kids. I don't call that a statement to gangs. I call that an exercise in slapstick.

"Frankly, before this morning, the worst thing I had done in my years on the force was bust a guy's nose once when I was off duty. I've fired my revolver a total of six times since I was a rookie. Never picked up a rifle. Today, not only did I have to pick one up, I had to blast six high-school students into 'American Bandstand' heaven. I don't call that good police work. I call that shit."

He stared at the mayor. The woman was stunned. Equating statistics on paper with images of blood and violence was something she wasn't used to. Her mouth began to move. No sound emerged.

Bweeeeeeep.

Broskey looked down at his blazer and began beating his pockets to locate the shrieking slab of metal. "I'll be right back. I'm being summoned by one of your employees." He shuffled away from the table, still emitting high-pitched squeals.

When he returned, the mayor had regained her composure. "I hope you didn't misunderstand anything I said, Lieutenant."

"No." Broskey sighed. "But I hope you understood everything I had to say. Now I'm afraid I have to cut lunch short. We just found another girl."

The mayor paused, midbite through a California roll. "Dead?"

"And then some. Apparently our boy got really creative last night. Found a wonderful set of designer carving knives. Decided to take up the pastime of whittling while his victim was still alive."

The mayor's eyes fluttered up toward some potted ferns suspended from the ceiling. She dropped her California roll. It hit the table and, after spinning a moment, took a header toward the tile floor.

Broskey offered a thin smile. "Good thing I didn't have a big lunch, huh?" he said.

He turned his back on the mayor and walked out of the sushi bar. He didn't even hear her when she fell.

Broskey stood, grimly, behind Goldstein as the forensics men took pictures of Claire Simmons's bedroom. They were careful not to step in any of the large pools of blood spattered on the wood floor.

"He's getting wilder," Goldstein said. "Nastier. If we don't get him soon, I'm afraid he's going to lose it totally. Start stalking his victims in an entirely new way."

"I'm supposed to be the psychologist," Broskey muttered.

"Do you agree?"

"Yeah. The guy seemed to have quite a time of it all right." He walked over to the bed and pulled the blood-soaked bedspread from the body. "He pulled her underclothes off so harshly, he left burn marks." He sighed. "He wanted to cause pain. Watch pain."

"Kev?"

Broskey turned around. Jake Mayer was at the doorway. "Medega told me what happened. He thought it would be a good idea if I showed up. Saw the crime scene with you guys. Holy shit!"

Mayer gazed into the bedroom, shut his eyes, and turned away. "That's *horrible!*"

"On a scale of one to ten, this is a twenty," Broskey said. He turned to Goldstein. "Who's interviewing the neighbors?"

"Two rookies. Brown and Warner. Nice boys. A bit squeamish, though. One of them was yanked off of canine duty. He seems confused at being around people."

Broskey offered a crooked grin. "I feel the same way most times."

"Lieutenant?" a feeble voice asked.

Broskey turned around. A blond-haired cop who looked like Dennis the Menace in blue shifted his weight from foot to foot in the doorway. "I'm Officer Michael Warner."

"I'm sure you are," Broskey said.

"Well, the thing is, sir, we found a neighbor who says he saw the killer last night."

Broskey brightened. Mayer's Adam's apple nearly collided with his lower lip. "It *can't* be," he said.

"Why not?" Broskey asked.

"Because this killer has been so crafty," said Mayer. "S-so careful. It's like he's a phantom or something."

"Everybody slips up once in a while." Broskey smiled. "Maybe our killer did last night."

"It's this way, sir," Officer Warner said.

"Lead the way, Warner," Broskey said, following.

"Mind if I tag along?" Mayer asked, grabbing his notebook. "I mean, it would make a difference to the series I'm doing."

"No problem," Broskey said. "Are you sure you can take the gory talk?"

"Are you kidding me?" Mayer cackled, lapsing into a Bela Lugosi tone. "Ven it comes to gore, I am ze master. I pour blood on my Rice Crispies in ze morning. Zey go 'snap, crackle, and owwww.'"

Broskey turned his back. Together, they followed Officer Warner to the apartment of the witness.

Twenty-eight

*A*mos Greene lived in the Shangri-la, a small geographical piece of the past. A white stucco-and-tiled castle, it had once been a posh watering hole where the elite of Hollywood cavorted after a hard day at the beach.

As Broskey walked down the hallway of its third floor, past the ornate light fixtures and framed portraits of Hollywood in its prime, he could almost imagine Valentino, Chaplin, Fairbanks, and Navarro darting in and out of its solid oak doorways. In fact, they had all done just that.

Now, it was an old age home.

On the plus side, it was very well kept.

"This is the place, sir," Officer Warner said, knocking on the thick door to apartment 3-G.

A frail but stately-looking man, standing over six feet tall, appeared at the portal. "Gentlemen?"

Amos Greene let Broskey and Mayer in. Broskey blinked. Greene was wearing a tuxedo. The old man extended a hand. "Amos Greene, screenwriter, at your service."

Broskey took the hand. It was skeletal. Greene's skin was virtually transparent, but for the liver spots. "Lieutenant Kevin Broskey, Mr. Greene, and this is my friend, a journalist, Jacob Mayer."

"A pleasure," the old man said, motioning them toward a

plush sofa. "Please come in. Please. Would you care for a gin and tonic? I find a gin and tonic to be very civilized on a hot and muggy day. It cures all that ails you."

"No, thanks," Broskey said, scanning the apartment. It was as if he had slipped into a time warp. The furniture was straight out of the 1930s, ornate and overstuffed. Every table boasted doilies. Framed movie posters from the 1920s and 1930s covered the walls. Buster Keaton's *The General*. Laurel and Hardy's *Sons of the Desert*. Chaplin's *The Tramp*. In the background, an old Victrola scratched through an ancient recording of Bing Crosby singing "Brother, Can You Spare a Dime."

"Please excuse the housekeeping," Amos said, easing himself into a chair. "I live alone these days and good help is so hard to find."

"I know," Broskey said, sitting next to Mayer on the sofa. "About the murder . . ."

"Ah, most unfortunate." Amos sighed, peering out from behind glasses thick enough to qualify for binocular status. "But I'm afraid that's the way this neighborhood is getting. Once, this was the crème de la crème of Bay City. All the greats lived here, or at least weekended here. Many of them, I had the good fortune to know and work with."

Broskey nodded, "Yes, but . . ."

"Yes," Amos agreed. *"But* things change. Tastes changed. The greats went to their eternal reward and I was left without a job. Children took over the motion picture industry and we old relics were sent out to pasture. A sad thing, that. It broke my heart to see the great Chaplin accept his Oscar after all those years. He was so frail. Hollywood had hated him for years, but when they thought he was about to die, they gave him the booby prize. A lifetime achievement award. I would hate to receive one, I tell you. It's like death coming to your door."

"About the death . . ."

The record stuttered to a halt. "Excuse me," Amos said, gracefully walking to the Victrola and changing the record. "I believe you will enjoy this one, Rudy Vallee and his Connecticut Yankees singing 'Life Is Just a Bowl of Cherries.' Lew Brown and Ray Henderson composed that one—a sadly underrated duo, I'm afraid."

The record scratched to life. Rudy Vallee picked up his megaphone and began to croon. Amos Greene returned to his seat. "I have seen death before, Lieutenant, but nothing like this. My first wife died where you are sitting. A self-inflicted gunshot wound. She suspected me of dallying with Veronica Lake. It was all purely innocent, I assure you. We were, I believe the phrase is, drinking buddies. And I assure you, she could drink me under a table.

"Terrible thing, losing a spouse that way. I managed to work a scene similar to that into the serial *Jungle Jack and White Pongo,* in the forties. It was left on the cutting-room floor, alas. The director thought it too strong for the serial crowd."

"Mr. Greene . . ."

"My second wife had a horrible end as well. She ran off with a Spanish dancer. The man could hardly speak English. This was back in the days, remember, when Spanish was considered the loving tongue and not the language of gardeners. Well, the dear boy drove as well as he spoke English. They became airborne somewhere over Mulholland Drive. Those are her remains in the base of that lamp over there." He pointed to a small, golden urn topped by a petite shade. "I always called her the light of my life, and now she is just that. Poetic, don't you think?"

"The murder!" Mayer suddenly injected. "Tell us about the goddamn murder. You say you saw it?"

Amos Greene heaved a heavy sigh. "Yes," he said, getting up and changing the record. "Glenn Miller and his Orchestra performing 'The White Cliffs of Dover.' Yes, I did."

He motioned Broskey and Mayer over to a window. Next to the window was a rocking chair and a pair of opera glasses mounted on a metal stand. "You see, gentlemen, I must confess, I'm a bit of a voyeur. Young ladies no longer find me attractive because I'm a little too old and a little too impoverished. As for women my age, why, who would want a woman my age?

"And, so, I will readily admit to the fact that very often,

late at night, I sit in the dark and watch some of the women in the apartment across the street undress. With my eyesight, much is still left to my imagination, but it does get the old heart pumping a bit quicker.

"That poor young lady who died last night brought a gentleman caller home. You can see the bedroom quite clearly from here."

Broskey peered through the opera glasses. In fact, he *could* see Claire Simmons's bedroom.

"Well, this fellow she was with just burst into her bedroom and did things to her that I never imagined could be done to a human being. It was quite dreadful. Worse than anything I ever wrote in *Dr. Terror's Killer Bats.*"

"Why didn't you call the police if you saw so much?" Jake asked.

"I'm afraid I am without a phone," Amos said, changing the record again. "Dick Powell, with the Warners Studio Orchestra performing 'We're in the Money.' Powell was quite a good singer, you know. A fine actor as well. Nice fellow. Cute little dimples. Cancer did him in."

"So, you're without a phone," Mayer said. "Why didn't you raise hell? Wake the neighbors."

"I'm afraid I fell asleep," Amos apologized. "It *was* rather late, you know."

"Oh, come on," Mayer said.

Broskey nudged him into silence. "Did you actually see the killer?"

"Oh, indeed I did." The old man smiled. He gazed at Mayer. "It was Hildy."

"Wuzzat?"

"You know!"

"How the hell should I know what you're talking about," Mayer fumed. "You lost me after Rudy Vallee."

"You being a newspaperman, I thought you'd know." Amos smiled at Broskey. "It was Hildy Johnson. *The Front Page?* The famous play that became a famous film. Not Hildy in the remakes but Hildy in the first, when Hildy was still a man. Pat O'Brien it was. Fine fellow. Nice man. Good Catholic. Better drinker. Hell of a lot of fun, that boy."

"I'm afraid I don't understand," Broskey said.

"The killer? I didn't get that good a look at his face, but he had a camera. It was flashing all the time. Right at the young woman. Right into my eyes. By the time the flash aftereffects would leave my eyes, he was on top of her. I'd try to focus my opera glasses and, then, flash, he was snapping again. He was snapping away like a good reporter."

Mayer's mouth dropped open. He began to titter. "Wait a minute. Basically, what you're telling us is that you saw someone in there with a camera. A fact which you could have gleaned from reading any of a dozen stories about the killer. And because the killer has a camera, he reminds you of Pat O'Brien who played a reporter in an old movie that you remember and love?"

The old man beamed. "Exactly."

Mayer turned to Broskey. "Great witness."

"I knew *you* of all people would see the connection." Amos grinned. "Being a newspaper man and all. In fact, you'd be *perfect* to star in a remake of *The Front Page.*"

"Mr. Greene." Mayer smiled. "I have enough trouble writing stories, let alone acting in them."

"Not so, not so." Greene smiled. "Look at Ronnie Reagan. I knew him when he was a boy. A complete turnip. He couldn't say hello without a cue card. Yet he managed to make a career out of being inept. Several, in fact." Amos turned and changed the record. "Hal Kemp's Orchestra performing 'The Boulevard of Broken Dreams.'"

"I'm afraid we'll have to be leaving now, Mr. Greene," Broskey said, standing.

"Oh, I'm sorry. I seldom get company. Since my second wife's death, I'm afraid I've become a bit of a recluse."

"When was that, Mr. Greene?" Broskey asked politely.

"Nineteen hundred and forty-nine, I believe. I can check the lamp to make sure."

"No, no. That's all right," Broskey said, pulling Mayer toward the door. "Thank you. You've been a great help. Thank you, so much."

Broskey and Mayer eased the door closed behind them.

"Nice witness," Mayer smirked. "That guy was Rod Serling's patron saint."

"He's just a sad old man," Broskey said, "but I do believe he saw something last night."

"What? The Ghost of Christmas Past? The guy's brain is locked into mental movie matinee time. He's probably still voting for FDR."

Broskey sighed. "You're probably right. Let's let Goldstein clean up the mess and head back to the campus."

"More sleuthing?" Mayer said.

"Yeah. There's a professor on campus I'd like to question."

"Fine. You take the professor, I'll check out his students." Broskey shot him a withering look. "Hey," Mayer pointed out. "I'm young, well, fairly young, attractive, well, fairly attractive, and single. Very, very single."

"Ever think of going to a computer dating service?" Broskey asked.

"I did." Jake shrugged. "I wound up seeing an IBM for two months."

Broskey laughed. "You never change, do you, Jake?"

Jake flashed a wide grin. "No, Kev. I do change. As I get older, I get better."

Twenty-nine

*W*hy haven't you called me all day? I've been worried sick!" Melanie exclaimed, grasping Broskey by the arm as he entered the campus newspaper office.

Stan watched from the sidelines, casting an arched eyebrow in Mayer's direction.

"I just thought I'd stop by while I was on campus," he said. "I'm here to talk to one of your professors, Roger Dante?"

"Old Jolly Roger?" Melanie laughed. "Why on earth do you want to talk to him? The guy is a total lech."

"That's why I want to talk to him."

Melanie stopped laughing. "Professor Dante? He's harmless."

"That's for me to find out," Broskey said.

"As for me?" Mayer said, "I want to interview as many students as possible, beef up the human-interest angle. Really get people *involved* in the feelings of the students."

"I can help you there," Stan volunteered. "What do you need?"

"Well, who's in charge of sorority and frat security? On campus, off campus?"

Stan thought a moment. "Basically, it boils down to two people, Jeff Golding and Roseanne Deemers."

Mayer shrugged. "Why don't we start with Roseanne?"

"Want me to walk you over to her office? She's on the Student Council."

"Naaah," Mayer smiled. "I'm old enough to walk across campus by myself, Daddy. Just give her a call and let her know I'm coming over."

"You got it."

Melanie took Broskey by the elbow. "Come on, I'll walk you over to Professor Dante's office."

Professor Roger Dante ran a hand through his mane of gray hair. He pushed his emaciated frame over his desk, perching himself like some great bird of prey.

"If this is a joke, Lieutenant, I don't find it a very funny one."

Broskey lit a cigarette.

"Do you mind?" Dante asked. "I hate smoking."

"So do I," Broskey said, "but I do it anyway. Let's talk about some of *your* filthy habits."

Dante sighed and slumped in his chair. "I should have known one of you bright types would look up my rap sheet. I know it doesn't look good for me. I *do* have a past, but, Lieutenant Broskey, I'm not that way anymore. I don't fraternize with my students at all. Especially the women. I'm too old, they're too young."

"That didn't stop you a few years ago, Prof," Broskey said.

"Things can change an awful lot in a few years," Dante sighed.

"Would you like to explain that?" Broskey asked.

"No. I'd rather not."

"Would you like me to take you in for formal questioning, Professor? Have you brought, in public, down to the station? Have you account for your whereabouts on every night a murder was committed?"

Broskey was baiting Dante. Dante didn't bite. He seemed defeated. He seemed dead.

"Lieutenant," Dante sighed. "The reason I don't fraternize with my students anymore is that I care about them too much. I am old, but still virile. True, I used to enjoy rough-housing with some of my female acquaintances in the past. Most of them agreed to it. Some had second thoughts and brought me in on charges, but, as you must know, I was never convicted of anything. Usually the women wanted the kinky details left out of the papers. We settled everything out of court. I would never do anything to really *hurt* anyone I cared about, Lieutenant, which is why I abstain from all sex these days. You see, Lieutenant, I am dying of AIDS."

Broskey's cigarette almost did a somersault out of his mouth. Dante laughed. It was hollow. "So much for your campus Casanova, eh?"

"I'm sorry. Does anyone know? Here on campus, I mean?"

"No. And I don't want them to know. I must have your assurances of that. I come into no physical contact with my students whatsoever. I still make the flirtatious remark, I still wield a mean double entendre, but I would never . . . could never . . ." Dante allowed his voice to trail off. "You see before you, Lieutenant, the ultimate product of a swinging society. I had lovers of both sexes in every setting imaginable: golf courses, elevators, bath houses; in every position imaginable. Taa-daaa. Now, I may have three months, three years, or three weeks. Who knows?"

Broskey got to his feet. "I *had* to talk to you, Professor. You understand that."

"I know. You're just doing your job. And believe me, Lieutenant, I really want you to catch this freak. You might say I have a vested interest."

"How's that?"

"I don't know how many people I may have killed without knowing it, or if I've killed anyone at all. But this freak? He kills. He destroys the act of lovemaking. Turns it into a butcher-block affair. That is something I would never have considered. When I die, and I *will* die, my only solace is that I will expire of wounds inflicted by the act of love."

Broskey left Dante in his office and walked out onto the

Bay City College campus. The sky was still steel gray. It was like walking across the interior of a gigantic mausoleum.

"I'm glad we talked this afternoon," Roseanne Deemers said, crossing her legs beneath her desk. "It actually made me feel better, opening up to someone about all this."

Jake Mayer nodded. "Hey, my pleasure. How often do I get to play father confessor to a campus queen?"

Roseanne laughed. "And how often do I get to talk to a Pulitzer Prize winner?"

"Ummm," Jake wondered, "once a week?"

"Come on," Roseanne giggled.

"Okay. Twice a week during months beginning with *J* and every other week during the rest," Jake countered.

"You're a kook."

He feigned shame. "Aha. You've found me out. I am a kook. An orthodox kook. In fact, I was brought up by a roving band of kooks who lived in the forests outside Cleveland. Before journalism, I made a meager living . . . selling meagers from door to door."

Roseanne laughed so hard she nearly slid out of her chair.

"Careful," Mayer cautioned. "You're on the border of an X rating."

Roseanne shook her long red hair back and forth. "Don't tell me you advocate censorship!"

"Only when it involves sex with Martians. I hate antennae."

He got up to leave, bowing down to kiss her on the hand. "And, now, my deah, there are other students to be grilled."

Roseanne blushed. "I've never met anyone like you before."

"Thanks." Jake grinned. "I think." He turned to leave. "Hey, if I want to ask you any other follow-up questions, where can I reach you?"

Roseanne smiled impishly. "Right here in the office."

"You have a home number, or is it locked away at Fort Knox?"

"Welllll," she teased, "it's not listed."

"We're talking name in the paper here, Roseanne," Jake teased back.

"Well, alllll right." The young woman sighed, scrawling her number and handing it to him. "But if you *do* call after school, don't call too late."

"Why?" Jake said. "Are you married?"

"No."

"Part of a harem?"

"Nope."

"Have a roommate?"

"Of course not. I have early classes. I *am* a student, after all, and most of us are losing sleep as it is, with all these murders going on."

Jake tucked the number into his inside blazer pocket. "Well, maybe I'll call you up and sing you a lullaby."

"Kook."

"That's the rumor."

Thirty

*B*roskey sat huddled next to Melanie in front of her phony fireplace. He was shaking.

She stroked his forehead. "Are you feverish?"

Broskey continued to shake. "I don't think so," he said glumly. "I think I've reached official overload status."

"You had a rough day," Melanie said, guiding her tiny hands over his furrowed brow. "That's all."

"No, it's more than that. I've reached total loser status."

"Come on," she chided.

"No, I mean it. Years from now, I'll be included in most of Henny Youngman's routines. You know, the kind of cop who falls on his back and breaks his nose? The kind of cop who's had the seven-year itch for eight years? The kind of cop who goes through life as handicapped as a cornet player with loose teeth?"

"Will you stop that?"

"Whose suit is so shiny, if it tears he'll have seven years' bad luck?"

"I'm warning you . . ."

"Who was once shipwrecked on a desert island with his own wife?"

Melanie began to laugh. "I have a frying pan and I know

how to use it!" She grabbed him by the hair and gave him a sharp tug.

Broskey winced. "What's the matter? Don't you like classic comedy?"

She kissed him on the lips. "Not from a classic knight in shining armor."

"Okay." Broskey laughed. "How about slapstick? I do a great pratfall. You should have seen me in front of the mayor this afternoon."

"That bad?"

"Worse. She tried to compliment me on my butchering abilities."

Melanie pursed her lips. There was nothing she could say.

"You know what the shittiest part of all that is?" Broskey asked no one in particular. "I never fired a gun at a person before. Today I killed six kids. They shouldn't have died no matter how screwed up they were, they didn't deserve to die. I'll wind up looking like a hero for killing six kids who should still be listening to rap records."

Melanie nodded and began stroking his brow.

"I mean," he continued, "up until today, I got things done by using my brain. It was one big puzzle. Today, I solved the puzzle by pounding the pieces together." He stared at his shaking hands. "I felt the gun slam into my chest. Right here."

He pointed to a spot below his right armpit. "The gun kept on slamming into me right there. I can still feel it, for Chrissakes." He shook his head from side to side. "And tomorrow, you just wait, I'll be written up like some sort of well-tanned Wyatt Earp. Doesn't make sense. I mean, I killed six children."

"The children could have killed those hostages," Melanie offered.

"But they didn't," Broskey countered. "They didn't want to. They were frightened. Scared. *And I killed them.* What does that make me?"

"A cop."

"Yeah." Broskey smirked. "Because I have a shield, I'm one of the good guys. Well, I have to tell you, I don't feel like one. I feel shitty. I killed children today. And you know what the sickest thing is?"

"No."

"I *really* wanted to cry."

"And . . ."

"And I didn't. I couldn't. My insides were crying but I couldn't get my outsides to cooperate. I don't know why. Maybe I was angry. Maybe I was playing adult. I don't know. But I wanted to cry. I *should* have cried. What's the matter with me, Melanie? What's the matter with me? Why can't I cry?"

Melanie began to massage his eyebrows. "You were born too late, my dear lieutenant. You were born into a world where there are no damsels in distress, no dragons to slay, no Sheriffs of Nottingham to stymie. You were born into a world of neon, Uzis, and film at eleven."

Broskey managed a slight smile. "You make everything I do sound so noble. I like that. I don't believe a word of it, but I appreciate it."

Jake Mayer sat amid the din at Music Max. His drinking partner was guzzling drinks like they were precious commodities never to pass his way again.

"Stan," he cautioned. "Stan. Slow down. You know you can't handle hootch."

"Hootch?" Stan gurgled. "I'm not drinking hootch. I'm drinking Cuervo Gold, slice of lime on the side."

"That's hootch," Mayer replied, sighing. "Why do I put up with you?"

"Because I'm smart," Stan declared. "I'm dedicated. I'm a wurmalist."

"Journalist," Mayer corrected.

"I'm co-editor of the college paper of the . . . the greatest, bloodiest campus in the nation. Waitress? Lady? Yo! Another round for me and my buddy."

"I'm not finished with this one yet," Mayer said.

"So . . . I'll drink it if you won't," Stan said, suddenly rearing his gangly torso like an offended ostrich.

Diminutive Mayer stared at the boy. "You're ossified."

"Damn straight," Stan said. "And the police are aware of that, too."

"What are you talking about?"

"I have my own theories about this killer." Stan smirked. "Annn everyone's too 'fraid to ask me about them."

"Uh-huh."

"Damn straight."

Mayer smiled at the drunken college student. "What's your problem, Stan?"

Stan shook his long face back and forth, resembling a truculent horse. "I don't haff no problem."

"Right."

"I mean, what she hanging around with that old cop for?"

Jake smirked. "Aha. It all seems clear to me, now. You're jealous of Broskey."

"What?"

"You have the hots for Melanie, don't you?"

"Dooonot," Stan crooned.

"And you're pissed off because she likes Kevin?"

Stan tried to screw his face into a semblance of a pout. His facial muscles, under the influence of tequila, formed instead a visage resembling the lead in a George Romero film. "Nope."

Mayer grinned. "Yes, you are. Hey, if it makes you feel any better, it'll never last. Kevin's too old. Melanie's too young. It's just a fling thing."

"Great," Stan mumbled. "Make me feel better, why don't you?"

"I'm trying to, man," Mayer said soothingly, reaching an arm across the table and grabbing Stan by the wrist. "Relationships are a bitch."

"She doesn't even know I exist," he moaned.

"Of course, she does."

"But she dropped me. Like that!" He tried to snap his fingers, but couldn't. "For that old . . . old . . . man!"

"He's not *that* old," Mayer said.

"Well he's older than I am!" Stan declared.

"Look, you and Melanie are buddies, right?"

"Right," Stan said, shaking his head limply.

"And now you feel like she's dropped you for a new buddy, right?"

"Damn right," Stan said, nodding so hard his chin nearly slammed into the table.

"Well, I know how you feel."

Stan brightened. "Really?"

"Sure," Mayer nodded. "How do you think I felt when Kevin moved west and got married? I mean, we were partners, man, *buddies.* Closer than brothers. We were like two sides of the same coin."

His smile faded. "And then, he left me. He wanted to find himself. Do something for himself. I'd been supporting us, you know. I was successful pretty much from the start. But Kevin felt he had to leave the nest, had to do things on his own. I understood, of course, but I mean, we'd been together since first grade.

"And, then, he met this slimy little bitch out here and married her. I was going to move west immediately, but wifey didn't like me. She made that quite clear. I waited until their marriage was on the skids to make the big move. I made sure their divorce was final. I mean, I know *exactly* how you feel. I was jilted, too, you know. Kevin wouldn't talk to me for years after the divorce. He blamed me for the whole thing. All I did was point out the basic flaws in his marriage. Sure, I helped his wife along a bit, introduced her to this stuffed shirt from England. I knew they'd like each other. They were both assholes. Kev's been alone ever since. He was *born* to be a loner, Stan old chum. Believe me, this new little fling of his won't mean spit in a few months."

"But that's *different,*" Stan wailed.

"What do you mean?"

"You and Kevin are *guys.* It's not the same. I mean, Melanie and I, I mean, we're girl and boy. That's different. I wanted to . . . I wanted to . . ."

Mayer nodded quickly. "I know. I know. Just trust me on this one, Stan. I know Kev. This will be over soon. I guarantee it." He glanced at his watch. "Excuse me for a minute, willya? I gotta make a professional call."

Stan nodded dumbly. Mayer scurried across the harried

dance floor of Music Max to the public phones. Plunking in a quarter, he dialed a number.

A female voice answered.

"Hi, there." Jake grinned. "Is this the queen of the hop?"

"Who is this?"

"Only Jake Mayers, Pulitzer Prize winner and journalist about town."

Roseanne Deemers laughed. "What do *you* want?"

"I'm polishing my story. Mind if I drop by to ask a few more questions?"

"Well, I was just getting ready for bed."

"Be still, my heart."

Roseanne giggled at the other end of the line.

"I take it I can come over?" Mayer smiled.

"If it doesn't take too long," Roseanne answered.

"Don't worry"—he cackled—"it won't."

"Well, okay. Here's my address."

He returned to the napkin-littered table at Music Max. Stan Webster was asleep, his head on the surface of the table, spit dribbling from his open lips. Mayer shook his head sadly. "C'mon, loverboy. Time to go bye-byes." He slowly lifted the love-struck college student to his feet.

"Huh?" Stan muttered.

"Not to worry," Mayer said. "Uncle Jake will get you home safe and sound. Just remember that I took care of you tonight, okay?"

Stan nodded dumbly. "Shhhhuuuuure."

He guided Stan toward the door. "Just remember, I'm your buddy, your big brother. You can trust me, Stanny. If you have a problem, you come to me, right?"

"Right." Stan nodded wildly.

"After all," Mayer continued. "That's what friends are for."

Thirty-one

Roseanne Deemers was rather flattered that a celebrity such as Jake Mayer would call her for a personal interview. When she hung up the phone after his call, the first thing that flashed through her mind was "publicity."

When he entered her apartment, satchel in hand, she was prepared for him, although not too flirtatiously. She wore a black leather mini, white blouse—first three buttons undone—and no bra. She *had* been voted Campus Queen, after all. Perhaps, with a man like Mayer on her side she could rise to the title of Miss Bay City or better. It wasn't long before the Miss California pageant. With enough publicity, there'd be no stopping her, perhaps Miss America, a career in modeling.

"Hi," she said, letting him into her apartment.

"Whoa." Mayer smiled, slithering into a chair. "You are the picture of postadolescent angst."

"Thank you." She smiled, running a hand through her long, red hair.

"No." He grinned. "Thank *you*." He placed his small satchel on the floor next to him.

She sat down across from him, not wanting to seem too coy. "What's in the bag?" she asked.

"Oh, just something I'm working on. A book."

"Can I see it?"

"Maybe." He shrugged. "If you're good." He whipped out a notebook. "Now, there are a few things I want to know . . . for my article, I mean." He gazed at her chest. "Now, a few of these questions may seem a bit personal."

"No problem." Maybe he'd send a photographer to the house.

"The murders," he began. "They've affected you a lot?"

"Oh, yes," she said. "I'm very careful about who I date now."

"Uh-huh," he said professionally. "And before the murders?"

"Well, I was careful, too. But, now, I'm *really* careful." She waited for him to reward her for a correct answer. He didn't.

"Let me see," he said. "What are your personal hobbies?"

"What?"

"I mean," he continued, "what do you do in your spare time? When you're not being a student, I mean."

"I don't understand."

"Do you like aerobics?"

"Well, I suppose. Yes, I do."

"And when you do aerobics, do you exercise in a co-ed gym?"

Roseanne cocked her head. She didn't understand. "Well, yes."

"Do men watch you when you work out?" he pressed.

"Well, I suppose they can, I don't really know," Roseanne replied, shifting uncomfortably on the couch.

Mayer stared at her legs, then at her breasts. "Well, I suppose they must, right? I mean, *I* would. Look at your legs, for instance. You have great legs."

Roseanne blushed. "Thank you."

"Oh, it wasn't a compliment," he said. "It was a statement of fact. Great legs. Great breasts. I mean, men must go crazy seeing those breasts."

Roseanne stared at him. What was he getting at? "I don't know that they do," she said.

Mayer smiled, allowing the woman to relax. "I didn't

mean they drooled over you, Roseanne. I just meant, well, you *do* have an amazing figure."

"Thank you."

"And you are a wonderful-looking young woman. Your breasts are full. Your nipples, right now, are stiff. Do you know I can see your nipples through your blouse?"

"Oh, Mr. Mayer."

"Call me Jake."

"I didn't know you would be looking at me *that* way." Roseanne tittered.

He laughed. "Well, I *am* a little older, but I'm not doddering and drooling yet."

"Oh, I know that," she said.

"The point I was trying to make, Roseanne, is that when women do aerobics, they appear naked to many men. Many men watch them, their breasts, their crotches, their behinds. They want to fondle them. They want to *do* them, Roseanne."

Roseanne was shocked.

"Sorry"—he smiled—"but it's something you should think about. There are many strange people out in the real world, love. You have to keep them in mind. Things that you do that you consider innocent may seem provocative to some young men."

"I'll . . . try to remember that, Mr. Mayer."

"Jake." He smiled.

"Jake," Roseanne repeated, feeling as if she was being lectured at by a preacher.

"Okay." He sighed, making notes. "That's all the advice you'll get all evening from wizened old Uncle Jake. Now we know you do aerobics. What else do you do?"

Roseanne thought hard. "Well, I read sometimes."

"Fine. You read. That's great. Very intellectual. Do you read at night?"

Roseanne frowned. "Sometimes. When I can't sleep. I read a romance novel to put me to sleep."

"That'll do it." Jake nodded, writing everything down. "Romance novels. Gotcha. And when you sleep, what do you wear?"

"Huh?"

"I mean, do you wear pajamas?"

"Pajamas are for men."

"Right. Right. So, you wear a nightie?"

Roseanne was growing uneasy, but she wasn't sure why. "Well, no."

"You sleep in the nude, then?" he asked.

"Well, yes. But I cover myself up with sheets and a comforter."

Mayer smiled. He was growing erect. "Hey, don't be nervous, kiddo. This is what I do for a living. I mean, if I was Barbara Walters, I'd be asking you what kind of tree you'd be if you could name your bark."

Roseanne laughed. "I'm just not used to being interviewed by a professional," she said.

He reached over a small table and patted her knee. "Not to worry," he said. "It's okay. Now, let's see. A lot of people accuse today's college students of being promiscuous. Do you think that's true?"

"No!" Roseanne declared.

"Okay. So, you don't like sex."

"I didn't say that!" Roseanne corrected.

"You *do* like sex," he amended.

"Sometimes."

"What kind?"

"Huh?"

"What kind of sex?"

"I . . . I . . ."

"Kinky?" Mayer asked, getting to his feet. "I mean, do you like to be subservient?"

"I'm . . . not . . . sure," Roseanne said, staring at him as he began to pace up and down before her.

"What about rape fantasies?"

"I . . ."

"Do you have them?"

"I don't think so. Look. It's getting late. Maybe I should just go to bed."

He laughed. "You're not tired, though, are you? You're

nervous. It's okay to be nervous. It's not easy to talk about these things."

As he walked by her, he stared down her blouse. Her nipples were hard. She was sweating. Good. Good. "Now, what about rape? Don't women have rape fantasies? Isn't it true that deep down, most women want to be violated?"

Roseanne laughed nervously. *"I* don't."

"Don't you?" He giggled. "I mean, wouldn't it be wonderful *not* to be in control? To have someone just walk in and sweep you off your feet? Tie you down? Rip off your clothes? *Do* everything to you you've always wanted, always feared?"

Roseanne was shifting in her chair. She wasn't sure what direction the interview was taking. "Maybe we should talk about something else."

"Of course," he said. "Sometimes I get carried away. Once I gave a very moving performance on a television interview show . . . the entire audience moved out of the studio."

Roseanne Deemers laughed. "I'm sorry if I'm not a good interview."

"No, you're great," Mayer said, moving back to his chair and to his satchel. "Maybe I should show you what I've been working on lately. I think you'll find it interesting."

Roseanne leaned forward. Jake continued to stare down her blouse. "I *know* you'll find it interesting." He grinned.

He opened the small satchel.

He stiffened.

He heard a key turn in the lock.

He spun around as another young woman, with frizzy black hair, entered the apartment. He turned quickly to Roseanne. "I thought you didn't have any roommates," he said, trying to keep his voice under control.

Roseanne blinked. "I don't. This is Bonnie. She's my friend. She's been so scared about these killings that she's bunking with me instead of in the dorm. It's just temporary."

Mayer snatched up his satchel and headed for the door.

"Howya doin' Bonnie?" he grinned, sweat forming on his chin. "Nice hairdo. Got any birds in there?"

"Bonnie," Roseanne said, slightly adrift, "this is Jake Mayer. He's a famous newspaperman."

"I don't read newspapers," Bonnie said. "They make me depressed."

"Smart girl." Mayer smirked. "Stick to those comic books. Betty and Veronica will perk you up every time. And how about that Jughead? He's a real scream, right? I'll see ya around, Roseanne."

"Don't you want to show me your work?" Roseanne asked, feeling as if she were losing control of the situation.

"Not now," he blurted. "Not now. Maybe some other time."

He ran out of Roseanne's apartment building onto the street. He was three blocks away from Bay City College. He was hot. He was aroused. He had to *do* something. It didn't matter with whom, to whom.

He'd fucked up.

He shouldn't have trusted her. She was an airhead. She had managed to catch him off guard. That wasn't good. He began walking blindly through the streets surrounding the college, talking to himself.

"Look at me," he muttered. "I'm losing it. I'm screwing up. In Las Vegas, I'd even lose money on a stamp machine."

He continued to chatter, marching toward the college. He couldn't control himself. He was burning. Burning. It was time to play. Time to play. But he had no playmate. His playmate had deserted him. He was all alone. He couldn't be all alone. He wanted company. He didn't care who.

Mayer blinked.

He found himself on the edge of the Bay City College campus.

He stood there, alone and frightened.

He glanced at the satchel in his hand. He had never tried this before. Everything had always been well planned. Well thought out. He peered across the campus. There were people strolling alone across the well-lit paths. In spite of the publicity, in spite of the warnings, women were walking alone to their cars, to their dorms, to their homes.

Mayer relaxed, wiping a lake of sweat off his brow. "Goddamn." He smiled. "It's true. It's really true. Ignorance is bliss." He strode across the Bay City College Campus feeling confident, his small, wiry form bouncing with each step.

This was going to be *new*.

He began whistling to himself.

Goddamn. Life was wonderful.

Thirty-two

"Do you know what I miss?" Broskey sighed, sprawled across the top of the bed, Melanie massaging his back.

"Uh-uh."

"I miss rain."

"It rains here."

"Not like back east. Big thunderheads whipping across the sky. Thunder and lightning. Sometimes it rains for a week. Yesterday, when it drizzled, there was some lightning out in the valley. A whole bunch of kids were playing baseball. They all ran under a tree. *Zzzzap*. Lightning hit the tree and the kids were all taken to a hospital with Afros.

"The funniest thing is, one of their *parents* led them to the tree. Back east, the first thing you learn when you're a kid is never run under a tree when there's a thunderstorm."

"Out here, we learn about earthquakes."

"But an *adult* leading them to the tree. 'I thought they'd need shelter,' the guy said. The kids could have been microwaved, for Chrissakes. This place is loony."

"*You're* loony."

"Yeah. That's probably why I fit in so well."

"Next"—Melanie laughed—"we have to teach you volleyball."

"No way. I'm holding out for Frisbee lessons."

Mayer stood in the shadows, satchel in hand. It shouldn't be too hard, he thought, fishing his blackjack out of the small athletic bag. He'd find someone, hit them over the head, maybe at the base of the skull, and knock them loopy.

He was near the student center. It was locked tight. Fortunately, Stan had given him a key. Well, not exactly *given* him the key, but he had one nonetheless.

It wouldn't be hard. He knew every inch of the building. After all, he'd been a regular on the campus before the killings. Now that he was practically representing the police, he had an even better knowledge of every office, every hallway, every lounge.

Boy, he would really blow their minds tomorrow.

The little darlings would flock into the student center, heading for the cafeteria, and there would be one of their own, suspended in time, never to eat glazed doughnuts again.

Mayer grinned.

It served them right.

College students, hah! The girls today, the way they dressed. They were asking for it. Sunday-school faces with Saturday-night ideas. Most of them had probably been on more laps than a napkin.

They wanted thrills.

He'd give them the biggest thrill they'd ever have.

He flattened himself against a wall. A co-ed was walking confidently down the pathway leading past the center. Nice. He smiled. A little tall for him, but nice. She had long blond hair that bounced when she walked. She probably had blue eyes. All real California girls had blue eyes. They loved to drink, to party hearty, to roller-skate in short shorts. They loved to tease, flirt, and entice.

He ran his tongue along his lower lip.

She was tall and willowy. He'd have to reach up to nail

her. That was all right. She didn't look heavy. He could drag her into the student center.

She was a foot or two past him before he jumped away from the wall.

He brought the blackjack down hard.

He heard it whistle through the air. He brought it slamming down on the girl.

Damn! It hit her shoulder. The girl did something Mayer hadn't expected.

She screamed.

She didn't teeter. She stood there, frozen, screaming. He leaped up in the air, trying to slam-dunk the blackjack onto her skull.

She was taller than he had judged.

The girl took the blow between her shoulder blades. She dropped her books and raised her hands behind her head. She continued to scream. He tried to hit her again. He caught her on the knuckles of her right hand.

Her screams sounded like a Civil Defense drill now. Mayer backed off, hearing voices and footsteps. He ran back into the shadows, grabbed his satchel, and skittered along the shadowy building, across a darkened pathway leading to the parking lot.

There were voices all around him.

Students were leaving their night classes, angry and alert. They were diving out of their cars and heading toward the center of the campus.

Somewhere, in the darkness behind him, he still heard the woman screaming. She sounded louder, now, than she had before.

He scrambled off the campus and found himself doubletiming it down a side street.

Damned Amazon. Why wouldn't she go down? Why didn't she fall? She had ruined everything. Standing there. Taking it. It wasn't normal. Probably a goddamned physical-education major.

He ran to his car. The engine roared to life. Mayer pulled the car away from the curb and drove aimlessly through Bay City.

This wasn't shaping up to be one of his better nights.

It would probably be best to head home, anyway. He'd been putting in long hours for the last couple of weeks. He needed his sleep.

He turned onto Pico and headed east, past Music Max, past Bay City College, past the ugly rectangular buildings that passed for storefronts. He spotted two young girls, they couldn't have been more than fourteen, hitchhiking. He slowed the car down.

He rolled down the window on the passenger's side. The teenagers approached the car. They had too much makeup on. Jake wanted to laugh. It was like watching the kids in Peanuts wear their parents' outfits.

"Heading for Hollywood?" one of the girls asked.

"Nope," Mayer said. "Don't you kids know it's dangerous to hitchhike this late at night?"

The girls rolled their eyes skyward.

"I mean it," he continued. "You're too young. You're in a lousy neighborhood, and besides, there's a killer roaming around."

"He only kills old women." One of the girls sneered. "College kids. We're safe."

"Are you going to give us a ride?" asked the other one.

"No," he said.

"Then, fuck off, Pop," the girl replied.

Mayer shook his head and pulled away, laughing. Kids, he thought to himself.

Broskey awoke in the middle of the night with a start. His beeper, still tucked away in his blazer, was shrieking. He stumbled out of bed and onto Melanie's floor.

"What's the matter?" Melanie called, her voice still confused by sleep.

"It's either a super-cricket or my beeper," Broskey said, fumbling in the dark. He finally got the little slab to shut up. He groped his way to the phone.

Within two minutes, he was gathering his clothes. "I gotta go," he said.

"What's up?" Melanie asked, turning on a light.

Broskey was caught with his pants at half-mast. He didn't notice. "The bastard slipped up!" he said. "He made a mistake. He panicked. Did something stupid. Something forced him over the edge. He tried it out in the open."

"Where?"

"The campus. He went after a girl right out in the open. Damn. That takes guts, as well as a good deal of stupidity. Talk about tempting fate."

"Did he . . .?"

"Nope. The girl is fine. Two broken knuckles and a few black and blue marks but that's it."

"Thank God."

"Thank whomever you want." Broskey grinned. "We *have* him. Don't you *see?* For the first time, we have a survivor. Maybe she can ID him. At any rate, the guy's on the ropes. We've forced him out of hiding. He's desperate."

"Why?"

"I don't know yet. But I intend to find out."

"Will you be coming back tonight?"

"Probably not. I'll wind up working all night, I suppose. But I'll definitely be back tomorrow." He leaned over the bed and gave Melanie a kiss on the forehead. "Until tomorrow night, my dear, this is Dick Tracy, signing off." He dashed toward the bedroom door.

Melanie smiled and, reaching under her pillow, pulled out a large ball of cloth. "Lieutenant?" she called.

"Yeah?"

"Are you aware of the fact that you're not wearing any undershorts?"

Broskey turned but didn't stop. "Who needs them? Besides, I've always been a freedom-loving kinda guy."

Thirty-three

*B*roskey sat, bleary-eyed, in Medega's office. Medega was gnawing on his mustache, which was not a good sign. The air conditioning was on full blast. Broskey fought back the urge to break out into a chorus of "Winter Wonderland." The presence of Mayor Gina Roberts, who was shivering in spite of her strawberry-colored jumpsuit, sobered Broskey up a bit.

He had spent the night with the survivor of the attack. She hadn't been able to tell them much. It was dark. The assailant had struck from behind. For some reason, though, his aim was off. She had the time to fend off the blows as she raised her hands. That cost her two knuckles. It could have been much worse.

Fortunately the girl, Lita Isaacs, had good lungs. She screamed loud enough for the whole campus to hear her. That frightened the attacker off.

Broskey had smiled when Lita said from her hospital bed, "My parents always accused me of having a big mouth. I feel like calling them up now to gloat about it."

Gutsy, Broskey had thought. It made him feel better. It was nice to know that not everyone in life was cut out to be a victim.

He spent the rest of the night poring over medical reports and pouring out vodka. He had managed to shave in the men's room before the mayor's visit.

He could tell by the way Medega was making a main course of his mustache that the meeting would have very little to do with law enforcement.

"The dead patrolman," the mayor said, between chattering teeth.

"McDonald," Broskey muttered.

"He will be buried with full honors, of course," she went on.

Medega nodded, his pockmarks glowing red hot. "Of course. He died in the line of duty."

The mayor shot Broskey a triumphant glance. "A very brave young man, taking on all those miscreants."

Broskey smiled sweetly. "Oh, very, very brave. Just like John Wayne."

"I want full media coverage of the funeral," the mayor said. "I've alerted my press secretary. Chief Medega, I'd like you to say a few words at the service."

"Me?" Medega blinked. "I'm not very good at public speaking, I'm afraid."

"If you don't improve your skills by tomorrow"—the mayor smiled—"you'll have good reason to be afraid."

Broskey squirmed in his seat.

"I'll speak after you," the mayor said. "I'll play up our tough, antigang stance. The officer made the ultimate sacrifice just to tell gangs that Bay City isn't their kind of town. That sort of thing. I would like you to play up the young man's valor. Stress his past achievements."

"He didn't have any past achievements," Broskey said, catching a stern look from Medega. What the hell, there was no way he was going to score brownie points with the mayor anyhow. "Getting blown apart yesterday was his finest hour."

"Actually," Medega interrupted. "I think it would be a lot more, um, *media*-wise to have Lieutenant Broskey speak at the funeral. After all, he *worked* with the young officer. He probably could shed a lot more insight on the boy's life. You know, play up the *humanity* of police work."

The mayor shook her head. "Ah, I don't think so, Chief. Nice try, though."

"I'm just trying to be helpful, Mayor Roberts," Medega said through clenched teeth. "Do you mind if I smoke?"

"Yes, I do," the mayor said.

Medega had already lit a cigar by the time the mayor had spoken and began exhaling clouds of smoke.

Mayor Roberts's cheeks took on the color of her jumpsuit. She turned to Broskey, rubbing a bruise on her forehead. A memento of her lunch with him the day before. "Actually, Lieutenant, I think you'll be too busy to attend the funeral."

"No doubt," Broskey said. "I've always been an overachiever."

"I understand there was an assault on the Bay City College campus last night," the mayor said.

Broskey nodded. "That's our boy." He smiled.

"I fail to see any humor in the situation."

"You're not looking at it from my perspective," Broskey answered. "From a police perspective, we've finally put enough pressure on this geek. He's losing it."

"I don't understand," the mayor said.

"Don't you see? He's gone from playing the Shadow, the emperor of the night, to the Three Stooges. He blew it last night. He came very close to getting caught. If we can keep the pressure on, he's going to get caught. I'm convinced of it."

The mayor shrugged. "Good. And I'm convinced that you will catch him within forty-eight hours."

Broskey's mouth dropped open. "What?"

"That's how long you have, Lieutenant. Personally, I find your holier-than-thou attitude about police work distasteful. You don't seem to be getting results, at least not the type of results I was expecting. If you don't arrest this maniac within two days, we can do one of two things. Since you are a bona-fide hero after yesterday's gang confrontation, I could reward you by granting an early retirement. I've already talked to the City Council about it and they will breeze the order through.

"If that doesn't seem attractive to you, then I can promote you to a lovely desk job in the department, where you can serve out your remaining time with a lovely view of the ocean." The mayor was grinning. She was having a great time.

Broskey smiled at her. "Mayor, personally I find you a pain in the neck, although many people on the force have a somewhat lower opinion of you. If you want an arrest in two days, you'll get an arrest. In fact, I'll try to take into custody every nutcase who's called the department to confess. We'll take statements. Check up alibis. Put extra men on the case. Go waaaay into overtime. And since I only have two days to deliver and since my career seems to be on the line here, I'm sure you can explain the bills to the council. After all, I'm working under *your* orders, right?

"And, if all the goons we bring in turn out to be bogus, well, I'm sure my successor will be able to sort out the paperwork in a month or two. In the meantime, I suppose we can put most of the looney tune crowd up in the city jail for a while. I mean, most of them would only be sleeping on the beach anyway. But I suppose that's not my worry. After all, I'll either be sunning myself in some tropical paradise or staring at the blue, blue Pacific from my penthouse office, right?"

He got to his feet. Medega seemed to be enjoying his cigar. The mayor did not seem to be enjoying anything. Broskey made a deep, chivalrous bow in front of her. "And now, Mayor Roberts, I must be off to my appointed duties. I have a really awful deadline to meet and ooodles of investigative work to do."

He paused in front of the air conditioner. "Bullshit." He sneezed.

"What?" the mayor asked.

"Excuse me, Mayor Roberts." Broskey smiled, turning to Medega. "Chief, you really should turn that air conditioner down. It's really irritating my cold."

Medega nodded. Broskey left the room. The mayor sat simmering in her chair.

"He's right, you know," Medega said.

"What?" the mayor replied, outraged.

"About the air conditioning," Medega replied, with a shrug. "It's a bad habit I have. My only vice, but I find that it keeps a lot of crap out of the air around me."

Thirty-four

Stan Webster sat in the student-center cafeteria and tossed his salad like it was a member of the Flying Wallendas. Jake Mayer sat across from him, watching the gangly boy sweat. "I tell you, Jake, I *know* I'm on the right track about all this."

Jake said nothing.

Stan continued. "I mean, think about it. The incidence, the frequency. As soon as the police got involved, the killings became more and more frequent. More and more savage."

Mayer nodded. "So?"

"It was like the killer *knew* everything that the police were trying. He had the information, the same information the police had *when* the police had it. Think about that."

He nodded. "Very interesting theory, Stan."

"And when the police actually moved onto the campus? When we had plainclothesmen roaming around talking to anybody, everybody, then the murderer really got going. You know what I think, Jake?"

"I'm all ears." Mayer grinned. "Like a donkey."

"I think we *let* the killer onto the campus."

Mayer bemoaned the fact that there was nothing stronger than beer served in the cafeteria. He quickly sucked his bottle dry. "Let me get this straight; you think that the killer is someone connected with the investigation?"

"*Has* to be," Stan said. "All the pieces fit. The killings were very sporadic before the investigation. After that, there were cops all over the place. They had access to everything, Jake. They could come and go as they liked. Now, all of the victims were murdered in their homes, right?"

"Right."

"No sign of forced entry, right?"

Mayer ordered another beer.

Stan abandoned his antigravitational lunch and concentrated on cracking his knuckles. "Well, who would have been let into any co-ed's apartment without question? Without fear? I mean, most of the girls on campus are scared shitless of letting even *friends* into their rooms. But who would they feel safe about meeting inside their homes, who would they *welcome* into their homes?"

Mayer got his second bottle and began sucking on it. "A cop."

"Don't you see? I'm on to something here. The only problem is, I don't know who to turn to. I mean, I can't very well go to the police about this."

"No. You did right in coming to me. One journalist to another, right?"

"I knew you'd understand." Stan smiled, relaxing for the first time.

"I really *should* go to Kevin with this." Mayer frowned.

"No. No," Stan said, scrunching his long back over the table. "I don't suspect *him,* of course, but if this killer is someone working with him and he made a remark about this, just in passing, we'd tip the killer off. He wouldn't get caught. He'd just stop for the time being. Maybe go into hiding for six months or a year. Then start up again somewhere else.

"Maybe he'd even leave the force. Go to another town. Join a police force there. The killings would begin again and no one here would be the wiser."

Mayer drained the second bottle. Things were getting out of hand, even for an optimist such as himself. Then again, the place where optimism flourished most was usually lunatic asylums. He was just having a run of bad luck, that's all.

"Let a smile be your umbrella and you'll wind up with a faceful of rain," he muttered.

"What?" Stan blinked.

"Nothing. Just quoting an old adage. Have you told *any*body about your theory?"

"No."

"Not even Melanie?"

"Especially not Melanie. I mean, she's shacking up with your buddy. All she has to do is breathe a word of it to him and we have a killer on the run."

He eased back into his chair. "I'm really proud of you, Stan. I think you've bested the police on this one. In fact, I think you've bested me."

Stan shrugged his shoulders in an "aw, shucks" fashion. "Naah. I mean, all the facts were there."

"But don't you see?" Mayer said. You little asshole. "You're the only one who noticed the obvious. All the facts were there for the police and me, too. But you're the only one who actually saw what was there. By God, Stan, you should feel proud of yourself."

Stan shrugged a second time. "So, now that we have our suspicions, how do we set about proving them?"

Mayer frowned. "Let me think about that for a while. Tell you what, I'll call you this afternoon, okay? We'll talk about this further then." He tossed a twenty down on the table. "My treat, Sherlock."

"Thanks, Jake." Stan beamed.

Mayer left the cafeteria and strolled across the college campus. He didn't know whether to burst out laughing or merely run up to a tree and start to gnaw on it.

He wasn't bested yet, but he was well on his way. And who got the upper hand on him? Some stringbean, a kid who'd have to climb Mt. Everest to reach a deep thought, who attended a college in Southern California that looked like a parking lot.

Mayer shrugged his shoulders. He'd find a way out of this.

He always did. He'd drive over to the police station and hang around with Kevin for a while. That always cheered him up. Kevin was a real pistol. Fun to be with. The best friend a guy ever could have.

Broskey showed Sergeant McGlory to the door. "So that's it, Mac. I'm on notice."

"It's not fair, Lieutenant," McGlory said. "You're a fine cop. My father and his father before him would have been proud to serve with you, and they were *cops.*"

"I appreciate that, Mac," Broskey said, not exactly knowing what the hell the guy was talking about.

"But won't we be wasting time, rounding up the perv patrol?" McGlory asked.

"No doubt," Broskey replied. "But if the mayor isn't going to give me the time to actually catch our boy, the least I can do is turn her life into a living hell for a few weeks. Think of it, Mac. More paperwork in a month than most shredders, including government ones, see in a lifetime. More drooling geeks in our jail than a dozen circuses. Makes you misty-eyed, doesn't it?"

McGlory was grinning. "You're a vengeful fellow, Lieutenant. I like that."

"Good. Well, take a few men, hit the streets, and waste some of the taxpayers' money and time."

"I'll do my best, sir," McGlory said, walking out.

Broskey returned to his desk. He needed time to crack the killer. He knew it. He was damned close to doing it. No way he'd do it in two days, though. It would be like pissing into a jet engine on full throttle.

"Lost in thought or has a butterfly kicked you in the noggin?" Mayer smiled entering the room.

"Ah. Comic relief. Sit down in my office, while it's still my office."

"Moving van on the way? Hiring starving students before they become planted pupils?"

Sergeant Fine stuck her head in the office. "Cheryl Williams is on the line. She says she wants to see you dead. Want to talk to her?"

Broskey rested his chin on his palm. "Nope. I think she's expressed herself quite nicely. What do you think, Jake?"

He thought for a moment. "Hmmm. Succinct. Simple declarative sentence. Offhand, I think she's topped her books."

Sergeant Fine was forced to laugh. "I'll cool her off."

"I don't know how you do it, Kev." Mayer sighed. "Dealing with psychoceramics all day . . ."

Broskey scratched his chin. "Huh?"

"Crackpots. A little humor, Kev, old boy. You're letting the job get you down. Actually, if you got any lower, you'd be gazing up at the undersides of snakes. What's the matter? Nutcases getting to you?" He got to his feet, imitating a sideshow barker's spiel. "Ya say you're tired of rubbing elbows with folks named Sanka? No active ingredient in the beans? Ya say yez is fed up with people who are fugitives from the brain gang? People who have a lot of backbone, but it's all above their eyes? Well, today's yer lucky day.

"I, Jake Mayer, bon vivant and all around journalistic whiz have an offer yez can't refuse. Let me take you to a chic restaurant in the center of Venice. That's right, lucky copper, you, too, can rub elbows with Dudley Moore, or elbow and earlobe as the case may be. See women who have actually played one of 'Charlie's Angels' and lived to tell the tale. Plus! Derelicts as far as the eye can see. Rivers of spittle of all race, creeds and colors will flow under our stunning rent-a-car as we pull into the driveway.

"Watch, stunned, as young men in red suits, who view English as a language resembling calculus, fumble with valet parking tickets and, before your eyes, reduce your transmission into the Latino equivalant of okra." Mayer rested his palms on Broskey's desk. "Now, let's see Vanna White top that for a prize selection."

Broskey laughed so hard his vision blurred. "I can't, Jake. I'm walking on death row, here."

Mayer slid back into his seat. "You got big probbies, Kevvy? Tell Unca Jake."

"Our esteemed mayor . . ."

"Of 'that was no garden hose, that was my date' fame?"

"One and the same. Mayor Roberts has told me that unless I catch our perp within forty-eight hours, I'm going to be facing either early retirement or a desk job that would make me the Mr. Greenjeans of the department."

"Can she do that?"

"Oh, she can." Broskey nodded. "And she *will* . . . 'cause that's just the kind of swell gal she is."

Sergeant Fine reappeared at the door. "Cheryl Williams is on the line again. She's fantasizing about the different ways she can kill you."

"When she gets to whips and cattle prods, give *me* the phone," Mayer said.

"Tell her when she has it down to a science, put it in writing and messenger it over," Broskey said. "I'll frame it and hang it next to my Official Hopalong Cassidy Fan Club Charter."

"Who's Hopalong Cassidy?" Sergeant Fine asked.

Broskey moaned. "Am I that old?"

Mayer turned to the blond policewoman. "A famous crippled cowpoke. Terrible accident. He had this crush on a cow, see? And then, when he tried the poke bit . . ."

"I don't want to hear about it," Sergeant Fine said, leaving.

"Well." Jake sighed, getting to his feet. "If the mayor wants you to catch the boy in two days, there's only one thing you can do."

"What's that?"

"Catch the boy."

"Fat chance," Broskey said glumly. "I'm not that much of an optimist."

"Good," Mayer declared, "because, as Ambrose Bierce once said, optimism is 'the doctrine that everything is beautiful, including what is ugly.' "

"Are you sure he said that?"

"It was either Bierce or our old landlord, Mr. Nastazzi."

"What a putz."

"And you don't need the advice of putzes," Mayer went on. "But you don't have to be an optimist to believe you can catch this guy. You just have to believe in yourself, Kev.

That's all. Besides, you have a lot of friends who are on your side. Friends you don't even know about."

"I'll think about that later and smile."

Broskey's friend walked toward the door. "Maybe. Maybe not. But I have a feeling you'll come out of this okay."

Broskey watched him walk out of his office, feeling, as usual, that he had spent the last few moments hanging on to the tail of a comet.

Mayer stood in the phone booth outside the Bay City police station.

"Okay, Stan." He smiled. "Here's the deal. I want to meet with you and Melanie tonight. Let's say eight. Okay. That's fine. Let's meet at her house. What's the address? Okay. Fine. Just tell her you have something very important to tell her about the case. No. No. Don't tell her I'm coming. Just tell her you have information you want to share. No, we're not lying exactly. I have a plan. It's only half worked out yet, so I don't want to run the risk of her mentioning anything to Kev. Right. Right. We don't want the killer to leave town.

"I promise you, I'll have everything worked out by the time I get there. That's right. Mum's the word about my being there. We'll surprise her. Okay. See you at eight." He hung up the phone, remembering his friend Broskey and the trouble he was in.

By tonight, all of his troubles would be over. He strolled along the sunny Bay City sidewalk, humming to himself. Of course, he'd bring his bag of tricks along, too. Kids loved surprises. He made a mental note to buy more bullets.

Thirty-five

Broskey watched the blue sky turn purple outside his small window overlooking Bay City. He heaved a deep sigh. Nothing was going his way. He was about to get kicked out of his job, thus allowing a maniac to go free. How had all this happened to him? He had more pipe dreams than an organist. None of them were about to become reality.

He quickly dialed the phone. Melanie answered. "This is an official obscene phone call," he said.

"Great," Melanie replied. "Start with Dream Whip and noodles and work your way up to barnyard animals."

"Actually I was going to go into heavy breathing for a while. Smoking causes emphysema."

"Oh, have it your way." Melanie laughed. "I'll just have to deal with the disappointment."

"It looks like I'll be over late tonight," Broskey said.

"Overworked?"

"And underappreciated."

"But not underloved, sport. What time do you think you'll be getting off?"

Broskey gazed at the stack of paperwork on his desk. "Well, I think I might have shafted myself today."

"That's illegal in Georgia."

"It's a crime in L.A., too." Broskey shrugged. "But in a vain attempt to hit the mayor where she lives, I have inadvertently saddled myself with about, ohhhhh, twice my weight in forms to fill out."

"Uh-huh."

"Are you mad?"

"Nope," Melanie said. "I knew it came with the turf. Besides, I have about fourteen literature courses to prepare for."

"Cliff Notes?"

"But of course. You wouldn't expect me to pay for hardcovers, would you? I mean, I'm a woman of desperate means."

"Maybe I could loan you some Classics Illustrated comic books."

"They stopped publishing ten years ago."

"I have them all," Broskey bragged. "In mint condition."

"I knew you were worth a fortune. After I'm done with them, we can auction them off. Buy an island somewhere."

"Near Maine."

"And wear black all the time. Call to each other saying 'thee' and 'thou.' I like that."

"I likest it," Broskey admitted. "I'd love to live in a place where the leaves changed colors in the fall."

"Dream on, Macduff. How late do you think you'll be?"

"Hopefully, I'll be outta here by ten," Broskey said. "I'll give you a call before I crawl out of here. Keep the home fires burning."

"It's a biological must," Melanie said. "I'll hold dinner. Stan said he might drop by. A journalistic coup, he said. That should take about eight minutes. Aside from that, I'll be pining for your arrival."

"You know what?" Broskey said.

"What?"

"I think I love you."

Melanie laughed. "I *know* that. I was just waiting for you to catch on."

"Always being kind to your elders, eh?"

"That was the way I was brought up," she said. "See you soon. Kisses."

Broskey almost licked the phone. "Ditto. Squared."

He heard the phone go dead. Sighed. Smiled. Returned to the litany of pervs that McGlory had brought in during the day.

The phone rang. "Broskey here."

"Jakey not there. Here," came a voice. "Can Kevvy come out to play?"

Broskey smiled. "Not tonight, Jake. I have plans. Even those are on hold."

"Having a bad time of it?"

"Paperwork up to my hairline."

"Good thing you're not going bald. What time do you think you'll be getting out?"

"Ten. Maybe eleven."

"Can I call you at home?"

"Nope. I'll be over Melanie's. What's up?"

"I may have a lead. I'm not sure. I'll call you after ten. Safe bet?"

"Safe bet," Broskey said, hanging up the phone.

Stan Webster guided his battered '78 Toyota to the front of Melanie Melnick's building. The car was a puke-green color, with a faded white roof. The engine guzzled gas like Nick Charles consumed gin. Someday, maybe after this story broke, he'd make enough to buy a decent car.

Maybe he'd even win the Pulitzer.

Then he'd be on equal terms with Jake Mayer. He'd savor that moment. All he wanted out of life was to be on an equal footing with one of the greats.

He bounded up the stairs toward Melanie's apartment.

He felt something odd at the base of his spine.

Something sharp.

A pain?

No. It was something long and round.

The barrel of a gun.

"Hello, Stanny." Jake smiled. "I just thought we should

walk in together." Jake cradled his bag of tricks in his other hand.

Stan nodded dumbly. What the hell was going on here?

"It's a gun. Just a little precaution. I want this evening to go as smoothly as possible."

"W-w-what's going on?" Stan whispered.

"Something you never even considered."

"I—I don't understand, Jake," Stan stammered.

Jake put a reassuring hand on the boy's shoulder. "Boychik, if you lived to be a hundred, you'd never understand."

Broskey dutifully filled out every form conjured up by McGlory's Wild West roundup that afternoon.

Maybe he should give Melanie a call.

Maybe he should tell her he'd be later than expected. After all, she was a part of him now. He was a part of her. He didn't quite understand how something so important had happened so suddenly, but what the heck, it *had* and he was enjoying it.

He made a move for the phone.

He froze suddenly, aware of another presence in the room. He glanced up at the doorway. Cheryl Williams stood there, a look on her face that reflected the thoughts of a one-track mind. He slowly tilted his vision downward. There was a revolver in her hand.

"Hello, Lieutenant Broskey." She smiled. "I finally settled on the way to kill you."

Broskey slid back from the phone. "On the one hand, Ms. Williams," he said, "I'm proud of you. It's about time you dealt with the real world. On the other hand, your method is fairly conventional." Williams shrugged. "Sometimes"— he grinned—"you can't fight old-fashioned values."

Melanie Melnick heard her doorbell ring. She tossed down the Cliff Notes to Thoreau's *Walden* and went for the door. She saw Stan framed in the doorway.

"Is this going to take long, Stan?" she asked pointedly. "I have my entire evening planned."

The tall, gangly student began to move his lips in strange, spastic directions. No sound emerged. Jake prodded Stan into the house. "Funny," he said to Melanie, "I have an entire evening planned as well."

"Mr. Mayer?" Melanie blurted.

"Call me Jake." He smiled. "You always used to call me Jake . . . or don't you remember?"

Broskey sat at his desk, entranced with the way Cheryl Williams tossed the gun from hand to hand, like a character out of an old Audie Murphy western. So Ms. Jonathan Livingston Seagull was really a tough cookie after all, a New Age moll. Broskey felt like he was watching a tennis match as the gun flew effortlessly from hand to hand. He had to fight to keep his head straight. If she kept it up, she'd put him to sleep. If he didn't do something soon, she'd accomplish that on a permanent basis once she stopped tossing the weapon and started squeezing it.

"So . . ." He smiled. "What's new?"

"What's new?" The perky hoofer-turned-actress-turned-best-pal-of-the-spirit-world sneered. "Do you know that you've ruined me?"

"No, but if you hum a few bars, I can fake it," Broskey said sweetly.

"You've sullied my reputation!" she barked.

"You seem to have done quite a nice job of that yourself, Ms. Williams," Broskey replied. "Look, I don't expect you to be really logical right about now, but you must have known that by schlepping off your prettier students to a sleaze like Rhodes, you were asking for trouble."

"Who knew?" Cheryl replied, still tossing the gun from hand to hand. "It was a few quick bucks. Do you realize how long it took me to put my metaphysical business into the profit column? For four years, I struggled. My first book didn't sell squat. I had to do something. Hell, I even did a series of aerobic videos. You know what happened? JanefuckingFonda put out *her* series and blew me out of the video market. I had to get money from somewhere. Rhodes gave me a fee plus a percentage of anything he made off the girls. There was no harm done."

"Until recently," Broskey pointed out.

"Until recently," Cheryl Williams repeated. Alley-oop, the gun went sailing again. "And you had no right to connect me with any of that. I had no idea what Rhodes was doing with those girls."

"Oh, come on, Ms. Williams."

"Okay," she admitted, screwing her pixielike face into a frown. *"Some* idea. But I never had the faintest inkling that any of those girls could wind up murdered. It wasn't my fault."

"I never said it was."

"No, but you *implied* it. I'm ruined, Broskey. Nobody comes to my channeling sessions anymore. They're all flocking to some new, goddamned spiritualist, the Movie Channeler. He tells your future in the voice of your favorite dead movie star! Can you imagine that! How stupid can people be! It's like Rich Little putting on a turban and telling people to have a nice day! It's ridiculous."

"You'll get no argument from me." Broskey shrugged.

"And my books? Down the toilet. They're practically remaindering my new book now. The publishers have canceled the contract on the one after that. Do you know what that means?"

"You'll have to get a normal job?" Broskey offered.

"What normal job! I was a dancer, goddammit. I used to dive for dollars in Vegas before I made it in Hollywood. And my acting career? The only reason I made it to the top was because my dresses didn't. I'm forty-three years old, Broskey. I'm not going to cut it when stacked against Demi Moore or Molly Ringwald or whatever embryo they're foisting on the public now. The New Age audience was my last chance. And *you've* taken that away from me."

She stopped tossing the gun around. She held it firmly in her right hand. "And, now, I'm taking *you* away from your audience. Say good night, Gracie."

"Look. I was just going to make a phone call. I had plans for tonight. Do you mind if I call and say I'll be late?"

"Are you fucking nuts?"

"I'll take that as a no."

Mayer smiled at the two students. He trained his gun on them. "That's very, very good. Just sit on the bed like good boys and girls."

"Jake?" Melanie asked. "What's the matter with you? I've never seen you like this before. Do you want me to call Kevin? Are you all right?"

"Right as rain. As a matter of fact, Kevin is the reason I'm here. I'm doing him a big favor. Stan gave me the idea this afternoon."

"I did?" Stan gulped. Melanie shot him a withering look.

"You did." He turned to Melanie. "Where do you keep your stockings?"

Melanie replied without thinking. "Top right drawer."

Mayer pulled out several pairs of stockings. "Good. Old-fashioned nylons. I hate panty hose. Stan? Here. Catch."

The gangly boy caught the nylon wad thrown his way. Mayer grinned. "Good hands. Now, I want you to tie Melanie to the bed."

"I—I can't," Stan stammered.

"You *will.*" He raised the gun toward Stan's head.

"Don't worry, Stan," Melanie assured him. "Everything will be okay."

Stan nodded dumbly. He didn't know what to do. Mayer rolled his eyes. "Nitwit. Tie one hand to one of the top corners of the bed. Tie the other to the other top corner. The feet get tied to the lower corners."

Stan did as he was told. Melanie was wearing a summery dress, loose fitting and blue in color. Her spread-eagled position caused the dress to grow taut.

Mayer noticed. "That can't be very comfortable for you," he said.

"No kidding," Melanie said.

He motioned Stan away, using the gun as a persuader. He carried the satchel with him to the bed, placing it on the edge of the mattress.

"Jake," Stan began.

Mayer casually raised the gun at Stan. "Shut up, kid." He grabbed one of Melanie's stockings and stuffed it down her mouth. "Sorry. I hate noise." He walked over to Stan, pulling up a chair from a dressing table. "Now, Stan, old boy. I want you to sit down. That's a good lad. Now, put your hands behind your back. Good boy."

Jake pulled two small slices of rope from his satchel. "Now," he said. "This may hurt for just a little while but I have to tie you around your elbows to the back of this chair here so you don't get any rope burns on your wrists."

"I don't get it," Stan said.

"You will later. Trust me, Sherlock. Everything will become clear. Now, I'm tying your calves in the same way because we don't want any burn marks on your ankles. I will now place this wonderful wad of hankie in your mouth to keep you from wimpering up a storm."

Mayer stepped back from the bound and gagged Stan. He returned his attention to the satchel, pulling out a blackjack, a soda bottle, and a Polaroid camera.

He smiled at Melanie. "You see, Stan here almost figured everything out this afternoon. He told me he suspected that your campus killer was one of the investigating team. He was *almost* right. Close enough for an A-minus. Not a member of the team, but a close personal friend."

Melanie's eyes widened. She tried to scream. She couldn't. She shook her head slowly from side to side. "Kevvy's working late tonight, so don't expect any interruptions." Mayer smiled. "I checked." He stood at the foot of the bed. He glanced at Stan. "And you, lucky sot, get to watch. You'll love the payoff. You really will."

He smiled down at Melanie. "Now, what? Oh, yes."

He slowly began to undo his belt. "This'll kill ya."

Broskey sat in his office, sweating. Cheryl Williams had the gun trained on his forehead, grinning like an idiot. She had been zeroing in on his temple for the last ten minutes, enjoying every minute of it.

"Won't you be late for dinner?" Broskey asked.

'I'm on a diet." She smiled thinly. "Besides, I'm having one hell of a good time."

Broskey sighed. He'd be getting over to Melanie's later than he thought. Cheryl Williams stood, grinning, over him, a well-coiffed gargoyle.

"Lieutenant Broskey?" a voice called.

Cheryl flattened herself against the wall as the man walked in. "Hi, Lieutenant Broskey," the man in the suit said, extending a hand. "I just called to thank you for everything you've done for me. The doctors at Saint Regis were very nice. They let me out early. I responded well to treatment."

Broskey glanced at Cheryl. She was clearly confused. Broskey shook Arnold Henry's hand. "Nice to see you, Arnold. But I'm afraid I already have a visitor."

Arnold Henry, the appliance killer, turned toward the woman with the gun. "Oh my God," he said. "Are you Cheryl Williams?"

The hoofer/actress/seer/moll shook her head. "Uh-huh."

"The Cheryl Williams?" Arnold enthused.

"Y-yes."

"Oh, my goodness, this is a *real* thrill. I've seen all your movies," the newly clean-cut and cured Arnold Henry said.

"You have?" Cheryl said with a smile.

"I even watched that TV series you did."

" 'Blair's Babies,' " she replied.

"Right. Right. I *hated* it. But *you!* You were fantastic. May I have your autograph?"

Broskey handed Arnold an interoffice memo and a pen. Arnold approached the woman. "This is such a thrill. I didn't know you knew the lieutenant. He's a great guy. He saved my life."

"He did?" Cheryl asked.

"Sure, he did. He's really something. Hey! Is that a twenty-two? I had a twenty-two." Arnold smiled. "Just ask the lieutenant. I was a pretty good shot."

Broskey leaned back in his chair. "Cheryl Williams, meet Arnold Henry. You have a lot in common. You're both nuts."

Arnold thrust the paper into Cheryl's free hand. "You want me to hold the gun?"

"No, no," she said. "I can manage." She raised a shapely knee and, placing the paper on it, began signing it.

"Not only have you seen all her movies," Broskey drawled, "you had a lot of her video tapes in your house."

"I did?" Arnold asked.

"Well, actually, I think your wife did," Broskey replied.

"I didn't know you had videos out," Arnold said, grinning.

"Uh-huh." Cheryl nodded, still signing the paper. "I did three aerobics tapes a few years ago."

Arnold stiffened. *"You* did aerobics tapes?"

"They were pretty good, too," she said, handing the paper back to Arnold.

He crumpled the autograph and tossed it aside. "Aerobics destroyed my family."

Cheryl cocked her head. "Wuzzat?"

Arnold raised his hands as if to choke the hoofer/actress/seer/moll/possible victim. *"Aerobics destroyed my family!"*

Cheryl's eyes nearly went into low orbit. "Broskey!" she called. "Get this creep away from me."

"Sorry." Broskey shrugged. "I'm a hostage."

"What?" Arnold said.

"She came here to kill me," Broskey informed Arnold Henry.

"First you kill my family! Then you try to kill my savior!"

Within an instant Arnold was upon Cheryl, his hands wrapped quite nicely around her neck. Cheryl let out a yelp that sounded like a terrier on a spit. She tried to raise her gun, but couldn't. She did manage to get off two shots, however. One of which turned Arnold's left foot into goulash.

Arnold grabbed the gun. "You bitch! You blew off my big toe!"

Cheryl didn't know how to react. "Sorry."

Arnold hauled his left fist back and hit Cheryl Williams with a haymaker that nearly sent her into the next county.

She rebounded off the wall and collapsed on the floor, her

jaw slowly puffing up to resemble a classic portrait of Popeye.

Broskey slowly got to his feet. He walked over to Arnold and put an arm around the man. "Arnold, you just saved my life."

Arnold was panting. Cheryl's gun was on the floor. Broskey kicked it under his desk. "I'll see that the chief gives you a special citation for this."

"I—I just came to . . ." Arnold panted. "She—she . . . my wife . . . my child . . . it's not fair, Lieutenant."

"I know," Broskey said.

McGlory came running into the room with two uniformed officers. "Lieutenant I . . . humma?"

Broskey pointed to the prone hoofer/actress/seer/moll/ KO'd assassin. "Her name's Cheryl Williams and she tried to ventilate my forehead. *His* name is Arnold Henry and he just saved my life. Can you get an ambulance for him and a pair of cuffs for her?"

The sergeant nodded to the officers. One grabbed Arnold. The other attempted to lift the petite Popeye clone.

McGlory stood there, ashen-faced. "What's the matter, Mac?" Broskey asked.

"I—I," McGlory whispered. "It's bad, Lieutenant. It's very bad. Your friend Jake . . . he called . . . the killer . . . the young lady you were seeing . . . I'm sorry, Lieutenant. I'm really and truly sorry."

Broskey felt the room buckle beneath his feet. McGlory's arms were there in an instant, lending support.

"Take me there, Mac."

"Lieutenant . . ."

"I want to be there!" Broskey yelled.

Thirty-six

Broskey stood, swaying, at the foot of Melanie's bed. He didn't want to look at what was left of her, but he couldn't help it. Blood was everywhere. It was on the pillows, on the sheets he had caressed her on.

He turned and stared at the far end of the bedroom. There was an overturned chair and the body of Stan Webster, his skull blown away.

Mayer stood next to him, shaking violently. "He lured me here, Kev. He told me he figured out who the killer was. I had pretty much pieced it together, but I wasn't sure. Once I got here, the son-of-a-bitch tied me up. In *that* chair."

Mayer displayed his wrists. There were rope burns on them. Broskey stared at the boy's body. He had been hit so hard his sneakers had flown off his feet. His socks had holes in the big toes. He had tucked them in between his other toes, so the holes wouldn't show.

"He wanted me to *watch,* Kev. I'm sorry. Goddamn. I'm sorry. The bastard made me watch. I couldn't get free in time. He had a gun. A blackjack. I'm so sorry, Kev. The things he did. *He took pictures,* Kev. God! I don't know how I did it, but I managed to get free. He was finished by then. I grabbed the gun. I blew him away, Kev. I *had* to. I called nine-one-one. I couldn't remember your number. I was a blank, Kev. Oh, God, Kev. I'm so sorry. I'm so very, very sorry."

A dozen or so Polaroid pictures were littered about the bed. Broskey couldn't look at them. Some of them were pink. Most of them were red. Two of them had splotches of white. Sneakers.

"I'm so sorry," a voice said. "I'm so very, very sorry." The voice spiraled down a deep tunnel, echoing off into the distance. The only sound was the beating of his heart. The quick in and out of his breathing. Sweat was dripping all around him. The world was ending. Armageddon had finally come.

"So very, very sorry."

Broskey nodded. He shook his head from side to side. He was empty. He had no thoughts. He had no feelings. There was only a great, empty void. It extended from the top of his head to the tips of his toes.

He gazed down at Melanie's face.

He slowly walked past Mayer, past McGlory, past Goldstein.

He stood on the small patio of Melanie's apartment. The plants would die now, he knew. No one would take care of them.

He grabbed hold of the metal railing.

His knuckles turned white.

He squeezed the metal railing.

He felt something surge up from within. It was not a whimper. It was something primordial, basic. It was pain, immense pain. The whine turned into a cry. The cry turned into a howl.

Broskey looked up at the full moon and opened his mouth.

A piercing sound emerged.

His body began to shake. He was racked by sobs, little-boy sobs. Tears cascaded from his eyes. He couldn't make them stop.

He felt an arm around his waist.

It was his best friend, Jake, leading him out of the apartment, away from the blood, away from the smell of death.

Broskey couldn't help himself. He cried all the way to Mayer's car.

He cried all the way home.

He cried for the next two days.

Thirty-seven

For the next two months, Broskey was in a stupor. When he wasn't drunk, he was trying desperately to be.

The shit hit the fan the day after Melanie's murder, with Mayer downplaying his role in catching the killer and playing up Broskey's. Broskey had been hampered by Mayor Gina Roberts, the story read, and thus had lost a lover to the killer.

Public sentiment turned against the mayor. There was a petition and a recall election. She was voted out of office and a Bay City councilman, an ex-spaghetti-western star named Cleve Stone, took her place.

Medega assigned Broskey a desk job, a job that was covered nicely by Fine and McGlory.

Broskey stayed at home and drank. And when he was done, he drank some more.

The recycling crew thanked him profusely for the amount of bottles he returned to the city. "You're making a real contribution," one kid told him.

His ex-wife, Janet, dropped by a few times with chicken soup and requests for more money. Fine, Medega, McGlory, and surprisingly, Officer Bluth, also checked in. Bluth had turned the corner. He wasn't into being a hotshot anymore. He'd become a good cop.

The days blurred into one another. Broskey had no concept of time. He lurched from bottle to bottle, from couch to floor. Mrs. Ramirez, seeing God floating over the street, ran out to touch Him and was killed by a speeding low-rider. Broskey heard none of it.

A package arrived sometime during the blur. Melanie's parents wrote him a letter. "Melanie would have wanted you to have these. She told us all about you. We were looking forward to meeting you. She told us you loved old music."

A package of Otis Redding albums and Eric Clapton's greatest hits.

Mayer stopped by often before he left town. "Los Angeles is just too damn violent for me, Kev. I've taken a job up north. Seattle. They have a great little paper there, the *Seattle Times.* They're paying me a fortune. I get to wear lumberjack shirts. Have a real house and get away from the smog. It's a perfect setup, Kev. Perfect. I want you to come visit me, okay? I want you to take some time off and visit me. It'll be like old times, okay, buddy? Please, Kev. Smile for me, willya? You're beginning to scare me. Smile, huh?"

Broskey spent a lot of time staring out the window, watching the sun play tag with the moon. Over and over, they sailed past the house, while Broskey's beard grew and the grass outside died.

The Santa Anas didn't bother him anymore.

But something did.

Eight weeks after Melanie's death, something jarred inside his head. A mourner died. A cop reemerged. There was something about the Co-ed Killer's death that didn't strike him as being *right.*

He didn't know what it was, but it was just too neat.

If Stan Webster was the killer, why would he turn against Melanie? She didn't suspect him in the least. In fact, she thought he was a geek.

And why would Webster suddenly turn against Jake? Jake claimed that he was putting the pieces together to catch the killer, but Jake didn't know anything more than the police did.

In fact, he knew *everything* the police did.

Broskey pictured Stan Webster in his mind's eye. A long-limbed kid who wanted to be a journalist. He had a strong grip but a weak face. He wore dumb clothes, his sneakers usually untied.

In the middle of the afternoon, Broskey jumped into the shower, shaved, put on a fresh set of clothes, and drove to his old office. Sergeant Fine was shocked. "Kevin? Lieutenant? Are you all right?"

"Uh-huh." Broskey nodded. "Bring me everything in our file on the killings."

"Everything?"

"Including the photos taken at Ms. Melnick's apartment."

He sat in his office for six hours. There was something strange about the photos. Melanie had been brutalized. He kept pushing back the nausea, gazing at the snapshots. They showed the bed. They showed Melanie. But they also showed the very tip of a chair positioned on the far side of the room. There was someone tied to the chair.

Someone wearing sneakers.

Jake hadn't been wearing sneakers.

Stan Webster had.

Sergeant Fine worked overtime, bringing him every file he requested. He read the statement from the woman who had been assaulted on the campus. The tall girl. The gutsy girl. Lita Isaacs. The assailant had missed her head. Why was his aim so bad? If he was short, he'd be jumping *up* at her head. If he missed, he'd be pummeling her shoulders.

"Sergeant Fine," Broskey said. "Get Goldstein down here."

An hour later, a very sleepy Goldstein stood before Broskey. "Nice to see you back, Lieutenant."

"Thanks." Broskey nodded. "Here's what I need. Remember that purse snatcher who was killed in an alley? I cuffed him?"

"Right."

"I want you to get the bullet that hit him and run tests on it."

"What am I looking for?"

"I want you to compare that bullet with the ones that killed Stan Webster."

"First thing in the morning?"

"First thing *now.*"

"But, Lieutenant . . ."

"Don't worry. I'll send out for coffee."

Goldstein heaved a massive sigh and paddled out of the room. Sergeant Fine stuck her head inside. "Do you just want coffee to rot your insides or would you like some lousy pizza, too?"

"Let's do the works," Broskey said, poring over the files. "You only die once."

Four hours later, Goldstein was munching pizza. "They match, Lieutenant. The bullets were fired from the same gun. The gun that killed Stan Webster."

Broskey put his pizza down.

"Jake," he muttered.

"Huh?" Goldstein replied, midchew.

Broskey rushed out of the room. "Thanks for coming down here, Goldstein," Broskey muttered.

"No problem." The bearlike man shrugged, chewing on his pizza. "What are friends for?"

Thirty-eight

The small house on the outskirts of Seattle was surrounded by trees and clean air. Beige in color, the single-family dwelling was picture perfect, adorned by a perfectly trimmed lawn and white picket fence. It was the personification of the American dream, a home of your own.

Inside, Jake Mayer sat at the kitchen table swilling a beer. The kitchen was bright yellow and cheerful. Mayer hated it. He emptied the bottle and went to the refrigerator for a second. The front doorbell rang. He put the second bottle down and swung open the door.

"Kev! Goddamn! It's good to see you. Why didn't you tell me you were coming? Come on in. Come on in."

Broskey walked into the house. It was the kind of place that would get a full-color spread in *Family Circle* magazine. Ma and Pa Kettle move to the Great Northwest.

"Come on," his friend enthused. "Have a beer. Boy, am I glad to see you. I mean, Seattle's okay, but in terms of excitement, it's right up there with Philadelphia."

"I don't want a beer, Jake," Broskey said solemnly.

Mayer sat down at the kitchen table. "Well, I can't offer you anything stronger. Sorry. Want some coffee? Milk? I have Twinkies in the house. Remember how Kevvy loves Twinkies?"

Broskey smiled faintly. "Yeah, I remember." He pulled out a large manila envelope and tossed it at Mayer.

"What's that? A present for Jake?" Mayer asked.

"Warrants," Broskey said.

"I don't understand."

"Warrants, Jake," Broskey repeated. "For murder. You want the exact count?"

"Is this some kind of gag, Kev?" Mayer said, astonished.

"No," Broskey said sadly. "Game's up, Jake. Seattle is going to cooperate with extradition procedures."

"You're not saying that you think that I . . ."

"I don't think, Jake. I *know.*"

Mayer calmed down. "You don't know anything, Kev. You only suspect."

"I can tie you directly to the murders of Melanie Melnick and Stan Webster, as well as the assault of Fritz Freeling."

"Who the fuck is Fritz Freeling?"

"The purse snatcher you winged," Broskey said.

Jake walked over to one of the kitchen cabinets. "Shit. I used the same gun I used on Stanny, didn't I?"

"Uh-huh."

Jake opened the cabinet and, spinning toward Broskey, displayed a .45-caliber pistol. "I got a new gun, Kevvy. Put yours on the table."

"I'm not carrying, Jake." Broskey sighed.

"Why not?"

"I thought I'd come in here and try to talk you out of it. I mean, what are friends for?"

Mayer sat across from Broskey, the gun trained on the policeman. "Are you shitting me? You came in here unarmed? Oh, Kevvy. You are acting veddy stupid today. You remind me of Whistler's Mother standing up. Very off your rocker."

Broskey nodded. "I came in unarmed. I didn't say I came alone."

"Bring a nuclear strike force with ya?" Mayer grinned. "Come on, you expect me to believe that you'd bring a posse?"

"Sergeant McGlory came up with me. He's been doing a bit of research on you. It seems that during the past six years or so, wherever you worked, there were lots of women being killed."

"Comes with the turf." Mayer shrugged. "I'm a crime reporter, remember?"

"I remember." Broskey nodded.

"McGlory outside?"

"He's outside. Twenty members of the Seattle Police Department are outside. High-powered rifles. Nifty scopes. Put a hole in you the size of a bowling ball."

Mayer laughed. "Bullshit. You're my buddy! My oldest and dearest buddy! You wouldn't do that to old Jake, wouldya?"

"I would."

"Naaaah. You're just putting me on. Just like old times. Remember the time you wrapped up that rubber chicken and had it hand-delivered to that woman who shot you down on that swanky date? Had it delivered to the Twenty-one Club for Chrissakes. Festively wrapped, as I recall."

"We're not playing games anymore, Jake," Broskey said. "You're going to serve time. You need help, Jake."

"The hell I do," Jake said, trembling. "The hell I do. I've never needed help from anyone in my life. Least of all, you. Man, where is your head at? I *carried* you for years. If it wasn't for me, you'd probably be some goddamned priest somewhere, diddling doughnuts under your cassock. Who taught you about life, Kev? It was *me!* That's who. I taught you everything.

"We could have been a great team, Kev. But, *no.* You had to go and become a fucking cop! Get married. Fuck me over. Well, I'm not the kind of friend who gets left behind, Kev. I'm not. And you're not the kind of friend who'd send me away, are you? Of course not. I mean, friends have secrets, right? Friends keep secrets. This will be our little secret."

Broskey shook his head from side to side. "Afraid not, Jake."

"Then, I'll kill you."

"And the police outside will kill you," Broskey replied.

"There are no police outside, Kev. Who the fuck are you trying to kid?"

"Nobody." Broskey leaned back in the chair. "The thing I don't get, Jake, is why? Why the hell would you do something like this? How could you? You have everything going for you. You're a success, Jake. People read your stuff. They *want* your stuff. You can get a job anywhere in the country just by snapping your fingers. You've won every award imaginable. If you want a lover, you can have one. Why?"

Jake bit his lower lip. "I don't know, Kev. I don't know. I—I've always felt so *alone,* you know? I mean, we're alike that way. We're loners. But you can deal with it. I—I can't. A few years ago, when everything was perfect, when I was on top, it suddenly occurred to me. *I'd done everything!* I mean, I'd been all over the world. I'd covered every kind of story you could imagine. I'd taken every kind of drug, sloshed back every kind of drink, been in every kind of cathouse.

"I was dead. I was a success and I was dead. I'd done everything illegal you can imagine. Just for kicks. Cock fights in Mexico. Kid boffing in Greece. Orgies? Man, I was in New York during the public-bath prime. There I was, Kev, people kissing my ass. People patting me on the back. And I wasn't even there to enjoy it. Then one night I saw this kid. She was hitchhiking. She got in the car. And I started to fantasize.

"We're riding along, right? And she's being really nice and all. And I'm thinking of all the things . . . all the bad things. I—I just don't know what happened, but it hit me like a thunderbolt. Here was something I hadn't done before." His face drained of all color. "Don't you see, Kev? There was nothing else *left* for me to do!"

Broskey shrugged. "Put the gun down, Jake, and we'll go."

Mayer uttered a harsh, guttural laugh. "Are you out of your fucking mind? Do you know what they'd do to me in prison? I'd be turned into a Mary Lou in about six minutes. I'm not the biggest, sturdiest man in the world, Kev."

"I'm not letting you out of here, Jake."

"But you have no gun."

"I have no gun."

Mayer got to his feet. "Then how are you going to stop me, Kev? You won't hit me. I know you. You're my pal."

"No, I won't hit you, Jake," Broskey said. "But if you walk out that door carrying that gun, without me, there are twenty police officers there who will send you into the next life in the blink of an eye."

Jake stood above Broskey. "Oh, Kev. Kev. You always were melodramatic. You always were a moralist. Well, I won't kill you. How's that for being a sport? But I *do* have to put you out of commission. I have to cross state lines, after all, and I don't have the best of cars."

Broskey looked up at his childhood friend. "I'm not bullshitting you, Jake. Step outside that door and you're dead meat."

Mayer cackled. He lifted a beer bottle from the table and smashed it down on Broskey's forehead. He watched his old friend fall, moaning, to the floor. "Sorry, Kev," he said.

Broskey hovered in and out of consciousness. His head was pounding. "I'm not," he whispered. Broskey heard Jake whistling, as he jogged toward the front door.

He heard the front door open.

He heard the shouts, the *crack-crack-crack* of high-powered rifles, the bullets whizzing, the front door splintering inward.

Then he heard the cry of surprise that was the last utterance of Jake Mayer.

Broskey tried to shake his head clear. There was blood trickling down onto his face. He heard the familiar voice of Sergeant McGlory.

"That was a stupid move, if you'll pardon my saying so, Lieutenant. I mean, fair is fair, but I don't know if you're a saint or a lunatic."

Broskey wiped the blood off his forehead. "Is there a difference?"

McGlory helped Broskey to his feet. "Now *that's* a

question that has been plaguing Holy Mother Church for years."

McGlory helped Broskey into a chair. Broskey glanced over his shoulder. The front door of the house was shredded. "Jake?"

"The little weasel looks like a slab of Swiss."

Broskey nodded. "Call the meat wagon and tell them we have an order to go."

Thirty-nine

*S*ergeant Fine and Kevin Broskey stood at his desk, gazing into the large box.

"Well, I guess your evenings are taken from now on." She laughed.

"Uh-huh," Broskey replied. "It's about time I dealt with real responsibility."

Medega coughed before entering the office. "Broskey, you should get an air conditioner in here. What *is* that smell?"

"I took your advice, Chief." Broskey smiled. "About improving my home life?"

"You bought a *dog?*" Medega gasped.

"Nope." Broskey smiled, opening the box. "I bought two. Pound puppies. Thirteen dollars each. The one with the weird ears is Gabby."

"Gabby Hayes?"

"Uh-huh. See those whiskers. The other one is Kate."

Fine glanced at Medega. "Hepburn fan."

Medega stifled a smile. "Two females, huh? You planning on raising a harem?"

"Nights do get lonely," Fine said, elbowing Broskey.

Medega glanced in the box. The puppies were cute, but they smelled awful. He pulled out a handkerchief and began daubing his eyes. "Nice work in Seattle, by the way."

Broskey shrugged. "It could have worked out better."

"I don't think so," Medega said. "By the by, the new mayor would like to see you tomorrow. Something about a commendation or some such bullshit."

Broskey glanced at the chief. "Will I get a bigger office?"

"I doubt it," Medega said with a wink, "but the department might spring for an air conditioner."

Broskey carried the box with the puppies up to his front door. His neighborhood was changing. It was quieter now. After Mrs. Ramirez's death, the whole family moved out of their two houses. Two yuppie couples moved in, repainted the homes, and took to playing soothing Windham Hill pap into the early evening. The rest of the old neighbors seemed intimidated by the sound of whale songs. Nobody played mariachi music anymore.

Broskey missed it.

He took no note of the Rolls-Royce parked across the street as he eased his door open.

He gaped at his living room.

There, newly uncrated, was a top-of-the-line stereo system, a forty-eight-inch television, a VCR, and thirty or forty hit-movie tapes. He placed the box down on the floor. He glanced at his coffee table. There was a Mr. Coffee machine on it. Next to it were ten pounds of Kona coffee.

Broskey had the sudden urge to run out of his house. He must have walked into the wrong bungalow.

"I told you I'd pay you back," said a voice behind him.

Broskey turned around. There, clad in a white cotton Nehru outfit stood Benjamin Holden, his recently grown-out hair pulled back in a ponytail.

"Bud?" Broskey asked.

"Hiya, Lieutenant." Bud, the former in-house transient smiled, stepping forward. "Do you like the stuff?"

"Like it? Sure I do. But, how. Why?"

Bud shrugged. "Sorry I had to borrow your old stuff, but I needed to pawn it to start my new business."

"But this is . . . it's too much, I—I . . . " Broskey began.

Bud smiled. "It's nothing, Lieutenant. I'm making money by the fistfuls, now."

"Financial adviser?" Broskey asked.

"Nope." Bud grinned. "Remember that talk we had?"

"I can't say as I do."

"You were telling me about the new spiritualism?"

"Oh yeah, yeah." Broskey nodded.

Bud spread his hands and gazed at the ceiling. "Behold Wotha, the Movie Channeler."

Broskey began to laugh. "You? *You?*"

Bud screwed his face up into a W. C. Fields smirk. "Ah, yes, the folks in Malibu simply adore getting fleeced by a blast from the past."

Broskey was giggling.

Bud sucked in his teeth à la Cagney. "And they, those dirty rats, they let me do to them what they do to their brothers. Stick 'em where it hurts. Their wallets, ummmm, yeah."

"Well, congratulations. Want to stay and have"—Broskey glanced at his table—"thirty gallons of coffee?"

"Can't." Bud shrugged. "I have wall-to-wall channeling today."

"This is all so incredible." Broskey laughed. "Bud, I am genuinely happy for you."

"I knew you would be, Lieutenant. When I was down, you were my only friend. You never treated me like a loser. I appreciated that more than you could know. Here. This is for you, too." Bud handed Broskey an envelope.

Broskey opened it slowly. His eyes widened. "It's a check for five thousand dollars, Bud."

"Just a little gift from Wotha. After all, you're the one who guided him toward the path of the stars."

"I can't take this."

"You can't give it back either," Bud said, turning into John Wayne. "'Cuz if you do, pilgrim, you'll have me to answer to and I'm not above wallopin' a cop, I'm not." He shrugged shyly. "Consider it a commission. Agent's fee."

"A gift from heaven?" Broskey said.

"Whatever turns you on," Bud said, running to the limo across the street. "My chariot awaits me. There are new fish to fry."

"Sheep to fleece?" Broskey called.

"It's a jungle out here, Lieutenant."

Broskey watched the limo pull away. He slowly closed the door behind him. Walking into his living room, holding the check, he felt a sudden pang of sadness.

He shook himself clear of the melancholy. He had to move on, right? That was the way things went. You can never stop moving. If you stumble, try to stumble forward.

He held the check up before his eyes.

Besides, maybe his life was changing. Maybe, from now on, things would go right.

He heard two small yips from the floor.

He glanced down toward his tattered rug.

The pups had gotten out of their box.

They had both decided to relieve themselves on his shoes.

He began to laugh, bending over the puppies and glancing around the run-down bungalow.

Some things never changed. He was glad of that.